THE MARKING

DESTINY DIESS

By Destiny Diess

Copyright © 2021 by Destiny Diess

All rights reserved.

This book or parts thereof may not be reproduced in any form, stored in any retrieval system, or transmitted in any form by any means—electronic, mechanical, photocopy, recording, or otherwise—without prior written permission of the author, except as provided by United States of America copyright law. For permission requests, write to the author at "Attention: Permissions Coordinator" at the email address below.

Any references to historical events, real people, or real places are used fictitiously. Names, characters, and places are products of the author's imagination.

Cover by: Amala Benney

Editing by: Jovana Shirley, Unforeseen Editing, www.unforeseenediting.com

Proofreading by: Zainab M., Heart Full of Reads Editing Services

Beta reading by: Kayla Lutz,

Destiny Diess

DestinyDiess@gmail.com

To everyone who has dealt with unaccepting family members or who has faced discrimination.

PREFACE

Warning: This is a paranormal romance with dark themes, including minor torture and sexual assault. If these are sensitive topics for you, please refrain from reading.

CHAPTER 1

MAE

A thunderous roar burst through the forest from behind Dad's Mercedes-Benz, conquering the light hum of its engine. Heart thrashing inside my chest, I stared into the rearview mirror with wide eyes, scanning the mammoth oak trees until I spotted the first few shadows of the wolves bolting through the forest behind us on their nightly run.

"Drive faster," I said to Dad, adrenaline rushing through my veins. I loved watching them run.

Dad pressed on the acceleration, jerking the car forward. I rolled down the window, letting the wind blow back my silver-blonde locks, and glanced out into Witver Forest, catching sight of the enchanting golden eyes of the largest wolf among them all —the alpha.

When he saw me, he howled to the setting honey sun and sprinted closer to the car with his pack, his claws scraping against the black asphalt with every leap. I reached out the window to stroke his fur, but before I could touch him, Dad rolled up the window, forcing me to yank myself back into the car.

I clutched my arm and frowned at their slowing figures in the rearview mirror, their snouts pointed to the sky and their howls reverberating through the car. All I wanted was to be able to run free with them in their forest and live in peace, but *someone* didn't find that acceptable.

Knuckles white on the steering wheel, Dad clenched his jaw and shoved his foot down harder on the acceleration, throwing me backward against his leather seat. "You know better than to touch those filthy animals, Mae," he sneered.

After balling my hands into fists, I flared my nostrils and glared out the window at the sunset as we flew by the thousands of trees and toward the city.

"Don't you?" he asked me.

Knowing that he wouldn't let this go, I sank further into my seat and mumbled, "Sorry."

While I loved Dad, I hated him sometimes. He couldn't see past his own prejudices.

A deafening silence spread throughout the car, the engine's continuous hum giving me some sense of peace and calmness among his madness. He relaxed his hand around the wheel and turned on Witver's most conservative radio station.

"Welcome back to our segment of Witver Without Wolves. All through the night, we've been keeping you updated on the riots that these filthy animals and their blind supporters are participating in throughout the city. And let me just say, they're digging their own graves out there, igniting towns with lies about the wolves, saying that they're civil creatures when all they do is kill. Our world is brainwashed. Werewolves should never live in a society with humans. Protect yourselves. Stock up on all the silver bullets you can get your hands on. Kill on sight. Our trusty police force is on our side. Those men and women are the true heroes, not those radicals trying to procreate with another species."

THE MARKING

Rather than listening to this bullshit, I clicked off the radio station and glared through the shiny windshield glass. Dad tightened his grip on the leather steering wheel once more and cleared his throat, merging onto the highway toward the city. If he didn't want to live with the wolves, I didn't know why the hell we lived in the middle of Witver Forest. He could live in a highrise with other humans in the city, but *no*, he'd had to find a gated neighborhood with people just as insane as he was.

"I'm glad you decided to join me for dinner with the Braxons," he said, thankfully not commenting any further on the Witver wolves. "I heard that Brett is going to be there tonight. He's been asking for you."

"Brett?" I asked, glancing over at him and raising a brow. "He's been asking for ... me?"

Brett Braxon was the biggest, sexiest flirt in all of Witver and my biggest crush since second grade, but too many other women and even some she-wolves fawned too heavily over him. I didn't have time for that kind of competition; I was too busy figuring out my life amid all these protests about the treatment of wolves.

"Are you excited to see Brett?" Dad asked, shooting his brows up and down.

"Dad!" I shouted, cheeks flaming. "Please, don't."

Since I'd moved out of Dad's suburban home and into a secluded apartment in the forest with my best friends, I rarely talked to him about these things anymore. He always tried to overcompensate for Mom being gone, asking me questions far too personal about my love life. It was all with good intent, but ... I didn't want to be sucked into all his drama and negativity.

I didn't really like human guys anyway. I had my eye on a certain someone already.

Turning off the highway, Dad parked in the lot to Tangled Orchard Winery. Overpriced and ritzy, Tangled Orchard Winery had large, bronze-cushioned chairs, white linen–dressed tables, and wall-length windows that flaunted the darkening honey-turning-violet sky. I hiked my cheap purse up my shoulder and stepped into the room, feeling out of place here.

Dr. and Mrs. Braxon beamed at us from a candlelit dark oak table.

Brett glanced over his shoulder with those sinful hazel eyes, his full lips curling into a smirk when he saw me. "Mae," he said, rising from the table and wrapping me into a hug. "It's been too long." Muscles rippling against my body, he squeezed me tight.

After awkwardly patting his back—not used to his proximity—I sat beside him, dreading tonight's conversation. All anyone had been talking about lately were the protests downtown and throughout the forest.

"Another one of those brutes was roaming around our neighborhood yesterday," Dr. Braxon said, halfway through dinner. He sipped on his Tangled Orchard Winery red wine. "A neighbor called the police on him."

"What don't they understand about that huge *Humans Only* sign outside our neighborhood?" Dad asked, shaking his head and scowling, accentuating the deep lines around his mouth.

I balled my hand around my fork until my knuckles turned white, knowing where this conversation was headed and wanting nothing more than to say something. Yet every single time I did, Dad would go off on a rant or just completely ignore me. Once he was set on believing what that stupid radio station had fed him, there wasn't any changing his mind.

"I bet they'd understand if they were locked in silver cages and force-fed some wolfsbane, but the government is too afraid of them to do anything like that," Dr. Braxon said.

"Hun," Mrs. Braxon said, shifting uncomfortably and smiling tensely. "Stop it."

"It's a shame," Dr. Braxon said to Dad, completely ignoring his wife.

My nails cut into the skin on my palm, and I leaned closer to Brett. "They really are closed-minded, aren't they?"

Brett scoffed. "Would you want a feral animal roaming around on your property? Those beasts attack anything they want for any reason they have. They have no sense of logic. If we're not careful, they'll destroy everything we've built."

I stared at him with wide eyes, even after he turned back to the conversation. This was coming from the man who occasionally flirted and slept with she-wolves, as if he only used them for a good time and didn't care what happened to their kind afterward.

Forty-five minutes of agonizing conversation later, I was itching to leave. All we had left was dessert, but I didn't want to spend a second longer listening to Dr. Braxon and Dad bad-mouth anyone else. It made me want to stab my ears out.

"Dessert?" someone asked from my left.

When I glanced up at him, my eyes widened. Standing at least six foot tall with a brawny frame, blond stubble, and vaguely pointed ears—one of the only distinguishing features of a wolf from a human besides their woodsy scent—a man stood with a platter of chocolate cake.

A wolf? Here? He looked so … so out of place among all the humans.

Dad scowled, his hatred for beasts making him ugly. "I am not eating that. Take it back."

"Have a *human* waiter bring it over, you dog," Dr. Braxon ordered.

Pupils dilating, the man tightened his grip on the steel platter. I inhaled sharply. Dad had warned me thousands of times that wolves' eyes darkened right before they released their inner beasts. What if this man shifted and attacked him? Dad would provoke him more—I was nearly sure of it.

Smiling nervously, I leaped from my seat and grabbed the platter. "Thank you so much! I'll gladly take this cake from you if nobody else here wants it." I sat back down with the entire cake in front of me, ignoring Dad's death glare, and grabbed my silver fork. "Chocolate cake is my favorite!"

"Mae!" Dad snapped. "What are you doing? Don't you dare eat that."

Stuffing a forkful of sweetness into my mouth, I chewed and smiled at the grinning waiter. "This is delicious. By far the best cake that I've ever had. Thank you so much." I didn't know why I couldn't shut my mouth. I just didn't want to give Dad the chance to belittle him even more. I swayed my fork in the air at him, signaling delight. "You deserve a raise."

Dad shoved his chair back, the legs screeching against the wooden floor, and snatched my forearm. "I'm sorry for her rude behavior," Dad said to the Braxons before dragging me to the other side of the room.

The waiter glanced over his shoulder at me one last time and then disappeared through a side door as other workers stared at him quizzically, like they had never even seen the man before tonight. A strong urge washed over me to follow him, but I couldn't do anything with Dad's grip.

Bracing for his scolding, I clenched my jaw and pressed my lips together. My logic failed every time against his closed-mind no matter what I'd say, he would never change his mind about people who differed from us. He had been scolding me for sticking up for them since I'd turned three years old and asked for a stuffed wolf instead of a stuffed doll at the store.

"Don't you ever do anything like that again!" Dad chastised, his grip so tight that my pale skin turned pink. "Do you know how embarrassed I am? You know better than to take anything from a brute. They are savage, disgusting, deadly animals; and they do not deserve to live in our society. We are better than them. We are higher class, Mae."

"Are you kidding me?!" I shouted back, unable to control my fury anymore. I ripped myself out of his hold and ignored the stares from the staff and other patrons. "Do you expect me to just sit around and do nothing while you disrespect an innocent person?"

He stiffened. I rarely argued with him anymore, but I couldn't stand his ridicule.

"Why do you think I moved out and I hardly visit you anymore? I'm so sick and tired of you and your goddamn disrespect for people who are different! News flash: Not everything you listen to on that stupid radio station of yours is true!"

Before he could even respond, I stormed away from him, snatched my purse from the table, and hurried to the exit without muttering a single good-bye to Brett and his family. They called my name, but I didn't turn around and run back to them. I didn't need them or even want to associate myself with them.

Flinging open the door, I rushed out and crashed right into a man's chest.

"Sorry," I muttered, glancing back through the closing door to see Dad shaking his head my way.

I needed to get out of here as soon as—

I glanced up at the man who hadn't seemed to move away and inhaled the sweetest honeysuckle scent ever.

With forest-green eyes that flickered gold every few moments, vaguely pointed ears, and a scar across his chiseled jaw, he was the most beautiful man I had ever seen. My heart stammered inside my chest, my mouth drying. The wolf from Witver Forest, the alpha who had run closer to our car and nearly let me touch him. It was him.

But what was he doing here? Wolves never frequented places like these.

After another moment, he stood straight and postured over me. "What are you looking at, *human*?" he snarled, his long canines extending past his lips.

If I wasn't slightly aroused, I would've almost taken it as a threat.

When he growled at me through them, I did.

All of the constant warnings my father had ingrained into me about wolves' dangerous behaviors suddenly rushed through my mind, rearing their ugly heads. I hated that man for instilling such vile thoughts into me. For the past eighteen years, I had been trying desperately to get rid of that implicit bias.

Yet, still, my heart raced at the sight of sharp and bared teeth.

"Why're you so scared?" he asked me, glowering at me. "Just a moment ago, I listened to you scream at your father about disrespecting wolves, and now, you're nervous, just standing in the presence of one."

Gnawing on my cheek, I stepped back but couldn't seem to look away from his huge teeth. While I'd originally believed that my nerves caused me to react this way in front of him, I ... I ... I couldn't stop thinking about the feel of his skin on mine, the way his teeth could slip inside my neck, and—

Gosh, no. What was I even thinking? Wolves and humans never mated.

Parting my lips, I tried to think of an excuse for my foolish behavior. When I realized no words were coming out of my mouth, I took another step back, wanting to put space between us because ... the closer we were, the cloudier my thoughts became.

He moved closer to me, almost ... *instinctively*, yet I stepped back again and plastered myself to the door.

Was it getting hot out here? Because my whole body felt like it was burning, scorching in flames even.

Placing both palms flat next to me, he trapped me between him and the door. I froze, gulped in fear that I'd do something stupid with Dad in the next room, and stared into those smoldering forest-like eyes that held so much passion, yet even more pain. I wanted to venture inside and peel back layer after layer of leafy facades and thick fortresses to see who this big, bad alpha really was.

He leaned down slightly and inched his face closer to mine, his honeysuckle aroma overwhelming my senses and his eyes darkening, just as the waiter's had. While I should've been terrified that this man would rip me apart, I felt oddly comfortable, like he and I were supposed to meet.

The door behind me swung open, and I stumbled back. He wrapped his strong arms around my waist and held me to his chest, a blazing fire erupting where his skin touched mine. My fingers curled into his taut chest, the energy charged between us. Dark strands of hair fell into his face, his honey breath fanning my lips.

"Get away from her!" Brett shouted from behind me.

A low, possessive roar erupted from the beast. He wrapped his large hands around my waist and placed me behind him, the muscles under his gray V-neck flexing through his shirt. Claws lengthening, canines extended, he held one arm back, as if to shield me from Brett. "And who are you?"

"I'm her boyfriend," Brett said, glaring at the animal.

Boyfriend?

I wrinkled my nose, the mere label sickening me. Where had that even come from? And why would he even say that? This wolf snarling between us wouldn't care what I was to him.

The wolf growled viciously this time and bared his large canines at Brett, his back muscles stretching and nearly tearing the threads of his V-neck. "*No.*"

Wanting to defuse the situation, I placed my shaky hand on the werewolf's forearm. He jerked himself out of my grip and yanked me in front of him, his callous digits digging into my shoulders. I yelped at the sudden movement, my heart leaping in my chest.

"Let her go," Dad spat, walking out from behind Brett. "Or I'll call animal control on you."

"You can have her," the wolf said, shoving me forward.

I stumbled into Brett, who enveloped me in his embrace and

stepped toward the door. But I didn't move from the spot. I didn't want to go back inside. I didn't want to sit through any more of their shitty conversation. I wanted to stay. I needed to know who this wolf was, why I felt this way toward him, and if he ... if he felt the same way.

He probably didn't, but ... I wanted to know what this meant.

I lived with a werewolf and didn't feel this strongly connected to him.

"You can try to keep her away from us," the wolf said to Dad, staring right at me with those golden-flaked green eyes, "but you can't stop the way she feels about us, nor the way she's drawn to *me*."

"My daughter doesn't like *any* of you." Dad seethed, lunging forward and flailing his arms around in an attempt to hit the man.

Swiftly dodging the attack, the wolf stepped to the left and smirked at my father. "Of course you think that. You can't smell her the way I can."

Though his words were degrading, I couldn't stop the heat clawing its way up the insides of my thighs. Forget everything I'd said about this man. He was an asshole that I never wanted to see again, especially after that last comment. He hadn't needed to sell me out to Dad like that.

Dad shot in for another punch, but I wrapped my arms around his waist and pulled him back.

"Stop, Dad. He's just trying to get you angry."

The wolf walked backward off the sidewalk and toward the street, as if he never planned on dining inside the restaurant tonight, as if he had come for a different reason entirely—me. Lips curled into a smirk, he winked at me. "Until next time, Kitten."

After he disappeared into Witver's busy streets, I stayed glued to the spot. I'd talked to many wolves before, but not once had a wolf drawn me in so effortlessly. Meeting this man had awoken an inner hunger that I hadn't known I even had.

A starved, feral animal rumbled inside of me, pleading for me to find him again someday.

And maybe, one day, I would.

Dad snatched my wrist and stormed with me to the car. "What's your problem? You know not to talk to wolves and certainly not to flirt with one like that. Do you not remember what happened to your mother?"

I ripped myself from his grip in the middle of the parking lot. "How could I forget, Dad? You mention it every other day."

Nostrils flaring, Dad shoved a hand into his pocket and pulled out a silver necklace with an off-white oval pendant hanging from the thin chain. In the center of the pendant, a red liquid substance sat within a small container. "I wasn't going to give you this now, as I wanted to keep it with me, but it seems you need the constant reminder every day."

"Are you giving this to me because it's silver?" I snapped.

Silver like these repelled wolves and would make them bleed from a single touch.

"No, I'm giving it to you because it was your mother's," he said. "She used to wear it and said something about it making her stronger during the blood moon. I hope it can make you stronger *and smarter* too. Maybe it will remind you of her death when you're out, hanging around those disgusting animals."

After ripping the necklace from his hand, I shoved it into my pocket. Nothing from him could ever just be out of simple love for Mom and me. Nothing could be sentimental anymore, not even my dead mother's necklace.

CHAPTER 2

MAE

"Goddamn, I can't believe we just walked five miles," Aaisha, one of my best friends, said, heaving as we walked away from the protest march around Witver city. She wiped the sweat off her brow with the back of her brown hand, her long hot-pink stiletto nails gliding against her forehead. "Mama needs something to drink, and some men."

Luca, my other friend, nodded to a bustling city restaurant that had a *No Wolves Allowed* sign on the door. "You can—"

"We ain't leaving you outside either, not with these crazy-ass people out here." She shook her head, her shoulder-length black banana curls frizzing in this heat, and walked ahead of us toward the Wolf District of the city. "Nuh-uh. We gotta go somewhere they aren't gonna kick us out of."

Cracked pavement, mossy clumps covering brick buildings, and boarded-up windows, the wolf sector of Witver's inner city wasn't large by any means. So small, in fact, that even the smallest percentage of city funding would drastically improve the neighborhood because just by walking across Hickory Avenue—from the human to the wolf side of Witver—it felt like entering a whole new world.

About a block away, a neon red sign flickered.

"How about we go to The Eclipse Bar?" I suggested.

"People get handsy in that bar, Mae. Why don't we get some liquor from the grocery store and go back home?" Luca said, placing one hand on my upper back and guiding me forward.

If I didn't know any better, I would've thought that Luca almost sounded ... possessive.

Not wanting people to get handsy with us ... or *me*?

I glanced up at him, a small smile creeping its way onto my face, my insides warming.

Aaisha turned around and arched a sharp brow. "I ain't waiting any longer. We're goin'."

In true Aaisha-fashion, she kicked the door open with the tip of her shoe and strutted into the hooting and howling room of wolves. Luca sighed and held the door ajar for me, his biceps flexing through his crisp white V-neck.

When we walked into the room, wolves sniffed the air, looked over their shoulders at Luca in disgust, and whispered to each other. I inched closer to him, not liking the way they eyed him up as people did to rogues. Luca might be a lone wolf, but he wasn't a rogue by any means.

Ignoring their judgmental stares, Aaisha strolled to a maroon-cushioned booth, sat, and picked up a menu like it was nobody's business. I awkwardly trailed behind Luca to the table, hating the attention, and slid in beside him—closer than I should have. But Luca had always been ... comfortable ... to me.

"Spill the beans," Aaisha said after the waiter dropped off three drinks for us. She wrapped her lips around the purple straw and leaned forward. "What happened with your dad the other night? You've been actin' weird all week."

"I might've met this guy." I drew my finger against an image of the Moon Goddess on the napkin and avoided eye contact with Luca, who stiffened next to me.

"You did?" Luca asked, gripping his cup tightly.

"Ooh, tell us all the juicy details!" Aaisha squealed. "What does he look like? Is he hot?"

Briefly glancing over at Luca, I swallowed hard, my heart jumping. "I was out to dinner with my dad, got into a fight with him about wolves, and stormed out of the restaurant and right into *him*. And … he's a wolf."

Aaisha bounced in her seat. "I'm so proud! My baby's growin' up so fast!"

Luca chuckled tensely and bumped his knee against mine. "You, uh, stood up for yourself for once?" he asked, thankfully directing the uncomfortable conversation elsewhere. He smiled at me, his brown eyes flickering amber for a second. "You're usually too much of a pushover."

"I ain't talking about that!" Aaisha said, cackling from the alcohol. "I'm talking 'bout Mae getting some sexy werewolf action!"

Those piercing green eyes of that mystery wolf flashed through my mind, and my arm hairs stood straight up. I brushed my fingers against the leather bracelet with small starry pendants that Luca had given me for my birthday last year. I hadn't taken it off for months.

"Okay, okay, that's enough," I said softly. Not only would I never see that wolf ever again, but wolves also didn't mate with humans. "You know nothing could even happen between us anyway. I'm human, and he's a werewolf. Our species don't date."

"Girl, you never know! You might be his"—she leaned across the table—"mate."

Luca grimaced. "Aaisha, that doesn't happen."

"Says who?"

"The Moon Goddess," Luca said, pushing the napkin with her image across the wooden table. "She chooses who our mates are, and she rarely, if ever, matches wolves and humans. A human doesn't typically survive the shift after a wolf marks them on the neck."

Aaisha held her glass of beer in the air. "Well, screw the Moon Goddess."

I kicked her under the table and shushed her as other wolves glared our way. The Moon Goddess was the most sacred being to the wolf species. They worshipped her every full moon, thanking her for another month on this earth. Wolf culture surrounded the moon, her rotations, and the Moon Goddess's innate powers to match two wolves to spend eternity with each other.

Aaisha rolled her brown eyes but then smiled at me. "For real, Mae, I'm glad you stood up to your dad. He deserves that and a kick in the ass sometimes." She scoffed. "And that Brett guy ... disgusting."

"I'm proud of you too," Luca said.

He leaned closer to me, his knuckles brushing against mine on the table, sending shivers down my spine. My heart leaped in my chest, thousands of what-ifs rushing through my mind. No matter how much I loved wolves, their Moon Goddess would never mate one to me, and I would never have the same kind of love that wolves shared in a mate bond.

Yet I couldn't seem to stop how I reacted to them, just as that mystery wolf had said.

Maybe in another life, I would be fated to be a wolf, to run free through the woods, and to love a mate. But in this one, I had been destined to fight for better lives, equal rights, and the ability to share beautiful friendships with them ... and to have the occasional hook-up, of course.

A tall, dark-eyed wolf appeared at the head of our table, a dragon tattoo covering the side of his neck. "Can I buy you a drink?" he asked Aaisha, staring down at her with hunger in his eyes.

Aaisha glanced up at him and then looked at me. "He talkin' to me?" she asked, pointing at herself for emphasis. After I nodded, she turned back to him with a huge smile, jumped up, and held out her hand. "Aaisha."

When they disappeared into the crowd, I sipped my drink and glanced over at Luca. "I want to go to more protests with you, but that was ... terrifying," I whispered, thinking back to all those men and women screaming at us and at the wolves for just ... being.

Apparently, it was a crime for wolves to be alive.

"That wasn't as bad as some other protests," Luca said, sipping on his drink.

"They threw wolfsbane into the crowd and snapped silver whips in front of the protesters," I said to him, fingers paling around my glass. If he didn't think that had been *that bad*, what was worse? What had those opposing protesters done to the wolves?

I gnawed on the inside of my lip and glanced up at the television in the corner of the room that played the nightly news. A wolf stood beside a fire outside the square, reporting about the latest protest that the *police* had instigated this time.

Luca leaned forward, placed one finger on my chin, and turned my head to look back at him. "Forget that for now," he said, amber specks floating in his brown irises. He drew his tongue across his lower lip, and I sucked in a breath. "We're here to relax, Mae, so relax."

Placing my elbows on the table, I tilted toward him and smiled. "And how do you suggest we do that besides getting drunk off this strong wolf beer that I *definitely* shouldn't be drinking?"

"If Aaisha disappears for the rest of the night, we'll have the whole apartment to ourselves," Luca said.

When Luca's eyes flashed gold, I sucked in a soft breath, my stomach fluttering at the sight of his wolf so close. We stared at each other for a few moments until, eventually, Luca pulled away and leaned back in the booth.

"We could, uh, watch that action movie that you've been wanting to," he suggested.

I looked away, my cheeks flushing, and gave a small smile. "Yeah, sure."

Two feisty she-wolves scooted into the empty booth where Aaisha had once sat, smiling at Luca.

"Hey, Luca," one purred at him, pressing her perky breasts against the table and toying with his shirt collar. "Haven't seen you in a while. How've you been?"

I clenched my hands into fists under the table as Luca tensed beside me. When the other girl dragged her claws across his forearm, I grabbed my empty glass and stood. "I'll leave you all alone. I don't want to intrude."

"Mae," Luca said, seizing my wrist. "You don't have to go."

"It's okay, Luca." I patted his shoulder like a friend would because that was all I could ever be to him. I gave the girls a tight smile, my chest tightening, and turned away. "I'm just going to get a drink ... or two."

Before he could convince me to stay, I hurried through the crowd to the bar. I didn't want to watch them flirt with my best friend, the man I ... I had wanted for so long. I couldn't stand to see them move their nails across his chest and purr at him—something I would never be able to do.

Sighing, I slid onto a leather stool that seemed to be cut and taped in the center and placed my glass on the bar. I wanted to look over my shoulder and watch Luca like a hawk, but I didn't want to feel this shitty anymore. I needed to just get over my stupid little crush.

Nothing would ever happen between us anyway.

"Mae!" Aaisha called, grabbing onto my shoulder and hauling herself toward me. Curly hair a wild mess, pupils dilated, and lipstick smudged all over, she grinned wickedly at me. "Hey, Mae!

We're going to get more *drinks!*" She exaggerated with a wink. "I might be back before tomorrow. Maybe. I don't know. Don't wait up!"

The man who had asked her for a drink wrapped his arms around her waist and mumbled something into her neck. She giggled like the maniac she was and wiggled her brows at me.

Before she left, I grabbed her hand. "Make sure to send me your location."

"Yes, *Mom*," she said, waving me off. "I'll be fine."

After she left, I slumped down in the stool and dared to look back at our booth. Luca had disappeared with those two girls, leaving our drinks and used napkins on the table. My phone buzzed in my pocket.

Luca: Get home safe with Aaisha.

My chest tightened at the thought of Luca going off with a couple of cute she-wolves for the night. It wasn't like this didn't happen often. I should be used to this by now. Ever since Luca's mate had rejected him and he asked to live with us, he had been sleeping with other girls to make himself feel better. I just … ugh … I wished that one night, one of those girls could be me. Maybe it would ease these feelings I had for him a bit.

Guzzling my drink, I listened to the rowdy music playing through the speakers and watched wolves grab she-wolves by their waists and sway to the steady rhythms together. I threw the glass back, thinking that if I got drunk enough, I could disappear into the crowd, too, and get snatched by the waist and taken home with someone.

"Kitten," someone growled into my ear from behind, his callous fingers sprawling around my hips. He trailed his nose up the side of my neck, which made me stiffen, my breath catching in the back of my throat. "I told you that I'd see you again."

CHAPTER 3

DAMON

I had been waiting to see that pretty human again for days. Fucking days.

After spinning on her maroon barstool, she smiled up at me with those rosy-red cheeks and piercing gray eyes. Between the alcohol running through my veins and my wolf on edge just from seeing her, I couldn't stop myself from grasping her face and feeling the tingles shoot up my arms.

She stared up at me in a haze, her eyes glossy from the Eclipse beer, and leaned into my touch, running her small and frail fingers over my larger ones. I growled at the gesture, knowing that I shouldn't be feeling this way toward a human—a damn human who would never be able to survive a shift into a wolf.

But I couldn't help myself.

When she tugged at the ends of my hair, I slipped my hands around her waist and stepped even closer to her. "Kitten, you don't want to see what happens when you get me excited," I murmured into her ear, wanting nothing more than to take her right here, right now.

She giggled and ran her hands down my abdomen, stopping right at the waistband of my jeans and hooking her fingers in the loops. "I think I do." After a moment, she blushed, her cheeks flaming red, pulled herself away as if she had never done something so bold before, and grabbed her drink.

Before she could take another sip, I took it from her and placed it back on the bar. "No more of this stuff. It's too strong for humans. Let's get you home," I said to her, not liking the way that some wolves from my pack glanced over at her. I grasped her elbow, scolding them through our innate mind link not to even look her way.

She was mine.

"Am I going home with you?" she asked, staring up with hopeful eyes.

I clenched my hands into tight fists, letting my claws slice right through the skin on my palms. If she were a wolf, I'd force her to come home with me. She wouldn't have a choice. But this woman was human, and I couldn't take the chance of bringing her home and losing all control of my wolf with her around.

If I accidentally bit her ... she'd die during the shift, just like my brother's mate had.

"No." I had to force the word out of my mouth.

Confusion crossed her face, brows furrowed. "No?" she asked, the confusion turning to fury. She ripped herself away from me and scanned the bar, turning back to her drink. "Then, I'm staying here."

"No, you're not. This is a wolf bar, and you're drunk. You're not staying here alone."

"I am not drunk," she said, hopping off the stool and nearly stumbling into me.

Growling, I grasped her upper arm to hold her steady and dragged her drunk ass out the exit with me. Goosebumps darted across my skin at our contact, and my wolf pleaded for power, begging to see her too. Yet I held him back, curled my fingers even tighter around her arm, and pushed her toward my car.

"Let me go! You can't do this!"

"You're drunk. I'm taking you home," I said, shoving her into my car.

There was no way in hell that I'd let her stay here with a bunch of rowdy, horny, and drunk wolves. While humans and wolves didn't mate, they still slept together whenever they could. And nobody was going to touch what was mine.

Nobody.

"You're not gonna do anything," she said, her words slurring.

I slammed the door and hurried to the driver's side before she could get out. When I slid into the car, I stiffened. Her sweet scent, trapped in such a small space, overwhelmed me to the point that my control almost slipped. *Almost.* I could feel my wolf on edge, ready to pounce on her whenever I offered the chance.

"Where do you live?" I asked, merging onto the road and heading toward the human sector.

She crossed her arms over her chest and glared out the window. "Let me go."

"Where. Do. You. Live?"

When she didn't say anything, I snarled and tightened my grip on the steering wheel. "Are you always a brat, or is it only when you drink alcohol?" I asked, letting the words slip from my stupid fucking mouth.

She turned toward me and narrowed those gray eyes. "Are you always annoying, or is it only when you talk to humans?"

Loving her attention—any attention that she gave me—I growled back and made a U-turn, driving to the forest. "I was just curious because both times I've met you, you've been very bitchy."

If she didn't want to tell me, then I would take her back to the pack house for the night. Just the night. She'd stay in one of the spare rooms, and I'd stay in control.

"WHAT? Was I bitchy when I stood up for your kind to my dad? Was I bitchy when you pushed me against the door? Hmm? Was I bitchy then?" she asked, flaring her nostrils and trying to look intimidating. It was almost cute.

I ignored her comments and drove home through the thick fog that lay among the massive trees. Under the shadows of monstrous oak trees, wolves raced across the cracked pavement streets and into the woods around us. I pulled up to my pack house—a large wooden cabin nestled in the center of Witver Forest—and parked.

"Come with me," I called over my shoulder to her as I walked up the stone path toward the front door. I needed to keep my distance because her scent—*her fucking scent*—was too much for me to handle for any longer.

When she stepped out of the car, some pack members glanced between us and whispered about her being a human. After what had happened to my brother and his mate, I had banned humans from my property, not wanting another human to die because of the innate yet forbidden decisions of one of my packmates.

But she wasn't just any human.

And she hadn't told me her address.

That's why I brought her here, I told myself.

After ushering her into the house and up the spiral staircase, I opened my bedroom door and gestured for her to walk in. I had other spare rooms that I should've brought her to. I should've. I fucking should've. But I hadn't. I didn't want her to sleep anywhere else. I wanted her in my bed with me, wanted her scent all over my sheets, lingering on everything she touched.

"What's this?" she asked, furrowing her brows and walking into the room, glancing from the large wall-length windows to the dim yellow lights glowing underneath my bed. She brushed her fingers against the beige comforter and then looked back over at me. "Why am I here?"

I placed my keys on the cherry-stained dresser. "You did say that you wanted to go home with me."

"That was before you called me bitchy. Now, I want to go home."

My wolf howled at the thought of her leaving. She couldn't. I couldn't let her go.

"I'm not going back out. You're sleeping here tonight."

"No, I'm not," she said, stumbling to the door.

Stop her, my wolf commanded.

Before I could stop myself, I stepped in front of her. She placed her palms on my biceps and shoved me backward, but I didn't move an inch. My talons lengthened slightly, and my canines extended, my wolf clawing to take power and claim the human before him. If I let her go, he'd surely take full control and force me to … to do something that I'd vowed to never do.

Huffing and puffing, she stomped to my closet and then into it, slamming the door behind her. I let out a breath that I hadn't realized I had been holding and slouched onto the bed, crossing my ankles and smiling at the door. She screamed inside the room and marched back out, her cheeks a rosy red.

I arched a brow. "Are you done embarrassing yourself?"

She snatched a blanket and pillow from the bed and tossed it on the floor. "You're so annoying."

"Are you seriously going to sleep on the floor?"

"Well, I'm not going to sleep with you," she said, twisting and turning on the hardwood until she finally settled on her stomach. She stared at the wall-length windows and out into the woods, lit with the moon. "I don't even know your name."

"Damon," I said, staring down at her, my wolf pleading with me to go sit by her, to lie by her, to touch her like we had at the Eclipse Bar earlier. The feeling of her skin on mine had been … fucking magical.

She hiked the blanket further up her shoulders to cover herself from me. "I didn't ask for it either."

I balled my hands into fists at her blatant disrespect and forced myself to breathe to calm down. Nobody in my pack ever dared to talk back to me like that, and if they did, I would put them in their place faster than they had time to say another word.

But I couldn't lose it in front of a human.

Yet when she turned around to face me, the moonlight bouncing off her gray eyes, and said, "I'm Mae," I couldn't stop myself from ripping the blanket off her, picking her up, and shoving her against those windows, my wolf in complete control.

With the scent of lilacs overwhelming me, tingles from her fingers against my chest electrifying me, her tiny gasp making me shiver in delight, I buried my face in the crook of her neck and drew my nose up the column of her throat. "Mate," I growled into her ear. "We found our mate."

CHAPTER 4

MAE

"Mate?" I whispered.

Part of me thought for just a moment that I was his mate. It would make sense. I had this odd attraction to him that I couldn't seem to quite shake.

I glanced at the tattoo on his chest of the woman in white—his Moon Goddess—which peeked out from under his shirt, and my heart ached. But as much as I wanted to be his, I couldn't be. It was impossible. Werewolves didn't mate with humans. Dad had told me, Brett had told me, Luca had told me—and he was a wolf, so he obviously knew.

With fury rushing through me, I slammed my hands into Damon's chest to push him back. "Why would you take me home? Why wouldn't you just leave me at the bar? Were you planning to sleep in the same bed as me, even when you knew who your mate was?"

Once mates met, they connected on such a deep level and latched on to every fragment of each other's existence that, it was believed, their souls merged into one. They were possessive and jealous creatures, craving their other half for themselves only. If a wolf found his mate with another, he'd lash out and be driven to the brink of insanity. I had seen it firsthand with Luca.

When Damon didn't say anything, I shoved him again, hating that I loved touching him with my fingers on his bare skin. "I thought you wolves actually respected your mates enough to not bring home another girl. You're not supposed to be like us humans; you're not supposed to cheat when you have the mate bond."

Damon growled, large and sharp canines glistening with saliva, and dark raven-colored flakes decorating his golden eyes. "We would never bring home another girl! We respect our mate."

"If you respected your mate, I wouldn't be here," I said flatly, curling my fingers into his chest and then dropping my hands by my sides, scolding myself for the way I felt for this man. It was wrong, so wrong.

"You're …" he started, his jaw twitching. Those beautiful, wolfish gold eyes flickered to green a few times and then eventually settled into their natural forest color. He shook his head and stepped back from me, canines shrinking into his human teeth. "You're right. I don't care about her."

Before I could stop myself, I asked, "Why?"

What had gone so wrong that he didn't love her anymore?

Suddenly, all emotions evaporated from his face, and he gave me a look so cold that I actually shivered in fear. He snarled at me and glared out the wall-length windows and into the woods filled with creatures of the night.

"She's weak. She could never hold the responsibilities of a luna, and help me run my pack."

My lips parted in disbelief. I didn't understand. How could he speak low of his mate?

"Listen, I don't want to talk about her anymore." He balled his hands into fists, veins protruding from his forearms, and tilted his head to look me in the eye. "I thought you'd be a good distraction from her for the night."

I slapped him across the face so hard that my hand stung. "You're disgusting."

Did I care that I was *just his distraction*? Maybe a little. Was I angry that Damon didn't care about his mate? Hell, yes. This man was nothing like the wolves that Luca had described. Damon didn't care about the bond, about how much that poor girl's heart must be hurting, knowing that her mate was out with other girls and trying to forget her.

The mate bond was so sacred, so damn sacred.

Hell, even though Luca's mate had rejected him, Luca *still* loved her.

How could Damon be so careless? Why was he acting this way?

Damon growled and rubbed his red cheek, glaring at me with such fury. Instead of being frightened by him like I had been at the restaurant, I'd had too much alcohol at the Eclipse Bar to really give two fucks about what he did to me. He might be an alpha, but he was a dick. A freaking big one too.

"Go to sleep. I'll take you home in the morning," he said between clenched teeth. Then, he stormed out of the room and slammed the door behind him, the harsh bang echoing throughout the house.

"You said that you'd take me home, not bring me out to breakfast," I said, crossing my arms and glaring across the Midnight Treasure Café table at Damon.

Outside the smudged windows, cars drove into the parking lot, dust propelling upward behind them. Black-and-white pictures decorated the walls behind the wooden coffee bar. Older wolves smiled at me from other booths and then grinned at their alpha, who studied the coffee-stained menu on the table between us.

"I wanted to bring you out," he said.

"Well, I don't want to be anywhere with you."

He growled and leaned forward, baring his canines at me. "Why are you still mad about last night? And why the hell do you care so much about the whole mate thing? You're not even a wolf."

I met his glare, leaning forward to get in his face and to not draw attention to us. "Because I think you should love, care about, and respect the person you're with or the person you're supposed to be with. She probably cares about you. You can't just treat her like she's nothing. Don't reject her, Damon. It'll break her."

"What do you know about rejection?" he snapped, green eyes flickering gold.

What did I know about rejection? I dealt with it every day with my best friend. Luca might act strong, but every time I looked into his brown eyes, I saw the sorrow. Hell, I could feel it. He slept with girl after girl to make himself feel better, but the next morning, he'd cry to me about it. I wanted to help heal him, but … but I couldn't, nor could I be with him either.

After shuffling my feet against each other, I grasped my glass of water and looked back at the menu. Luca wasn't any of Damon's business; I wasn't about to blab to anyone about the heartbreak that he had been going through for the past three years.

I glanced back up at Damon to see those piercing green eyes watching me carefully and a stupidly adorable, lopsided grin on his face. I shifted in my seat and forced myself to look away because if I didn't, all that talk about respecting his mate would go right out the window.

"Why don't you look at the menu and not at me?" I suggested.

"You're not on the menu?"

Cheeks flaming, I flared my nostrils and looked down. "Funny. Really funny."

"Morning, Alpha!" a she-wolf waitress said, walking up to our table and running her fingers up his forearm. She glanced over at me and smirked behind Damon's back at me, as if to say, *You're not the only one who gets his attention.*

I turned myself away, giving them privacy. What Damon did with her wasn't any of my business. It was obvious that he didn't care about his mate, whoever that poor girl was. And I didn't care about him or about the way that she-wolf ran her nasty fingers all over him. I really didn't. Damon might be the most attractive man I had ever had the pleasure of meeting, but it didn't matter.

"Let me know if you need anything, Alpha," she purred, not sparing me another glance.

When the she-wolf left, I found myself just staring at Damon, unable to pull my gaze away, and I couldn't fathom why. I ached to uncover the secrets he had spoken with his eyes and the memories he had seen with them, the hurt and pain and heartbreak within them.

He propped his elbows on the stained table, rested his chin on his palm, and leaned closer to me, his minty breath on my lips. With his other hand, he reached out and rested it next to mine, brushing his fingers against my knuckles, sending a rush through me. My breath caught in the back of my throat, the electricity between us awakening that inner hunger in me again.

I hated it. Hated the way I felt for him so much.

Yet I didn't pull away.

He trailed his fingers across each hill and valley of my knuckles, his claws just barely dragging against my skin. And I let him because ... I didn't understand how, after everything I had learned last night, I could still feel this way for him.

Was it wrong to lust after a man who had a mate? Was it wrong to crave his touch and to find comfort in it too? Was it wrong that I didn't *want* him to stop, that I didn't want this breakfast to end? What was Damon doing to me?

~

"I didn't pin you for a girl who lives in the forest," Damon said, parking in my driveway after breakfast. He sniffed the air as if he smelled something unusual, and then he shook his head and averted his attention back at me. "You seem like you'd live in the suburbs with that bigot father of yours."

"Ew, no." I scrunched my nose. "I can barely handle having dinner with him."

He paused and lightly brushed his thumb down my bottom lip. "Good, Kitten."

"Have you forgotten my name already?" I asked, arching a brow.

"No, I just like the nickname," he said, giving me a breath-taking smile—unlike that scowl he'd had last night when I brought up his mate. He hopped out of the car and leaned down to peer at me in the passenger seat. "It fits you."

A small smile tugged at my lips as I got out. "You don't have to walk in with me. I think I can make it twenty feet to the door without getting lost."

Damon shut the passenger door behind me and chuckled. "There are monsters in these parts of the woods, Kitten. I can't have anyone else trying to eat your sexy little ass."

"Anyone else?" I asked, arching a brow. "I don't recall—"

"*Heeeey girl!* Is this that hot wolf guy you were telling me about?" Aaisha shouted out from the upstairs window. "Wait a minute! Let me come down and meet him. I'm sure he's fine as fuck!"

With flushed cheeks, I pushed Damon back to the driver's side. In less than a minute, Aaisha would be down here, cracking inappropriate jokes to Damon, and asking me how good he was in bed right in front of him. Both things I *never* wanted to happen.

"You need to go," I said to Damon.

He leaned against the car and smirked. "You think I'm hot?"

"No," I lied, opening the door and shoving him toward it. "Now, you need to go."

"I want to see you again," he said, eyes shimmering as he stared down at me.

"Fine, fine," I grumbled, looking back at the front door.

She would just embarrass me, and I didn't want to inflate Damon's ego even more. It was already big enough for some ungodly reason.

"As long as you leave before she comes down."

"I'll pick you up tomorrow at seven then."

"Fine! Now, go!" I said, ushering him into the car.

He shut the door, rolled down the window, and smiled at me. "It's a date."

It's a date.

A date?

A date.

He drove off the driveway and down the street, his car disappearing into the forest. My eyes widened at the thought of agreeing to another date with the damn Witver devil. I'd just agreed, so he would leave and not have to meet Aaisha.

Aaisha threw open the door with one set of fake eyelashes glued on her right eyelid and the other set glued between her pointer finger and thumb. "Where did he go? I wanted to meet his cute ass."

"He is no cute ass," I said, walking inside and up the stairs to our second-floor apartment, of which she'd left the door wide open. "More like an annoying asshole."

She fired off questions in my direction, sulking at my brief replies. If I babbled on and on about him, she would fabricate this grand romance between us that would never happen. I refused to step in the middle of the drama between him and his mate. We'd go on one date, and that would be all.

If he actually appeared to be enjoyable, I would consider being friends with him.

But nothing more.

"So, what about you and that guy you left with?" I asked her, hoping to avert the attention elsewhere.

She walked into the bathroom, fixing her lashes and swiping five excessive layers of mascara onto them. "Best sex that I've ever had. I'm seeing him again tonight because Mama needs another dose of f-i-n-e." She shivered in delight and shrieked so loudly that our downstairs neighbors probably thought that this alpha was up here, having his way with her.

I grabbed her hair spray from the closet and let her go to town with styling her hair in a cute, curly updo, watching anxiously from the door because the fumes made me choke. I slumped against the wall, letting my mind wander back to the alpha I'd spent last night with. I had barely known that man for twenty-four hours, and I couldn't get him out of my racing thoughts.

And while I didn't want to admit it, I couldn't wait to see that man again.

CHAPTER 5

LUCA

I slammed my bloody, bare fists into the heavy bag until the scabs on my knuckles split open. The hanging black bag swung back and forth under the dim Dynamo Gym light, the grainy sand shifting around inside.

What was wrong with me? What had I done to not only make my mate reject me, but Mae too?

When those two she-wolves had approached me at the Eclipse Bar, I should've said no and pushed them away. I shouldn't have left with them, just to make myself feel fucking better. Because now, two nights later, I hadn't had the courage to make it back home and face Mae. I should've stayed with her, the one damn woman who actually made me smile after that pathetic rejection.

Sweat rolled down my abdomen—or maybe that was blood from my knuckles. I couldn't tell anymore, and I didn't quite care right now either. I pivoted on the bright red-and-blue mats, pounding away at the bag in hopes of making myself feel less shitty.

When she—I couldn't even think her damn name—had rejected me, I'd lost fucking everything. My pack. My lands. My dignity. And when I'd finally found someone who could be my entire world, I had blown it because ... because a wolf like me could never mate a human.

I was too terrified that she wouldn't be able to survive the shift.

In the past hundred years, only a handful of humans had.

Not only that, but Mae had already lost her mother. If she wanted me, and her father found out, he'd never talk to her again. Hell, he might even try to kill me. It wasn't that I was scared of him—I could probably tear him in two—but I didn't want Mae in the middle of that kind of drama.

I swung my leg in the air and smacked it against the bag, sending it flying so high that it nearly hit the ceiling as I cursed so loud that my voice echoed through the empty gym. The door behind me opened, and Mae's lilac scent drifted into the room.

"Luca?" she called.

Continuing to beat the bag to death, I desperately tried to ignore her because my wolf was out of control and had pent-up anger. I didn't have it in me to resist her like I usually did.

She flicked the light on and sighed. "Luca, I've been looking for you everywhere. Why didn't you come home last night?" she asked me from behind, probably nervously tugging on a strand of her silver-blonde hair.

When I didn't answer, she walked onto the mat, her figure appearing in one of the many mirrors. "Luca, are you okay? I know how you get the morning after you go home with *someone*. Do you want to talk about it?"

Not wanting to unleash my anger on her, I punched harder and let the blood seep down my fingers and onto the black leather bag.

Why hadn't the Moon Goddess given me an easy life with a

mate who loved me? Why had she given me rejection and heartbreak, and then someone I could never be with?

"Luca," Mae whispered, brushing her fingers against my back.

"WHAT?" I growled, ripping myself away from the bag and turning on my heel to glare at her. My canines extended past my lips as her bare neck drew me in closer, like it always did. I shook my head and pressed my lips together, letting my sharp teeth cut through my gums, making them bleed.

Gray eyes wavering, she swallowed and parted her lips but didn't say anything.

Guilt washed over me for snapping at her, and I sighed and glanced down between us. "Sorry, I just ..."

She moved closer and pushed some brown hair from my face. "It's fine. Are you okay?"

My lips quivered.

Was I okay? Was I fucking okay? I hadn't been okay for three fucking years now.

I knitted my brows and glanced up at her, one fat tear running down my cheek. Shifting my face away from her, I pushed it away, not wanting her to see me, out of all people, cry *again*. I wanted to protect Mae, to be strong for her, but all I felt was weakness.

Mae wrapped her arms around my sweaty waist and pulled me closer. "Luca, it's okay," she whispered, drawing her fingers across my cheeks to push away more tears that I couldn't seem to stop. "It's okay. It's okay."

My body heaved forward, my stomach tightening and my heart fucking aching. "Why doesn't she love me? Why doesn't my mate love me?" I asked, feeling nothing but pain shoot through my body. "Why can't she love me?"

I hated being so weak in front of her. I hated it.

"Luca," she said, intertwining her fingers with mine, "there are so many people who love you. I know it's not the same. I know that"—she glanced down at our hands—"you'll never feel the same way about anyone else. But Aaisha and I are here for you. We care about you." She looked back up at me and gave me her best smile, though I could see the heartbreak inside it. "We love you too."

After a few moments of tense silence, I smiled as best I could. "You want to get something to eat? You're all dressed up."

"Oh, um …" She tugged on a strand of her silver-blonde hair and chewed on the inside of her cheek. "Actually, I'm going out with someone I met at the Eclipse Bar the other night. I kinda just got roped into it."

"A wolf?" I asked, my canines lengthening slightly.

"It's just a one-time thing," she assured, shrugging but not holding eye contact with me.

"You're going to hook up with him?" I asked. I had no right to be jealous of Mae going out with someone, not after I had gone home with two girls the other night, but I couldn't stop myself from asking. I wanted—*needed*—to know.

She pulled away from me, her cheeks flaming, and turned back to the door. "No! We're just friends—I don't know if you can even call us that. He's kinda annoying."

I balled my hands into fists and grabbed my gym bag, watching my bloody knuckles heal slowly, thanks to a wolf's healing abilities. "You like him," I said, not as a question, but as a statement.

Mae was blushing and blushing damn hard.

I never saw her like this, except with me.

"No, I don't like him," she lied.

Pushing my hands into my black gym shorts, I walked to the door to hold it open for her. "All right." I gazed out into the deep thicket of Witver Forest and laughed so emotionlessly that I knew she saw right through it. "Well, I'm going to jog then. I'll see you back at the apartment after your date."

"It's not a date," Mae called after me, but I had already started sprinting through the forest, not having a destination but needing to let my wolf free for a few hours.

CHAPTER 6

MAE

"Having second thoughts?" Damon asked after pulling up to the side of a dirt road and parking near part of Witver Forest that I didn't recognize. He held the door open, arched one brow, and looked inside the car at me, waving one of his callous hands in front of my face. "Mae?"

Shaking my head to try to rid myself of thoughts of Luca, I jumped out of the car and aimlessly followed Damon through the woods to wherever the hell he was taking me. My chest tightened. When Luca had asked me to dinner, I'd wanted to go out with him so bad. I loved spending time with him more than I probably should because nothing could ever happen between us.

Which was the reason that I'd ditched him there altogether.

I had built a friendship so strong with Luca that sometimes I mistook us for something more. And … I couldn't anymore. I needed to keep my distance, no matter how much I wanted him. It would just end in heartbreak or … death.

"You okay?" Damon asked, pulling some overgrown mossy vines back from a deserted path for me to walk through.

"Where are you taking me?" I asked, following him despite the nervousness inside of me. It probably wasn't the smartest idea to get in the car with basically a stranger and not pay attention while he had driven through the most deserted part of the woods. "This place looks abandoned."

"Don't worry, Kitten."

After walking a few more minutes—while I was definitely worried—we came to a barbed-wire fence with a large *Danger: Wolves* sign attached to the metal wires. Damon walked about twenty feet to our right and pulled back part of the fence big enough for me to crawl through.

I eyed it, sighed through my nose, and crawled underneath. If he brought me here to kill me, I was already fucked. I wouldn't be able to outrun him in these woods, especially since he was a wolf. I'd have to pray to their Moon Goddess that this man wasn't a psychopath.

"It's just a bit farther up," Damon said, continuing forward.

About a quarter mile ahead, a large brick warehouse covered in thick vines and grassy moss stood within the curve of a flowing river. Ears flat against their heads, three wolves drank from it and looked up as we passed them. Almost instinctively, Damon wrapped his arm around my waist and led me to the door.

The closer we walked to the building, the more nervous I became. Damon wouldn't kill me, right? *No.* This was just Dad getting in my head, years of listening to him drill into me that all wolves were out to get us. But not all werewolves were bad. Luca surely wasn't.

Still, I found myself peeling his hand away.

He replaced it and clutched my waist tighter this time, fingers jabbing into my sides. "Kitten, please, let me."

"No," I said, ignoring my racing thoughts.

"I like feeling your touch."

"I-I don't care."

Picking up my pace, I hurried toward the building. Something inside me told me to stop, to turn around, and to run as fast as I could, away from this unknown place and back to my apartment with Luca. But I wanted to prove my father's views wrong. Damon wasn't going to kill me, and he wasn't a horrid creature, like my dad thought.

He shoved his opinions down my throat so much that I feared part of me had actually started to believe them. It had taken so long to undo all the damage he had done to me, and I hated that I still had to actively try to repair myself.

Damon grasped my hips again, turned me around to face him, and pushed me against the side of the building, trailing his nose up the column of my neck and sending shivers down my spine. "Kitten, don't act like you don't love my touch. I can smell how excited you are for me, just like the night I met you." He buried his head in my hair and inhaled my scent.

Suddenly, he tensed and sniffed me again, a growl rumbling from his throat. "Why do you smell like another wolf?"

My eyes widened, my breath catching in my throat. He must've smelled Luca all over me. But why was he getting so ... so possessive all of a sudden? So possessive and so frightening, staring down at me with those blazing golden wolf eyes.

"Answer me."

I wrapped my arms around my body and stared down at my shoes, unable to get any words out. If I told him it was Luca, someone I lived with, who knew what the hell Damon would do or how he'd react? I'd never seen him or even Luca like this ever.

"Who was it?" he snapped, vein pulsing. "I will kill him."

Placing my trembling hands on his chest, I took a deep breath. "I wasn't with anybody. I promise, Damon. It was nobody," I said. Yet when he still didn't calm down, I found myself pressing my back against the building and sliding to the ground, heart pounding. "Please ... please don't hurt me."

After a few moments, his eyes began shifting to lighter shades of gold until they became completely green. He crouched, reaching out his fingers to touch my shoulder, but I flinched away, terrified and afraid.

"I'm not going to hurt you," he said. "I'm sorry you had to see me like that. That was my wolf. I lost control of him for a second. I'm sorry."

"Why?" I whispered, hugging my knees to my chest. "Why did you get like that?"

He sat down beside me, about a foot away, and sighed. "Sometimes, my wolf gets ... jealous."

"Sometimes? The way you forced me out of the Eclipse Bar the other night, the way you acted at the diner the other morning, just now. It seems like every time I'm with you, you're like this."

He brushed his knuckles against my cheek, and for some ungodly reason, it calmed me. "My wolf can't control himself around you."

"Why not?" I asked, wanting him to be straightforward for once. When he didn't answer, I shook my head in disappointment and gazed out into the mossy forest. I didn't want to be here with him, not after that. I mean, I did, but I couldn't. "I want to go home."

"Give me a chance and let me show you that werewolves are better than what your dad has made them out to be."

"I don't listen to anything my dad says about them. I know there are good ones and bad ones, just like there are good humans and bad humans," I said to him, glancing over into those beautiful green eyes that I just wanted to get lost in for days.

"Then, let me show you I'm one of the good ones."

Knowing that I wouldn't be able to say no to him, I crossed my arms. "You get one chance, Damon. Don't mess it up."

He jumped, grabbed my hand, and led me to the entrance. Above the door, someone had spray-painted images of wolves, the moon phases, and a naked woman with long silver hair and a white aura around her. She seemed so real that her hair looked like it could come off the building and blow in the breeze.

The Moon Goddess, goddess of the wolves, was absolutely beautiful.

Damon placed a hand on my shoulder and led me into the noisy warehouse, where groups of young humans and wolves were laughing together and flinging axes at battered wooden targets. My eyes widened slightly, and the cheers and howls and camaraderie from everyone together made me actually smile.

This was the future of Witver. This was the future I so desperately fought for.

Wolves and humans mingling and celebrating together.

"Welcome to ax throwing!" Damon said with a huge, lopsided grin.

"You brought me here for our first date?" I asked, brow arched. The words had come out faster than I could stop them, and I slapped a hand over my mouth. "I mean ... to hang out for the first time?"

He led me to an empty lane, his smile even wider somehow, and seized two axes hanging from a shelf. I took the smaller ax from him, ignoring the way my fingers tingled as they grazed against his.

He rocked back on his heels and watched me. "Give it a chance, Kitten. You'll like it. I promise."

After demonstrating the proper way of throwing the ax, he hurled it at the target, launching it so forcefully that the tip of the ax cracked the wood down the center. Damon cursed under his breath and jogged to grab the broken pieces of wood.

"How'd I know you'd do that again, Damon?" a human said behind us, shaking his head and approaching us with another circular wooden board. The human tossed the board to Damon and walked closer to me, crossing his arms and smirking. "I'm Dylan, one of Damon's…"

"Friends." Damon grinned.

"*If* you could call us that," Dylan said, sarcastically. "You'd better kick his ass and put him in his place. He's too arrogant for his own good sometimes."

Damon waved him off and gestured for me to line up with the target. "Your turn."

Grasping the ax in my hand, I stood about fifteen feet from the target, drew it back over my shoulder, and hurtled it forward. Instead of hitting the target, the wooden handle smacked against the concrete wall and dropped to the ground.

"Try it again," Damon said, handing the ax back to me. He stood behind me, placed one hand on my hip, and wrapped his other over mine to steady my grasp on the ax. "Bring it over your head and focus on the target, Kitten," he murmured in my ear, his warm breath fanning my neck.

I closed my eyes, unable to focus when he stood this close to me.

"Now, step forward and release," Damon said, moving forward with me.

Following his movements, I chucked the ax and cracked a smile when it hit the upper-right corner. A rush of adrenaline coursed through my veins when Damon clapped his hands together and then wrapped one arm around my waist, pulling me closer.

"I told you that you could do it, Kitten. Next, I'm going to teach you how to break the board."

"You'd better not!" Dylan called from somewhere in the warehouse over the howling.

"We just won't tell him," Damon said, yanking the ax off the board and handing it back to me.

〜

"So, how was it?" Damon asked after parking in my driveway.

I picked at the calluses from gripping the wooden handle so hard on my palms. We had thrown axes for almost three hours, never stopping once, and I'd had an … amazing time. Better than I'd imagined it could be.

"Good," I said.

"Good enough for a second date?" he asked from the driver's side, the moonlight bouncing off his green eyes.

"Sure, but I wouldn't call it a date."

"But you did call it a date earlier."

Frowning, I pulled my gaze away from him. Sappy feelings were creeping up on me, slowly seeping into my veins, becoming even more intense than my feelings for Luca. I needed to put a barrier between Damon and me, but I didn't want to stop seeing him.

"Well, it wasn't," I said. "Calling it a date would mean that there is something romantic between us, and you have a mate," I said, glancing at the way his knuckles paled on the steering wheel, golden specks appearing in his green eyes. "Damon, you know that I'm right."

He sighed deeply. "As long as I get to see you again."

"Of course!" I said a bit too excitedly, but I should've told him no.

"Tomorrow?"

"I can't tomorrow. My dad and I are going to see my mom."

"Where does your mom live?"

"We're visiting her grave," I said, tearing a callus off my palm. Before he could apologize or sympathize, I held my hand up. I didn't like to be pitied over her; I didn't even remember her. All I had left of her memory was what Dad told me. "I have accepted her death. I don't need you to say that you're sorry or something like that. Don't pity me."

"Yes, girl! Get it!" Aaisha hollered out from the second-floor window again.

Damon gazed out the windshield and chuckled, breaking the awkward silence. "She's something else."

"Get it! Get it!" she shouted even louder, her voice screeching.

Damon squinted at her. "Is she talking into a megaphone?"

Unable to hold myself back, I burst out laughing, clutching my stomach and leaning over onto Damon for support. Tears slipped down my cheeks. No matter what she was going through, Aaisha never disappointed.

"There is literally never a dull moment with her."

"Kiss her!"

When those words came out of her mouth, my laughter died down, and I glanced over at Damon to see those golden eyes of his wolf again. My breath caught at the thought, though we couldn't kiss. I reached for the door handle to make a quick exit and to avoid the awkward tension, but he locked it like the creep he was.

"Let's give the lady what she wants," he said, brushing his fingers against my knee.

Heat rushed up my thighs. I placed a hand on his chest to stop him from leaning closer to me. "No. You know how I feel about this. You have a mate."

"I also know how you feel about me," he murmured, tucking a strand of hair behind my ear. "You feel something between us, something more than the friendship you keep insisting upon. I know that you want it just as much as I do. Stop denying yourself something so pure and simple."

"Nothing about this is pure or simple."

"It's just a kiss, Mae."

"Just a kiss? I barely know you!"

"You went on a date with me and slept in my bed already. What more do you need?"

"Nice try, but that doesn't count." I crossed my arms and ignored the warmth in my core.

"Tell me how you feel about me after one kiss. If there is nothing, I won't push this anymore. I promise."

One kiss. That was it. It wouldn't hurt. It wouldn't change my feelings about him and about this situation. It would just be one simple kiss to prove to myself and to him that we didn't have the connection that I kept thinking about.

"Fine," I whispered. "As long as you're serious about leaving me alone."

"I'm serious about it," he said, jaw clenching slightly.

Lacing his hand into my hair, he pulled my face closer to his, his honeysuckle scent overwhelming my senses. I swallowed nervously and closed my eyes, waiting for his soft lips to touch mine. Before he kissed me, he pulled away slightly, leaving me feeling rejected.

"I have to clarify something first, Kitten. When I said I would leave you alone, I really meant that I wouldn't pursue you romantically, but that doesn't mean I won't still bother you. I still want to be your friend ... at the very least."

"Well, that's what I assumed. I didn't think I could get rid of you that easily. You're very persistent and annoying, like a gnat."

"A gnat? I'm not as annoying as those little things."

"Yes, you are."

"No, I'm not."

"Damon, you're definitely more annoy—"

"*What the heck are you waiting for? Stop stalling!*" Aaisha screamed through her megaphone, her voice echoing through the quiet and dark Witver Forest.

Heart pounding, I placed my hand on his stubble and inched closer to him until our noses grazed together. Before I could pull back or change my mind, he closed the distance between us and pressed his lips onto mine. A rush of adrenaline shot through my veins, my bones, my very being.

Hesitant at first, I didn't kiss him back. This feeling wasn't anything I'd ever experienced before, and it scared me. I didn't understand how a simple kiss could ... drew me even closer to him somehow.

When he pulled back, I drew him near and kissed him even harder, parting my lips and slipping my tongue into his mouth. This kiss was supposed to be just a peck on the lips, but ... I didn't want him to stop. I wanted his lips all over my body, in places that nobody had explored before.

He trailed a hand up my thigh, and goose bumps darted across my skin. While our situation, my dad, and the stigma around werewolves and humans had always held me back from pursuing a mixed relationship, with him ... I just couldn't explain it. With a single kiss, I surrendered all of my fears and was left craving more, turning into a starved animal.

Finally pulling away, I pushed his hand off my thigh and tried so desperately to breathe. *Was it hot in here, or was it just me?*

Eyes shifting from green to gold and back to green, Damon gripped the steering wheel hard and stared right ahead, as if his wolf was fighting for dominance.

"I-I, uh ..." I panted, not knowing what to say. Though I wanted to kiss him again and again and again, I refused to admit that I'd liked it. I couldn't do that to his mate. I just ... I couldn't. So, I leaned over him to unlock the door from his side and slipped out with my awkward self. "I have to go! See you sometime later. Hopefully, a lot later! Not soon! Ha-ha."

After I ran to the apartment and slammed the door closed, Aaisha jumped up and down and squealed beside me, blocking my escape to my bedroom. "*Yas, girl*! I can't wait until you two give me babies soon!"

I rested my back against the door.

I'd kissed Damon. I'd really kissed him.

"I'm beginning to think that you're his mate!"

"Come on, Aaisha," I said, shaking my head to get the thought out of my mind even though I sorta, kinda thought it too. "You know that can't happen. Werewolves and humans can't be mates. Luca even said it."

"But what if he's wrong?" she asked.

"I know it sounds magical or whatever, but don't drag me into this fantasy world that you thought up about werewolves and humans mating with each other. We don't mate and can't. The Moon Goddess never pairs humans with wolves."

But ... what if she was right? What if everything I had been told was a lie, thought up by humans to stop our species from mating? So many humans wanted to keep our blood pure and believed associating with werewolves would taint our existence. *Maybe I really am his mate. That would explain our bond so well.*

After mulling over the thought, I shook my head. It was stupid. There was no way I could be his mate. Werewolves, especially alphas, always claimed their mates right when they found them. If I were Damon's mate, he would have taken me as his already, and he hadn't.

CHAPTER 7

LUCA

"Luca, you're back!" Mae said, jumping up from the couch as I walked into the apartment. She wiped her tired eyes and padded over to me in the kitchen, leaning against the counter and yawning.

I flicked the light on and stared down at her, brows furrowed. "Did you wait up for me?"

"Maybe ..." She grabbed my hand and pulled me back toward the front door. "Come on. I wanna get ice cream with you. Splitz's Creamery down the street closes at twelve. If we leave now, we'll make it there in time."

Pulling my hand away from hers, I stuffed them into my jean pockets and ignored the ache in my heart. From the urgency in her voice, I could tell that she wanted to make up for leaving me earlier tonight. But she didn't have to make up for anything; we weren't an item.

"Luca," Mae drew out, tugging me down the stairs. "Stop moving so slow."

After sighing, I picked up my sluggish feet and walked with her down the street to Splitz's Creamery to see someone closing and locking up the doors.

Mae pulled me along, her short legs moving fast, just to a jog. "Wait! Do you have time for two more?"

The she-wolf held the door open ajar, giving me a small smile and bowing her head so slightly that I didn't think that Mae picked up on it. "Sure. But two more, and that's it."

Mae pulled me into the creamery, bouncing on her toes in front of the twenty flavors of hard-served ice cream. She usually spent ten minutes gazing at all the flavors, but she always settled on...

"Vanilla," I said, glancing down at Mae with a small smile. "Two vanilla cones, one covered in rainbow sprinkles and the other without it." When the woman started making them, I bumped my shoulder into Mae's, leaning closer to her. "You know you're so plain."

"Says the guy who runs for fun," her smart mouth said back.

"Hey, what's wrong with running?"

Mae grabbed her vanilla cone. "I'm just saying, there are other forms of cardio you're missing out on."

Once I grabbed my sprinkled one and paid, I walked out into the humid summer night with Mae. "Like what?"

"Like—" She stopped mid-sentence, cheeks flaming, as if she'd thought of something dirty, and then looked down at her feet. "Like ... I don't know, uh ..."

My lips curled into a smirk as I listened to her fumble over her words. If she had just come out and said it, I'd have been more than happy to try it out. With her. Goddess, I had been waiting for years now.

"You can stop stuttering, Mae," I said, sitting on a bench outside of Splitz's. "We both know what you really mean."

"And what do I really mean, Luca?" she asked, biting her ice cream.

"You want to fuck me."

Breath catching in the back of her throat, she stared at me with wide eyes and let some ice cream drip down her cone and onto her fingers. "I don't want to ... to ... do that with you," she said finally, voice quiet. After another moment, she tore her gaze away from me. "You know that ... we can't. *I* can't."

Neither she nor I had to say it for us to know that we could. We definitely could, but we'd both catch feelings for each other once it happened. We wouldn't be able to keep our hands off each other. Hell, I had to hold myself back now from touching her every chance I got.

I leaned my forearms onto my knees and looked down at the cracked pavement, diverting the attention elsewhere. "How was your date tonight?"

She stayed quiet, kicking her legs back and forth under the bench because they weren't long enough to reach the ground. "It was fine."

"Just fine?"

"Just fine," she said quickly and with finality so that I wouldn't push it.

"Are you going to see him again?" I asked, unable to stop myself.

"Luca," she whispered, "don't do this."

I tightened my hand around the cone, almost hard enough to break it, and sat back on the bench, annoyed and pissed the fuck off that this guy—whoever he was—was taking Mae from me. It might only be a hook-up, only a few-nights fling, but it still fucked me up.

After another couple moments of silence, Mae stared out into the dark forest. "I'm going with my dad tomorrow morning to visit my mom's grave, and I'm dreading it. After the other night at dinner, I haven't answered any of his calls. I don't want to listen to another earful about wolves."

Crossing my ankles, I leaned back further and watched the

moonlight make her silver-blonde hair glow in the night. "Do it for your mom. She would've wanted you to try to get along with him even though he's a dick."

She glanced back at me with those gray eyes, licked some ice cream from her fingers, and reached into her pocket to pull out a silver necklace, the metal so strong that it almost immediately repelled me. Wolves could spot silver just by its metallic glint; it was too dangerous for us to even touch, or we'd burn.

"He gave me her necklace the other night. I kinda wanna wear it, but … I'm afraid that he's lying about it, and it's just to repel wolves," she said, taking the circular pendant between her fingers. Though the pendant was silver, it looked almost like a capsule that held a sort of reddish liquid inside of it.

"It looks … familiar," I said, not knowing where I'd seen this type of pendant before but sure that I had. After studying it for another moment and coming up with nothing, I nudged her. "If it's hers, you should wear it. It's the only thing that you have left of her, isn't it?"

She frowned. "I guess so …"

Tossing the rest of my cone in the metal trash bin beside us, I went to grab for the necklace. "Let me help you put it on."

"But it's silver. It'll burn you."

"I don't mind it for you," I said, taking the silver chain and wrapping it around her neck. My fingers blazed, the skin searing off at the mere touch. But for Mae, I pushed through the pain and clasped it around her neck. "Perfect."

Again, she grasped the pendant in her fingers and smiled at me. "Thank—" She glanced behind me, stopping suddenly, and frowned. "Wait." She abruptly stood up, gaze still focused on Witver Forest surrounding us.

"What's wrong?" I asked, grasping her hand.

She looked back at me. "I saw the man who my dad insulted last week at the restaurant. I wanted to apologize to him for it."

I peered around the woods, unable to pinpoint another wolf

or human, even with my enhanced sense of smell and hearing. "Where is he?" I asked, standing beside her, ready to attack in case someone really was stalking the woods.

She looked behind me and frowned. "He-he was right behind you."

After glancing around us once more and still not spotting anyone, I ushered Mae back to the house. "It's probably just your lack of sleep, Mae. You can't be staying up all hours of the night, or you'll end up seeing people who aren't there," I reassured her.

But something didn't feel right.

If there really was someone out in the woods, why couldn't I sense them?

CHAPTER 8

MAE

Fog hung heavily around the cemetery, woven around the gravestones, and sitting feet off the muddy grass. Rain pounded down onto our black umbrellas like a gloomy serenade. I held Dad's umbrella as he knelt before Mom's gravestone, his body doubled over and his head in his hands.

He drew his finger over the indentations of her name and placed a single moonflower—Mom's favorite—on the grave. The flower emitted a white glow—the only sense of hope on this dreary afternoon—gleaming and glimmering under the downpour.

Dad's lips trembled, tears spilling down his cheeks. I knelt beside him and hugged him to me, like I did every year. I didn't remember Mom; she'd died when I was merely three years old, so coming here didn't affect me like it probably should've.

"I miss her so much," he cried. "Every day, a bit more, Mae."

I patted his back, lost for words. "It's okay, Dad. You've made it this long without her."

"It could've been longer if that wolf hadn't killed her!" he cried, ripping himself away from me and staring around the forest, as if he was looking for one to kill too. "I hate them. I hate that one took her. She didn't deserve it."

Pressing my lips together, I sat my ass right on the mud, Mom's necklace swaying around my neck, and rubbed his back, forgoing the umbrella. It wasn't really keeping us dry anyway. Hair matted to my head, I looked up when I noticed two gold eyes staring at us from deep in the woods. If Dad saw him, he'd blindly run after that wolf as retribution.

"Dad, just because one werewolf killed her doesn't mean that they're all bad people."

"How can you even say that, Mae?" He shook his head and scowled at me. "How can you stick up for people like that? For people who killed your mother?!"

Fury running through my bones, I asked, "What if it were humans who'd killed her? Would you hate humans too?"

"Humans aren't savages! We don't kill people for no reason at all! Only they do that."

Deciding that I would never be able to convince him, I ushered him to the car and sat in my muddy pants all the way back to his house. As much as I loved and wanted to be there for Dad, I didn't want to hear this. It was the same shit every year, every day even.

When Dad pulled up to the house, he stormed out of the car, as if my presence disgusted him, and pushed his house key into the lock. I followed him up the stairs and picked up a large blue ceramic pot covered in sheets of plastic that the mailman must've delivered while we were out.

"What's this?" I asked Dad, stepping into the house.

He took it from me, placing it on the wooden side table and pulling the plastic off. Suddenly, he stopped and gasped, his eyes widening. "Moonflowers," he whispered. "Your mother's favorite …"

A bouquet of fifty moonflowers sat in the pot, glowing so brightly against Dad's fair skin.

"Who are they from?" I asked.

Dad grabbed the small note attached. *"Mr. Cogan, I am greatly sorry for your loss,"* he read. Suddenly, he stopped reading and crumpled the note in his hand, his jaw twitching. *"Alpha Damon."* He gripped the pot so tight in his hand that I thought he'd break it to pieces.

My insides fluttered, and a smile stretched across my face. Damon had sent Dad flowers and not just any flowers—moonflowers. Even though Dad hated him and had insulted him the other week, Damon had decided to be the bigger person and send him flowers on the anniversary of his wife's death.

Dad hurled the pot at the wall beside me and let it shatter, small, sharp fragments raining down on the ground and a piece impaling my shin.

I screamed and grabbed my leg, blood gushing out of the wound. "What the hell, Dad?! What was that for?"

"It was from one of those things! What did you expect?"

"I expected you to not act like *one of those things*! You're always saying how savage and dangerous they are, and then you go act like one." I shook my head at him and hobbled to the hallway. "What the fuck is wrong with you?"

Dad flared his nostrils, his bushy brows furrowing. "Don't you EVER compare me to one of *them*."

"Or what, Dad? What are you going to do? Throw another flowerpot at me?"

He slammed his fist down on the side table, rattling his keys and phone. "Mae! Stop it now! I can't believe you keep defending them. You're just like your mother. She always had a soft spot for those disgusting beasts. I just can't believe that you would have one too, even after they killed your own blood."

I sighed, tired of having this conversation over and over

again. He was blind with rage; he couldn't see that I was in pain, that blood was pouring down my muddy leg.

"Dad, not all of them are bad. I keep trying to tell you this. Damon is not a bad guy. If you got to know him, he is actually sweet and—"

"Are you friends with him, Mae?! I thought I'd raised you better than that!"

The doorbell rang, and I exhaled sharply and yanked open the door.

Brett stood under an umbrella with a big smile on his face and chocolate cake in his hand. "Hey, Mae and Mr. Cogan." He glanced between us, sensing the tension. "I, uh ... sorry I came over, unannounced. I thought you both could use some company and some sweets, but I'll leave you alone."

After giving me the most ruthless glare, Dad turned to Brett and smiled—*freaking smiled*—like there wasn't a piece of ceramic impaled into my shin. "Thank you, Brett. At least someone has some sense around here."

"Right. I don't have any sense." I hobbled back to the hallway and shook my head. "Come on in, Brett. I'm going to go get cleaned up and then leave. You can spend time with my dad because he doesn't want to spend that time with me, obviously," I said, gesturing down to my shin.

He would rather scream and yell about the beasts than acknowledge what he had just done.

"Why don't you go help Mae?" Dad said to Brett.

I cursed him out under my breath, the blood rushing down my leg in a red trail. After running a towel under warm water, I squatted on the toilet and wrinkled my nose as I wiped the blood off my leg.

Brett knelt beside me, taking the towel and gripping my calf to hold my trembling leg still. I tugged my dress higher up my legs, so he could wash off all of the blood, and winced when his gaze flickered upward for a moment.

Preparing to remove the jagged piece from my shin, he placed a hand on my thigh and held his palm open for me to take. "This is going to hurt. If you need to, you can hold my hand," he said.

Instead of taking his hand like he wanted, I balled my hands into fists and took a deep breath of air. When he lightly tugged on the piece, a sharp pain shot up my leg. I wrapped my hand around his and dug my nails into his palm until he pulled it out.

After wiping off more blood, he wrapped my leg in gauze. "There you go."

"Thanks," I said, giving him a small smile.

"Let me drive you home. I'm sure your dad needs some time to cool off, and you need a ride back, don't you?"

Though I didn't want to leave Dad on the most sorrowful day of his life, I couldn't stand to stay here any longer. So, I grabbed Brett's hand and accepted his invitation to drive me home. Brett might have the same opinion of wolves, but at least he wasn't as forward about it.

I could get through a simple car ride with him, couldn't I?

CHAPTER 9

DAMON

I leaned against my parked car in Mae's driveway with my arms crossed and my heart fucking racing. Mae was in insurmountable pain; I could feel it deep in my bones that something had gone wrong at her father's house. My wolf hadn't stopped aching since this morning.

If it wasn't a human-only neighborhood, I would've gone straight there to find her.

Now, I was stuck, waiting for her to—

A white BMW drove up the driveway, Mae in the passenger seat and as close as could be to the window, as if she didn't want to be anywhere near the driver. And when I saw that loser who had claimed to be her boyfriend the other night behind the wheel, I didn't blame her.

He parked beside me and glanced over at her. "I wanted to ask you if you'd like to get coffee with me sometime," he said, placing his hand on her thigh.

Ripping the door open, I pulled Mae out and pushed her

behind me. "She doesn't. You can leave," I said, slamming the door closed and waving my hand for him to back the fuck out of her driveway and get out of my sight before my wolf lost control.

Yet he had the damn audacity to get out of his car and walk toward us. "So, this is why your dad got mad, huh? You've been hanging out with this animal..." He flicked his tongue toward me and shook his head in disgust. "Shouldn't you be off, killing some rogues or pulling ticks out of your fur or something?"

"Brett!" Mae scolded, gray eyes wide.

I stepped forward, my canines and claws extending. I swore to the Moon Goddess that I'd kill him one day—one day that Mae wasn't frightened and hurt behind me. I would rip him piece by piece and smile in all the glory of it.

"Damon, please don't," Mae said, grabbing my hand. "I don't want you going to jail."

Brett postured. "You should be on a leash."

Mae grabbed my bicep and pulled me to my car, glaring back at Brett and pleading with him to leave. Deciding not to put up any more of a fight—because he'd fucking die against me—he hopped into his car and sped off down the road.

"Damon, what are you doing here?" Mae asked, a silver necklace gliding across her neck.

I balled my hands into fists, claws slashing through my palms. "What was he doing here? Why were you in his car?"

"He was bringing me home. I'd gotten into a fight with my dad."

"And you called him to bring you home? You could've called me."

Mae placed her hand on her hip. "First off, I can have friends other than you. Secondly—"

"No," I said, feeling the jealousy and possessiveness creep up into my veins.

"No?"

"You're mine," I growled.

She huffed. "You know what? I'm done talking to you."

"You're right," I said, grabbing her hips and shoving her against the car, burying my face in the crook of her neck and inhaling her sweet lilac scent. I'd claim her here one day. I'd fucking do it, so Brett wouldn't even think about touching her again. "We're done talking."

Unable to control my wolf, I laced my fingers into her silver-blonde hair and kissed her as hard as I could, waves of ease washing through me. Yesterday, the soft brush of her lips had sent tingles throughout my body. But today, my rough lips dominated hers in any way that they could.

Despite her hesitation, she brushed her fingers across the stubble on my face and pulled me closer. When she parted her lips, I slipped my tongue into her mouth and trailed my fingers down her body, wanting to touch every inch of her already.

My brother and his human mate flashed through my mind, her harrowing screams tormenting me every time I thought about taking Mae. As much as I wanted her, we could never be together like that. So, I pulled away and rested my forehead against hers, breathing raggedly.

"You ..." she started, drawing a finger against the corner of her lips. "You don't get to kiss me whenever you want. We made a deal, remember? You have a mate, and I'm just a human. We can't be together."

Maybe not, but I couldn't leave her alone. It wasn't that easy.

"I distinctly remember that you liked the kiss," I said.

"I never said that I did!" she said, tugging at her silver necklace. After huffing and puffing, she crossed her arms. "Why are you even here anyway? I told you that I was busy today and couldn't meet you."

I scratched the back of my head, feeling a couple of last raindrops from today's storm smack against my forehead. "Something told me that you were in trouble and hurt. I needed to see if you were okay."

She stayed quiet for a few moments. "You felt my pain?" she whispered.

Not wanting her to pry into *why* I'd felt her pain, I shrugged. "Why were you in pain?"

Glancing down at the ground, she held out her leg, wrapped in gauze.

"Who did that to you?" I seethed, feeling fury boil inside me again. "I'll kill him."

"It was an accident," she said quickly.

"Who was it?" I growled.

"My dad."

My canines extended even more, and I balled my hands into fists. "He will pay for this."

"Damon, please, just forget about it. I can't deal with any more drama today, please."

Though I nodded in response, I couldn't just let it go. If her father had no problem doing that to his own daughter, only the Moon Goddess knew what else that man was capable of, and I didn't want my ... *mate* to be in danger.

After convincing Mae to come back to the pack house, I opened her car door and led her to the backyard. An aroma of burning charcoal and piquant barbeque drifted around the yard, light smoke wafting up from the grill. Small pups ran around the lawn, tackling each other and staining their pants at the knees with mud and grass.

Wolves smiled and bowed their heads to us, and I wanted so badly to announce that I had found my luna. I had looked forward to this moment for years, yet I couldn't claim Mae and risk her life like that. My brother had done it to his mate, and now, they were both dead.

Instead, I grabbed Mae's hand and led her into the pack

house, where Mom sat at the dining table with some higher-ranked wolves in my pack.

"Hey, Mama," I said, kissing her graying hair and then pulling out a seat for Mae across from her.

Mae eyed the chair and fiddled with her necklace. "Damon, I don't think that—"

"You need to eat," I said, raising my brows and gesturing for her to sit. "Eat with us."

"But—"

"Sit."

Inhaling sharply, she sat and briefly glanced up at Mom, her cheeks flushed. I sat beside her at the head of the table and brushed my foot against hers to calm myself and her. She peeked over at me and gave me a small smile.

"Damon, would you like to introduce us all?" Mom asked, grabbing some food from the center of the table.

The higher-ranked wolves stopped chatting and looked over at us, all their eyes studying Mae.

"This is Mae." I placed my hand on Mae's shoulder. "Mae, this is my mom and my beta, Samuel," I started before introducing every one of my high-ranked wolves with their names and titles, knowing that she probably wouldn't need to remember everyone. She couldn't be my luna after all.

When I finished, Mom leaned closer to me and to Mae, grinning widely, as if she was excited. She never was excited about meeting any girls I brought home. Maybe she saw something in Mae, or maybe she could just tell that Mae meant something more to me than anyone else had.

"Would you like to tell us anything else about Mae?" Mom asked.

Tensing, I looked down at my food. I didn't want to answer the question aloud.

"Is she your mate?" Mom clarified.

My wolf howled inside of me, clawing for control to claim

that Mae would be my mate and my pack's luna. I wanted to so desperately, but when I closed my eyes, I saw my dead brother's body in the bath with an empty bottle of wolfsbane floating beside him.

"No," Mae said politely. "I'm just a friend."

Mom looked at me, expecting me to refuse. Instead, I clenched my jaw and nodded along with Mae. She might be my mate, but I couldn't take her. I just wanted to spend as much time with her as I could. Because whether I claimed her as a mate or not, our love would be short-lived.

"Oh, that's all right," Mom said, shaking her head and plastering a fake smile on her face.

Mom had wanted me to find my mate for so long, and I hated lying to her. But … I couldn't let my pack down, not after how far we'd come since Dad had run us into the ground.

Mom sipped on her wine and looked back over at Mae. "Mae, that's such a beautiful necklace! Where did you get it?"

"It was my mom's," Mae said, drawing her finger across the silver.

"Well, it's beautiful," Mom said.

"Yeah, Mae. It looks really good on you," my beta, Samuel, said, smiling at her.

Unable to stop myself, I growled at the compliment that my beta, my most trusted man, had given my mate. Everyone quieted down once more and stared over at me with wide eyes, especially Mom.

"Don't compliment her," I said through the mind-link to Samuel. *"She's … she's …"*

I wanted to say that she was mine, but I couldn't get the words out because, really, she wasn't. One day, I would have to set her free and take another woman as a mate, a woman who was a wolf and not human, like her.

CHAPTER 10

MAE

*D*inner couldn't have been more awkward. I didn't know anyone; few wolves would even look in my direction after Damon growled at Samuel for complimenting me; and all that mate talk had been beyond uncomfortable.

"Where is everyone?" I asked as Damon led me down a dirt path an hour later.

Squirrels scurried around before us, scrounging for nuts and berries and picking at some moonflowers that blossomed along the pathway.

Damon took my hand and continued forward through the tall oak trees. "Do you like Samuel?" he asked after tense silence.

My eyes widened. That came out of nowhere.

"Why would I like him?" I asked.

Instead of responding like any normal person would, he pressed his full lips together and led me to the end of the trail to a glimmering lake. Bundles of moonflowers floated on the surface next to lily pads. Large pale wooden boards of the dock lay over the teal-blue water, which was surrounded by hundreds upon hundreds of dark pine trees.

My eyes widened, never before having seen something so beautiful. I tugged him to the edge of the dock, pulled off my shoes, and dipped my feet into the water. He sat next to me, posting his palms behind him and leaning back to admire the scenery. The wind curled up the edges of his hair and blew it against his forehead.

I kicked my feet around slightly and watched the water ripple. "Why did you send my dad moonflowers?" I asked.

"Because it was the right thing to do."

"But why moonflowers?"

"Moonflowers symbolize the moon, and us wolves worship the Moon Goddess. If you haven't noticed, my pack has an abundance of moonflowers." He picked a flower from its bundle floating on the lake and lifted it to my nose, so I could inhale its refreshing earth fragrance.

Under the moonlight, Damon's eyes glimmered gold.

I glanced down at the water, my fingers curling around the edge of the wooden dock. "Can I see your wolf?" I asked, gnawing on the inside of my cheek.

"My wolf?" Damon asked, lips tugging into a smile. "Really?"

After I nodded, he jumped up and jogged behind a tree to strip off his clothes. The quiet Witver Forest filled with the familiar sounds of hundreds of bones cracking and shattering. Then, a few moments later, Damon walked out from the tree, his black wolf massive in size and his eyes even more golden somehow.

Before I could stop him, he playfully jumped at me and knocked me back onto the dock, his breathing heavy as he licked my neck, careful not to touch the silver necklace. I giggled, my stomach light and fluttering, and stared up at the moon. Damon lay on top of me, his paws on my chest and his snout resting on top of them.

I stroked my fingers through his fur and inhaled his honeysuckle scent, letting it relax me.

We might not be mates, but I didn't want this night to end.

As bad as it sounded, I wished that, just this once, the Moon Goddess had broken her rules and matched us together. But that was a dream that would never come to fruition.

A tree branch suddenly snapped behind us, and Damon lifted his head, ears pinned back and snout pointed to the air. When another snap echoed through the forest, Damon stood up and stiffened, his canines dripping with saliva.

Moments later, a naked woman appeared behind a pine tree, her brown curls blowing against her muscular olive-colored shoulders. With piercing green eyes, she smiled down at Damon as he shifted into his human form.

I sat up and inhaled sharply. Maybe this was her. Maybe this was his mate.

"Damon," she said without using his alpha title, looking him up and down.

"Alexandra," Damon said, stiffening.

My stomach tightened at the exchange. I glared at the ground and bit my lip to hold back my anger. I didn't know why I felt so … jealous over this woman. I had known from the beginning that Damon had a mate; he had told me about her. I should've been prepared to actually meet her at one point. I'd just thought …

Ugh, it didn't matter what I'd thought.

This Alexandra was his mate, his real mate.

She straightened her back. "Alpha Richard is here for your meeting about the pups being kidnapped. He says that this is urgent, and he needs to talk with you as soon as possible. More pups from packs surrounding us have been taken."

"Has anyone seen or heard anything?" he asked her, brows furrowed.

"No. We've had increased security around our borders and had people sniffing for rogues all day." She pushed some hair behind her shoulder, letting the wind take it back. "Alpha Richard says that he hasn't heard much anyway, but he fears his pack is next."

After Damon nodded to her, she gave him one last smile and disappeared through the woods without sparing me a single glance. He stared at her departing figure with both lust and fury in his eyes.

Sorrow twisting my bones, I glared at my lap and felt so damn stupid. He'd told me he didn't want his mate, that she wasn't good enough for him, and then he'd acted like that around her. But I had known the mate pull wouldn't let a wolf leave their mate that easily.

Three years after Luca's mate had rejected him, he still ... still fucking loved her.

And again, I was left heartbroken.

Hopping up, I brushed past Damon and back down the path toward his pack house.

"Mae, is everything all right?" Damon asked, tugging on his jeans and hurrying after me.

"Yes." I forced a smile on my face, stepping into the pack house and wanting to disappear from his life forever. "I have to get back home anyway. Go to your meeting. I'll see you tomorrow."

With that, I walked up to his bedroom, shut the door, and texted Aaisha to ask her to pick me up. I would've called Luca, but ... I was with another guy, and it would have been wrong. As I waited for her, I stood in front of the mirror and let a tear roll down my cheek.

God, why am I so stupid, so freaking stupid? A wolf could never love a human.

Another tear raced down my cheek and landed on my chest. When I went to wipe it away, my necklace shifted around my neck, and I noticed a crescent-shaped red mark on the center of my chest, where the necklace had rested.

Eyes widening, I leaned closer to the mirror to examine the necklace. Once filled with a red liquid, the pendant now only held a couple small droplets inside. The damn thing must've leaked out and seeped into my skin.

I'd worn Mom's necklace for less than a day, and I'd already ruined it. Dad was going to kill me.

After licking my finger and furiously rubbing the mark, it *darkened*.

What the hell was happening? Why wouldn't it come out?

Blowing out a deep breath, I refused to let it bother me now. It wasn't like I could magically put the liquid back inside the pendant container. It was gone now, just like Mom was. So, rather, I set the pendant back on the center of my chest and gasped when the pendant and mark formed a perfect oval.

My heart raced. Too fast. This must … must just be a coincidence.

It would come out. It had to.

Three days later, I stood in front of my bathroom mirror and blew out a deep breath. Rays of sunlight glared through the small bathroom window, illuminating the room. Unlike the past two days, today would be the day I woke up without the stupid red mark on my chest.

After stripping off my nightshirt, I stared at my reflection in the mirror and screamed.

Three days! Three fucking days! And the mark had done nothing but darken.

I splashed some cold water on my face. I had to be seeing things. That was definitely it.

But when it still hadn't disappeared, I drenched a towel in

soap and water and furiously scrubbed the marked area. After fifteen minutes, my skin was raw and burning and darker. I hurled the towel at the mirror.

"What's all the ruckus?" Aaisha asked, peeking her head into the bathroom.

My eyes widened, and I clamped my hands over my naked chest. "Aaisha, please leave."

She raised an eyebrow at me and smirked.

"Aaisha!"

"Are you hiding a hickey?!" she squealed, eyes widening when they landed on my chest. She looked down the hallway and grinned. "Luca! Come see this! Mae is hiding a hickey, and it's freaking huuuuge."

A moment later, Luca looked over Aaisha's shoulder. I groaned and rolled my eyes. God, nothing was ever secret in this house. Everyone had to know everyone's business. Aaisha stalked toward me and gripped my arms, pulling them away from my chest.

"Aaisha! Stop, please. This is assault! I am naked!"

"Girl, shut up. It's not like we haven't both seen you naked before."

"When have you seen me naked?" I shrieked, eyes wide.

Both of them smirked at each other and then at me. I wrinkled my nose at them and shook my head. Couldn't even be naked in private around here either. I would have to dead bolt my bedroom door or something.

Suddenly, Aaisha slammed her heel on my toe, and I immediately cradled my toe.

"Aaisha, what's wrong with you?"

Aaisha placed her hands on her hips and leaned close. "Damn. That is one dark hickey. He must be good! Get it, girllll!"

After throwing me a towel, Luca dragged Aaisha out of the room and told me to meet them outside once I finished dressing. From the look on his face, I could tell that he wasn't too happy about this *apparent hickey* on my chest, which definitely wasn't a hickey at all.

"Let me see it again!" Aaisha said when I stepped out into the living room.

"Don't be creepy, Aaisha," Luca said, pulling her away. "Let me see it."

"Stop, you guys. It's not a hickey. I have no idea *what* it is."

"How'd you get it then?" Aaisha asked, narrowing her eyes.

After sighing, I collapsed onto the couch next to Luca and threw my head into my hands, explaining to them that Mom's necklace had somehow broken and the sanguine-colored liquid had seeped into my skin. And that this hadn't come out since then.

Luca leaned closer to me, brushing his thumb across the mark, careful not to touch the silver pendant, sending shivers down my spine. "That's weird. It forms a perfect circle. And it won't come out?" he asked.

"It hasn't even faded a little," I said, anxiety twisting around my veins. "I've had it for three days." I gnawed at the inside of my cheek and looked between them. "How are you guys not freaking out that it hasn't come out?"

"It should come out eventually," Luca said, glancing up at me with those big brown eyes.

Aaisha cocked her brow. "I still think it's a hickey. But, hey, girl, I'm just saying. You should hide it though if you're gonna go see your man later tonight. Don't want him getting jealous and thinking Luca did it or something." She winked.

As Aaisha walked to the kitchen for breakfast, I glanced over at Luca, my breath catching.

Luca glided his tongue across his teeth, brown eyes flickering from my mark to me. "Wouldn't want that, huh?" he asked.

I swallowed hard and pressed my thighs together. "No," I lied, "I wouldn't."

Luca took a deep breath, canines extending just past his lips. "Me neither."

CHAPTER 11

MAE

"Is Damon here?" I asked Samuel when he answered the pack house door.

All morning, I'd debated on whether or not to visit Damon today, but when Luca and Aaisha both left the house, I'd decided to just come here because I didn't want to be alone.

And I might've wanted to see him.

Samuel nodded down the hall toward Damon's office, and I hurried in that direction. Since I'd met Alexandra, Damon's mate, I had wanted to both spend every waking second with Damon and to leave him alone so he could be with her. I didn't want the drama, but something kept drawing me to him.

As I was about to open the door, I heard her voice inside.

"Let's talk about it during a run together. I know running helps to clear your mind."

"Alexandra." Damon sighed.

I could hear the pain in his voice. I waited and waited and waited for him to say no, to reject her; it was what I wanted him to do because—I hated admitting it—I kinda liked him more than I should've.

But when he said, "Fine, we can go for a run," I slumped my shoulders in defeat.

"Thanks so much! I love you!"

My heart raced, and I leaned closer to eavesdrop on them even more. If he said those three little words back to her, I … didn't know how I'd feel. Even when nothing could happen between us, even when other females flirted with him, I wanted him, and I hated it.

After a few moments of silence, I dug my nails into my palms and walked to the kitchen.

Wearing a compression shirt and a pair of loose sweatpants, Samuel stood over the stove, bobbing his head and humming. He glanced my way and grinned. "Someone's moody this morning." He filled a dish with eggs and bacon and then handed it to me. "Would you like some breakfast to calm you down?"

He sat across from me at the granite table and nodded. "Eat your food."

I stabbed my fork into my eggs in jealousy and took an angry bite. Why had I come here, expecting to feel any different, knowing that they were mates? Because I was a stupid human, vying for the attention of a man who wasn't mine—that was why.

"Do you want to know a theory that I have about females?" Samuel asked, a smirk crawling onto his face as he finished chewing a bite of egg. "My theory is that you can cure a woman's moodiness by feeding her."

"What?" I asked, the corners of my lips curling up.

"Women and she-wolves always get so moody, but then you just offer them food, and *bam*, they're happy again." He leaned closer to me and grinned. "See! You were moody. I gave you food. Bam! There's a smile on your face."

"I'm not smiling because I'm not moody," I said, poking fun at him. "I'm smiling because you're being stupid."

After chuckling for a moment, Samuel looked behind me and dropped his smile. I glanced over my shoulder to see a furious Damon behind me with a scantily clad Alexandra digging her claws into his bicep. Her spandex shorts looked so tight that they were basically riding up her vagina.

"What's going on here?" Damon growled, golden gaze fixed on Samuel.

"Good morning to you too," I said, ignoring Damon's intense glare and returning to my food. "Samuel just made me some really good breakfast, and we were chatting. Is there something wrong?"

A low hiss escaped Damon's mouth.

"Damon, calm down." Alexandra placed a hand on Damon's shoulder, and his body instantly relaxed under her touch.

His eyes, however, still blazed his wolfish gold. He glared at Samuel and then stormed out of the house with Alexandra following, slamming the door behind them.

Samuel pushed his seat out and threw the rest of his breakfast in the garbage. "Well, I have to train."

"Can I come with you?" I asked, knowing that if I went home, I'd be alone.

With the little summer I had left, I wouldn't start college back up for another few weeks; Aaisha and Luca were off doing who knew what; and Dad was … well, I didn't want to see him after what had happened the other day.

"No."

"Please?"

"He already doesn't like me talking to you," Samuel said, thrusting his hands into his pockets and blowing out a deep breath, a piece of his dark hair flying up. "If he saw us hanging out, he'd kill me."

"He has no right to kill you," I said, annoyed with Damon's jealousy.

He could spend time with Alexandra, but I couldn't spend

time with another guy without him getting angry? What kind of logic was that? It was one of the many reasons that I hadn't told Damon about Luca yet. He'd flip out for no reason at all.

"Please, Samuel. I know Damon has found his mate. He has no right to get mad."

"Damon's told you?" Samuel asked.

"It's Alexandra, isn't it?"

Samuel blew out another breath and shut his eyes, frowning. "Mae, it's complicated."

Though I'd expected his answer, my heart tightened. Maybe I had been hoping he'd reassure me that I was making a huge deal out of nothing.

Why couldn't Damon have just told me from the beginning? He still hadn't admitted that his mate was Alexandra, and it irked me.

"Well, he has no right to be mad. He has a mate that he should care about," I said.

After running a hand through his thick brown hair, he sighed and headed out the door. "You can come with me but just this once." He glanced over his shoulder and smiled at me. "Come on."

I scraped the rest of my eggs into the trash and followed Samuel out of the house. We went down a dirt path toward a large field that doubled as a training area with soft workout mats, free weights, and squat racks. Large groups of wolves raced by us, small pups chasing after them, as if they were training too.

Samuel laced up his shoes. "Do you want to practice?" he asked, glancing over at me with a smile. "Might as well since you're here with me and have nothing else to do because you're boringgg."

I rolled my eyes but leaped forward in excitement, wanting to learn. Luca invited me out sometimes, but he usually trained alone. I kinda, sorta wanted to impress him with new moves the next time I worked out with him.

"Okay, we will start with the basics," Samuel said, lowering his chin, assuming a boxing stance, and rhythmically hopping back and forth. "So, to throw a punch, you want to hurl your hands forward while you rotate your hips, like this ..." He punched forward and rotated his hips, making the wind whistle around me.

"Samuel, I've thrown a punch before."

When Luca had moved in with Aaisha and me, it was the first thing he'd taught us to do to defend ourselves.

"You?" Samuel laughed. "You've thrown a punch before?"

I crossed my arms over my chest. "Why is that so funny?"

"I just didn't expect *you* to have thrown a punch before. You look weak."

"I'll show you weak," I said, throwing my fist forward and colliding into his abs. As soon as it hit, I pulled my hand away and shook it out, pain shooting up my arm.

Samuel stood there with the blankest face, as if it hadn't even affected him.

"You wanna play dirty, Mae?" he asked, whipping a fist through the air at me.

I ducked under it and hurled an uppercut at his jaw, making direct contact and listening to the crack.

Backing away, he moved his jaw around slightly and popped it back into place. "Damn, didn't expect that one."

After he lunged faster and struck me in the abdomen, I roundhouse-kicked him in the side and sent him stumbling back a few feet.

I smirked and jogged a few more feet away from him to keep my distance. "Is that all you got?"

"Barely."

Fists firing rapidly at me, he landed devastating blows all over my body. My skin ached at the sudden contact, and I sidestepped a jab he had thrown to my face and landed a counterattack on his cheekbone. Following up, I hurled a fist across to his face, but he ducked and lunged into me, wrapping his arms around the backs of my knees and wiping my legs out from under me so I landed on my back.

I wrapped my arms around his neck, trying to hold him close to me so he couldn't attack me further, but he fastened my hands above my head.

"Is that all you got?" he said, watching me squirm under his hold.

"*Barely,*" I mocked.

Kicking out Samuel's knees, I rolled him over, straddled his waist, and snaked my legs around his ankles to stop him from moving. With our bodies pressed together, I tried damn hard to keep him pinned to the ground.

But he easily gripped my chin, said, "Too easy," and flipped us over again. "Did you really think you could get me with that?"

"With what?" I said, my eyebrows furrowing.

"Grinding your body against mine?"

"I wasn't doing that!"

"I know; I know. I was kidding," he said but still didn't let me move. He placed more weight on my stomach and slowly crushed me with his muscle. "You're a lot stronger than I thought."

"And you're a lot heavier than I thought," I said, trying to muster up the strength to push him off of me.

But before I could, he was ripped off me and flung to the opposite side of the mat.

Damon stood over him with blazing gold eyes. "SHE'S MINE!" he growled, stalking closer to him, wrapping his hand around his neck, and slamming him onto the mat again, Damon's wolf in full and utter control.

Samuel scurried out of his grip and scooted away, bowing his head in submission.

I sprinted up next to Damon and grabbed onto his arm, hoping to calm him down. "Damon! Please! Don't hurt him!" I pleaded.

Damon pushed me away, and I stumbled to the ground. "I'm

not going to hurt him. I'm going to kill him." Leaping into the air, he shifted into his beast and lunged at Samuel, who stood quickly, dodged Damon's attack, and shifted.

The two massive wolves stared at each other, Damon's beast looming over Samuel. He lunged forward and sank his teeth into Samuel's leg, puncturing his fur and letting blood seep out of him, soaking Damon's snout. Samuel howled in pain, not fighting back, but Damon continued, jerking Samuel around.

"Damon! Stop! It was my fault. Samuel didn't do anything."

Damon released Samuel's leg, and I sighed in relief, thinking Damon had proven his point. But then he pounced on Samuel and dug his claws into his belly, ripping fur and skin away and letting him bleed out profusely.

Unable to watch this anymore, I sprinted to Damon. As blood splattered on my clothes, I punched Damon right in the snout. Damon turned to me and stalked dangerously in my direction, blood dripping from his teeth. Heart racing, I staggered away until I hit the edge of the platform and fell onto my back.

"Damon! STOP!" Samuel shouted, shifting back into his human form and cradling his stomach. "Damon! Look at who you're about to attack. Don't be stupid."

I squeezed my eyes shut and winced away, not wanting to watch him kill me, my fingers digging into the grass. Suddenly, a shrill of bones cracking echoed throughout the forest, and I squinted my eyes open. Damon stood in front of me, covered in Samuel's blood, and scooped me up into his arms.

"Don't you ever touch her again!" he growled at Samuel. "Or I'll kill you next time, and she won't stop me."

After Samuel bowed his head, Damon carried me into the pack house without saying a single word. My heart thumped heavily in my chest, my thoughts racing.

What was Damon going to do to me? Where was he bringing me? I didn't want to die and didn't even want to be in the presence of this man. Not now. Not when he was high off adrenaline.

Once he walked into his bedroom, I scrambled out of his arms and scurried to the opposite side of the room. "Damon, it wasn't what it looked like. I-I …" I parted my lips to continue but couldn't find any words. I didn't even know why I was trying to defend what had just happened. We had done nothing wrong.

"You what?" he growled, stalking closer to me with those golden eyes.

With every step he took toward me, I took one back until I hit the edge of his bed. When I didn't answer, a deep growl rumbled from his throat. I stood no chance against this beast in front of me. He could easily tear me apart any way he liked.

"Do you know what the fuck it looked like to me?"

"No," I whispered, fear twisting around my body, nearly suffocating me.

"It looked like my beta was about to seduce my mate! That's what it looked like!" he shouted, his eyes drinking in my fear. He snatched my chin and strummed his fingers across my jaw. "Kitten, don't act all scared. This was what you wanted, wasn't it? You've always fantasized about what it would be like to be with a beast like me."

With his other hand, he grabbed my hip and pulled me closer to him. Massive canines brushed against my sweet spot, and I unconsciously tilted my head away from him, giving his beast full exposure to my neck.

How did he make me this weak? I was just a human after all.

He growled in my ear again, laced his hand in my hair, and pulled it roughly, so I gazed up into his blazing golden irises. After a few moments of silence, he brushed his callous palm against my jaw. "Well, Kitten, you're *mine* whether you like it or not."

CHAPTER 12

DAMON

She was my mate.
Mate.
Since the moment I'd met Mae, that word had been thrashing around in my mind like a caged fiend, dragging me closer and closer to her before I could seize it by the throat and destroy it.

And her neck...

I licked her lilac-scented flesh... and it tasted so good.

Good enough to mark.

Mae shoved her fragile hands into my chest and pushed me away. "What do you think you're doing?"

"Marking what's mine," I growled, eyeing her like prey and stalking closer to her again.

I pushed her down onto my bed and trailed my nose up the side of her neck, making her shiver. She relaxed under my touch for a few moments, a blissful sigh escaping her lips, but then her entire body tensed.

After smacking me with a pillow, she crawled to a kneeling

position and swatted me again. "You can't keep doing this to me! You can't lead me on, then flirt with another girl, and then tell me that I'm your mate! That is not how it works, Damon!" Every swing of her pillow was filled with blinding anger.

I ripped the pillow out of her hands, throwing it to the other side of the room, but she grabbed another.

"Mae!"

"You almost killed Samuel!"

Smack.

"You made me cry!"

Smack.

"I hate you!"

Smack.

Once I yanked that pillow away from her, too, she stormed to the door with tears in her eyes. I slapped my palm across the door to hold it closed because I wasn't going to let her run off on me just like that. It had taken everything inside of me to hold back until this moment. I wasn't going to let her go that easily.

"Let me go home, Damon. I don't want to be here."

"Mae, I'm sorry that I did all of that," I said. "But you can't leave."

She glared up at me. "Are you really sorry?"

Sighing, I reached out to grab her hand, but she pulled it away from me.

"Don't touch me," she snapped. "I can't have you touch me, not after that. You'll ... you'll lose control and mark me, and I'll ... I'll ..." She stared down at her feet, cheeks flushing, and pressed her lips together, almost as if she didn't want to admit that she'd like it.

Whether she admitted it aloud or not, she'd wanted me to sink my canines into her neck and claim her.

Instead of doing just that, I walked toward her, took her hand in mine, and slumped down on the bed. "Yes, Mae, I am sorry."

"I'm really your mate?" she asked, irreplaceable shock washing over her face. "Me?"

"Yes."

"What about Alexandra?" she said, not pulling her hand away this time.

"What about her?"

She clenched her jaw. "Don't act clueless, Damon. I don't understand your relationship with her. For over a week, you hid the fact that I was your mate. Why are you trying to hide your relationship with her from me too? Is she also your mate?"

"Did you not just hear anything I said to you?" I asked, anger twitching inside me. "If you weren't my mate, I wouldn't have brought you home the second night we met, I wouldn't have taken you out on dates, I wouldn't have almost killed my beta for you," I growled, my fists clenched by my sides and my jaw tight. "If you weren't my mate, Mae, I wouldn't want you here with me."

"That didn't answer my question. Who is she to you?"

Guilt washed through my body, but I held myself together so that it didn't show. "She's nobody that you need to worry about," I said. When Mae parted her lips to protest, I continued, "Mae, please, drop it. I don't care about her like I care about you. I don't want her like I want you. She could never complete me like you could."

But she meant something to me, something that I couldn't quite admit to myself yet.

Surprisingly, Mae clamped her mouth closed and dropped it. Though I could tell that I wasn't getting out of it that easily. If I didn't tell her, Mae would probably start asking around my pack for more information, figuring it out herself.

"Kitten," I drew out, curling my finger around a strand of her silver-blonde hair. I trailed my nose up the side of her neck, sending goose bumps across her skin. "Let me show you how much I care about you."

After a few moments, she sighed softly. "Fine."

"You won't regret it, Mae. I promise you."

"Where are you taking me?" Mae asked, grasping my hands that covered her eyes.

After I had taken a shower to wash off Samuel's blood, I'd decided to bring her to the one place I always imagined raising a family—my secluded cabin on the outskirts of my property, where I had a personal ax-throwing range and a cozy living room that I knew she'd love.

I hadn't brought anyone there before, not even Alexandra.

"Patience, Mae."

We continued down the dirt path lined with moonflowers, steering clear of the training field. I didn't need to pass the field to smell Samuel's blood and feel like shit about almost killing my beta. I had just lost control for a second because he had been all up on my mate, my one and only. I'd check on him later tonight.

Sitting on the curve of the teal lake that I had taken Mae to the other day, my cabin glimmered under the setting orange sun.

I stood in front of it and peeled my hands away from her face, admiring the way she squinted to readjust to the light. "This is my cabin, where I hope to raise a family with you."

"Raise a family with me?" she asked, taken aback.

"We'd live in the pack house until our oldest became alpha, but—"

She chewed on the inside of her lip and shook her head. "You're talking like we're going to have children soon. I know that wolves usually do once they find their mate, but can't we just ... enjoy life? I don't even know if I *like* you, never mind want to have children with you."

I growled, "Mae, I want a family soon."

"I literally found out that I was your mate a few minutes ago. Don't you think you're rushing it?"

"No"—I balled my hands into fists—"I'm not. Most alphas would have taken their mates to bed already."

"Their mates are also wolves," she clarified for me. "If you can't see, I'm not a wolf. Most humans don't just jump into parenthood after a little over a week of knowing each other."

And she was right. She was fucking right. I just didn't want to … I didn't want to believe it or force myself to let her go. I had known that I could never, ever mark her from the beginning. I had fucking known it, yet I couldn't stop myself from pleading with her.

"I need a family, Mae."

"And if I don't give you one, then what?"

My wolf suddenly took hold of the conversation. "I'm an alpha. My mate will bear my pups whether she likes it or not. Your stomach will be swollen before the full moon with my children."

"Excuse me?" She narrowed her eyes at me and poked a hard finger into my chest. "Listen, this isn't going to work if you can't stop being a jerk. You can order around all of your other wolves, but that isn't happening with me. Stop being a dick and show me how much you actually care or else I'm leaving. For good."

Exhaling through my nose, I pushed the cabin door open for her and let her walk into my home—my real home. With huge glass windows, a small crackling fire, vanilla-scented candles burning throughout the house, it was much more homely than the big pack house, which housed many high-ranked wolves.

Glancing around, Mae strolled over to the large back door window, paused a moment, and then looked back at me. "You throw axes back there?" she asked, eyes lighting up with excitement.

I grazed my fingers against her lower back. "Do you want to throw?"

"Maybe we can later, and then I can beat you at it—again." She winked.

"You wish," I said, padding to the kitchen to pull out bowls from the cupboard.

She stayed by the door, staring out at the small squirrels scurrying between trees with their mouths filled with nuts.

Mae froze, cheeks paling, and inched closer to the window.

"What's wrong?" I asked, grabbing some pasta.

"I thought I saw …" She shook her head and turned back to me. "I just thought I saw a waiter that my dad had insulted at Tangled Orchard Winery. I, uh, saw him a couple days ago too. But … it must've been someone else. Wolves' golden eyes all look too similar to me."

Sighing quietly to herself, she walked over to the sink to wash her hands. I wrapped my arms around her waist and rested my chin on her shoulder, lips brushing against the soft spot on her neck.

"You're beautiful," I murmured against her and placed a kiss on her ear. "Especially when you laugh."

"When I laugh—"

I curled my fingers into her sides and tickled her silly.

"Damon! Pl-please stop! Oh my goodness." She giggled, her knees buckling beneath her. She threw herself back against me, a huge grin on her face, trying to push me away.

For a second, I stopped tickling her and tucked a strand of hair behind her ear. "You're mine, Mae," I whispered.

And in that moment, that was what she was. But soon, she wouldn't be, so I would enjoy this for as long as it lasted.

CHAPTER 13

MAE

*A*fter dinner, I stared out the back door window and admired the moonflowers' gleam against the trees. Something about it seemed so magical that I didn't question Mom's reasons for those being her favorite flowers.

My gaze wandered throughout the forest again, as I hoped to see that blond wolf who had eyes just like the waiter at the restaurant again. Though I'd told Damon I didn't think I actually saw him, I knew that I had. I couldn't have pictured that twice.

Yet when my eyes landed on Alexandra standing out in the woods and watching us closely, I balled my hands into fists. Not the person I'd hoped to find in these woods tonight and definitely not the person I wanted to ruin my quiet, fun night with Damon.

But I needed answers.

So, I turned on my heel toward Damon, who was finishing washing some dishes in the sink, and crossed my arms.

"We need to talk about Alexandra," I said to him, flinching

when her name rolled off my tongue. It tasted so sour in my mouth.

Damon blew a breath out of his nose and shook his head. "Why now? We're having a good night, Mae. Don't be childish and ruin it."

"Childish? Childish!" I shouted, unable to believe those words had just come out of his mouth. "You're the one being childish. You're the one lying to me about Alexandra. You're the one who wants me to have your children after just two weeks of knowing you. Two weeks, Damon!"

"I told you that she means nothing to me," Damon snapped, jaw clenched hard.

"Then, why can't you look me in the eyes and tell me that? Why can't you talk about her without your wolf begging to come out?" I asked him, feeling nothing but pain in my heart.

I had spent years seeing the hurt in Luca's eyes from his heartbreak, and now, I was seeing it in Damon's too. I just wanted him to be honest with me.

He shrugged and turned away from me. "I don't know."

"*I don't know* isn't good enough. You do know."

He crossed his arms over his chest and walked to the door. "Why can't you just drop it?"

"Why can't I drop it?! What kind of dumbass question is that?" I asked, rage rushing through my veins.

Damon looked down at his phone, cursed under his breath, and opened the front door. "I need to go to my meeting. I am done talking about her. You should be too. Go lie down and forget about it," he said, walking out the front door.

Not accepting him just walking away, I followed behind him to the pack house through the path of moonflowers. "You aren't going to get off that easily, Damon. You're going to tell me who she is to you, or I'm going to find out myself."

"Damon!" someone shouted to our left. The tall man who Aaisha had gone home with the other night approached us, holding a couple of manila folders. He smiled at me and joined us in walking to the pack house. "You must be Mae. Aaisha has told me so much about you. I'm Richard."

"Treating Aaisha good?" I asked, still peeved at Damon. Aaisha had *very briefly* mentioned that she was still hanging out with who-was-supposed-to-be a one-night stand.

Richard smiled even wider somehow, eyes glimmering. "Of course I am."

When we reached Damon's office in the pack house, Damon told Richard to wait for him inside and stopped me outside. "We need to chat about the missing pups," he said to me. "Go to my room and sleep off this"—he shook his head as if he didn't want to deal with me—"whatever it is."

Before I could enter, he slammed the door in my face and locked me out. I banged on the door, demanding him to let me in because I wasn't finished chewing him out. I needed answers, and I needed them now. I didn't want to be led on; I had seen what that did to Luca.

For years, I'd dreamed and fantasized about being with a wolf. I loved their protectiveness, strength, and beauty. And while Damon fulfilled my craving for a feral romance, I couldn't stand these secrets and his blatant disrespect for me when I asked him to just tell me who Alexandra was to him.

But werewolves loved their mates more than anything. Maybe if I gave him some time, things would change. Or maybe, if I gave him another chance, he'd disappoint me again, and nothing would change.

Stomach growling still even after dinner, I walked to the kitchen and pulled out my buzzing phone.

Luca: Can you meet me at Splitz's? I need to talk to someone.

My eyes softened for a moment as I stepped into the kitchen. When I looked up from my phone, I saw Alexandra leaning over the counter, spraying some whipped cream on her finger and sucking it between her red lips. She looked over her shoulder, excessively rolled her green eyes, and turned away.

"Alexandra, I need to talk to you," I said.

She looked me up and down, raising an eyebrow. "Who are you?"

"You know who I am."

"Oh, no, I really don't. Are you another one of Damon's whores?" she asked, head tilted.

I clenched my jaw and sneered at her, "Sorry, you must've mistaken me for yourself."

An empty laugh escaped her lips. "That's what you think I am? Do you think I'm the pack slut or something?"

"Why don't you tell me who you are then? What is going on between you and Damon?"

"You really have no idea, do you? He hasn't told you?"

"Told me what?" I asked through gritted teeth. When she didn't say anything, I repeated, "Told me what?"

"I mean more to him than you think," she said, walking around me, her smirk growing, as if I were her dinner and she had been starved. "I *am* his everything. His life. His night. His day. I'm his mate."

Reeling with anger, I dug my nails into my palms and clenched my jaw. "You're not his mate. I am."

She cackled. "Did he tell you that? Poor you. You actually believed him too?"

Crossing my arms over my chest, I glared at her, not wanting to believe her but unable to stop myself. She slithered into my mind, sank her ugly fangs into my thoughts, and poisoned me with fear. Damon had hidden that I was his mate from me, he continuously lied to me about Alexandra, and ... and he hadn't claimed me like he'd even admitted most alphas do.

If I was his mate, what was Alexandra to him? Another woman that he didn't want anymore but still had feelings for? I needed to know, and nobody—*freaking nobody*—would tell me the truth.

Though something had been off about Damon and Alexandra the first time I saw them lock eyes. I wanted to trust him, but how could I trust someone who couldn't be completely honest with me?

"Damon and I have a long history together," Alexandra said, rubbing it in where it hurt. "He has killed for me, and I have sacrificed so much for him. No matter what he tells you, Mae, you will never be his. So, stay away from him."

CHAPTER 14

LUCA

Standing in front of Splitz's Creamery, I stared down at my phone and hoped that I hadn't disturbed Mae. I had avoided her as much as I could these past few days, knowing that I couldn't handle seeing her with someone else. And I wouldn't have bothered her tonight either since she was out with her new *fling*, but I felt myself slipping.

Slipping fucking hard.

And Mae was the only person who could help calm me back down.

"Luca," Mae shouted, hurrying down the street toward me. "Is everything okay?"

I took a shaky, deep breath, inhaling her scent and letting my shoulders slump forward. If she hadn't come, I would've gone back to the Eclipse Bar and found another she-wolf to do something that I regretted with. Even after three years, my mate's rejection still weighed heavily on my heart. And I wanted to finally move forward and stop feeling like shit all the time.

Before I could respond, she enveloped me in a hug, resting her head on my chest. I relaxed even further, drawing my arms around her shoulders and pulling her closer to me, the desire—the blatant *need*—to feel loved by someone suddenly ... filled.

It was stupid. It really was. But Mae ... Goddess, she was different from all those other girls I brought home. Mae didn't want me for any sort of title or abilities; she didn't know about any of that. Mae wanted to be here because she loved me whether it was as a friend or not.

After nodding, I ushered her toward the creamery, knowing that it would close soon. It was nearly eleven thirty p.m.

"Two vanilla cones," I said to the server, leaning against the white-sided building and smiling down at Mae. "I just wanted to see you."

She furrowed her brows and pushed some hair behind her shoulder. "Are you sure?"

"Yeah, I'm fine," I lied. "How's, uh, your *boyfriend*?"

She rolled her eyes. "One, he's not my boyfriend. Two, I don't want to talk about him right now. It's so much drama that I need to talk to him and set some things straight, if he ever wants to hang out with me again."

Regretting asking her about him, I grasped her jaw and tilted her head to the side to gaze at that deep red mark still on her chest under the dim yellow streetlight. "You still have the mark?" I brushed my thumb against it, using it as an excuse to touch her. "I thought it would have gone away by now, but it looks like it's gotten bigger."

"Bigger?" Mae asked with huge gray eyes. "What if I'm possessed?"

"Mae, you're not possessed. Just think of it as a tattoo."

"Two vanilla cones!" the server said, giving Mae one and me the other.

After handing her a few dollars, I walked with Mae back down the street to our apartment, my arm grazing against hers.

How I felt for her … there wasn't a way to describe it. She wasn't my mate, and I didn't think she'd ever be, but I loved her. More than a friend should.

"A tattoo that I didn't ask for," she said, licking her cone.

"Well, let me know if it goes away."

She narrowed her eyes. "And if it doesn't?"

"Then"—I playfully bumped my shoulder into hers as we walked up our driveway—"I'll get a tattoo that matches yours, so you won't feel like a weirdo anymore."

Pointing a finger at me, she smiled and opened our apartment door. "You'd better not be lying because I'm going to hold you to that. If this nasty *tattoo* thing doesn't disappear"—she curled her fingers into the center of my chest—"I want you to get one right here."

Stopped in the doorway with a flickering light the landlord hadn't fixed yet, I stared down at Mae and her glimmering gray eyes under the moonlight, something pulling me to her. Almost as if she felt it too, she stared up at me, vanilla ice cream dripping down her fingers, and glanced between my chest and my face before her eyes lingered on my lips.

I leaned down slightly, just a few inches, and tucked some hair behind her ear. "Mae," I whispered.

Though I expected her to move, to push me away, to tell me to stop because we could be nothing more than just friends, Mae sucked in a sharp breath and balled my shirt into her fist to pull me closer.

"Mae! Luca!" Aaisha called from upstairs. "You guys home?!"

Cheeks flushed, Mae pulled away from me, glancing between my lips and my eyes to the stairs that led up to our apartment. I silently cursed at myself for not just leaning down and pressing my lips to hers. I'd had the perfect fucking chance.

"Coming!" Mae shouted, running up the steps and leaving me at the landing.

When she disappeared into our apartment, Aaisha shouted, "You too, Luca!"

Jogging up the creaky wooden stairs, I followed Mae into the apartment and stopped dead in my tracks when I saw a big red mark on Aaisha's neck.

Hopping on the couch and clapping her hands, Aaisha grinned at us. "I have a mate! I have a mate! I have a mate!"

My eyes widened, fear rushing through my veins. Aaisha had been marked by a werewolf, which meant that during the next full moon, her body would try to force her to shift. And ... less than a single percent of humans survived that shift.

"Alpha Richard marked you," I stated, unable to believe it myself. He had been way too into her at the bar, it had to be him. "He marked you."

She jumped off of the couch and smacked me in the head with a pillow. "Hey, I was supposed to tell her that! It ain't your information to tell." She turned to Mae and grinned. "I'm an alpha's mate!" Whirling around on her heel, she raised a sassy brow at me. "As for you, I knew that humans could be mated to werewolves!"

"I never said that it couldn't happen, Aaisha," I said, anger rushing through me at Richard's senseless decision. "All I said was that it doesn't happen often. Hell, I don't even know the last time it did. You could d—"

"Do you hear that, Mae?!" Aaisha said, completely ignoring me. She suggestively wiggled her eyebrows at Mae. "Now, that hot werewolf guy who keeps trying to hang out with you might be your mate! You guys have been spending a lot of time together."

I sighed and tossed my ice cream cone into the trash, slumping down on the couch and throwing my head into my hands, desperate to think up a plan to reverse this or ... to make it so Aaisha wouldn't die during this shift. Mae would be devastated if her best friend went through a pain like that.

Mae frowned. "I don't want to talk about him right now. He causes too many problems."

"But he—"

"Aaisha, please don't. Not right now," Mae said, almost a bit too quickly, peeking a guilty glance at me. She sat by my side and furrowed her brows. "So, what's gonna happen to Aaisha now that she's marked?"

Blowing out a deep breath, I shook my head. "During the next full moon, she will complete her first shift." I paused for a few moments, not wanting to continue. But this was our reality now. Once a wolf bit a human, there was no turning back. "There is a chance that she will be too weak for the shift."

Mae slackened her jaw, cheeks paling.

Aaisha turned to me, her eyebrows furrowed. "What do you mean by that?"

"Human bodies are not made for shifting. They're a lot weaker than werewolves. There is a chance that you won't make it," I repeated, loathing the words as they tumbled out of my mouth, but she had to know what lay ahead of her.

"H-how do you know that?" she asked me, tears welling up.

"I've watched one human try to shift during the full moon for the first time," I started, remembering his screams and cries of pain.

Someone from my old pack had bitten a human during one full moon when that wolf couldn't seem to control himself. That man had died, half-shifted, with a snout like a wolf but the limbs of a human, a disgusting and terrorizing animal.

"What?" she whispered, jaw quivering.

"If you're not properly trained, you could die," I said. "We need to train you to be strong both mentally and physically. I'm not going to let you go out the same way that he did. I ... I can't."

Fury quickly replaced her tears, a fire burning in her eyes. "Oh! That stupid little piece of ... why would he mark me if there was a chance I was going to die?!" She hurried to the door and turned around. "I'm gonna wrap my hands around his freaking neck and squeeze the life out of him if I die. I'll haunt his freaking wolf every freaking night."

After she slammed the door behind her, Mae turned to me with glossy eyes. "Please, don't say it's true," she whispered, swallowing hard and wrapping her arms around me. "I know it is, but … but I … I don't want her to die. She's my best friend, Luca."

I stroked her soft silver-blonde hair. "Well then, we have three weeks to make her strong."

"Three weeks?" Mae asked with unease.

"I think she can do it," I said. At least, I hoped that she could do it. I didn't want to lose her either. "She's strong and stubborn. We just have to get her back in the gym to build up her endurance and strength because the first shift, especially for humans, is the worst. I'm just thankful that Richard marked her before the blood moon."

"Why?"

"Because nobody, not even werewolves, survive shifting during the blood moon."

"What's so different about the blood moon?" Mae asked.

"Well," I started, pulling her into my arms, "as you know, during a full moon, a she-wolf goes through heat. She becomes much, much more physically and sexually aggressive, and she gets cramps—bad cramps. However, during the blood moon, no female wolf has ever reported a heat. Also, during blood moons, wolves can't shift, we're more sensitive to silver, and if a she-wolf is pregnant with a pup, she loses the pup. Humans bitten before the blood moon usually try to shift but physically can't and die."

She widened her eyes in horror. "Well, it's good she's marked now, I guess, so she has a better chance of making it through the shift. I just wish that she'd thought it through before letting Richard mark her."

My lips curled into a frown. "She probably didn't let him. He took and claimed her himself. A mate bond is stronger than you think, Mae. Wolves do senseless things for their mates. And alphas, especially, don't wait to claim their mates unless something is stopping them."

CHAPTER 15

MAE

After my chat with Luca last night, I showed up to Damon's house the next morning, looking for answers. Alphas claimed their mates as soon as they met them unless something was stopping them. And right now, Alexandra was the woman in Damon's way. She had to be.

For the past twenty minutes, I had been sitting across from Damon at the breakfast table, trying to figure out what to say to him. Every time I brought her up, he always—*always*—diverted the conversation elsewhere. While I wasn't about to be led on, I really, really liked him. Maybe it was just the mate bond affecting me too.

Heels clacking against the ground, Alexandra brushed her fingers against Damon's back and sat next to him and some other warrior wolves, who turned away from her. "Thanks for running with me last night and this morning," she purred. "It really helped me out and cleared my mind. I couldn't be more grateful for you, *Alpha*."

I gripped my plate tighter, unable to force my gaze away. She had some nerve.

Damon nodded and smiled, his green eyes filling with golden flakes of his wolf, though I couldn't tell if his wolf enjoyed her company or loathed it. Deciding that I would get nowhere with her sitting right next to him, I pushed my plate to the center and walked out of the room to be alone for a bit.

All night, I had thought about what I could say to him, and I still didn't know. Part of me wanted him to tear his canines into my neck and claim me while the other half thought it'd be best to … keep things this way because humans rarely survived the shift.

"Mae!" Damon called after me, but I ignored him. "Mae!"

Collapsing onto his bed, I closed my eyes and sighed. From Alexandra to Aaisha to the mark still on my chest, my mind was all over the place today. I should've just stayed home and thought of a plan with Damon before blindly coming over here just because my body ached whenever I wasn't near him. It was stupid, and I hated it so much, but I guessed I kind of understood Luca's position now and how much his mate rejecting him had hurt.

Damon appeared at the door with a plate of food. "Mae, you need to eat breakfast."

"I'm not hungry," I said.

"Well, you're going to eat."

"No, I'm not. Don't tell me what to do," I snapped.

This was an endless game of push-and-pull with him that I couldn't stop, nor did I want to.

After placing the plate of food on my lap, he sat beside me and pressed his lips into a tight line, probably still annoyed that I'd left last night without telling him first. It wasn't my fault Luca had needed me.

"Lunas need to eat, so they can be strong."

My hands tightened around the plate. "Well, then, why don't you go feed your luna?"

"That's why I'm here."

Anger rushing through me, I jumped up and hurled the plate of food at his chest. How dumb did he think I was? Did he really think he could continue to lie and hide things from me? I needed to know now. I couldn't hold back my jealousy and anger any longer.

"What the hell was that for?!" Damon growled, the food smeared all over and dripping down his shirt and onto his lap. "If you weren't my mate—if you weren't even human—I would punish you for that. Don't you ever even think about doing that again! Do you understand me?"

"I'm tired of your lies. I'm tired of you leading me on. I'm done with you, Damon. Take me home. Now. I'm not going to just sit around and watch you flirt with Alexandra. She is the girl you should be with. She is who you want to be with, Damon. Just let me be. Stop trying to for—"

Before I could continue, Damon grabbed the sides of my head and pulled me closer to him, crashing his lips down onto mine, sending a wave of innate need through me. I found myself relaxing, all that anger boiling away in those few moments, and I moved my lips back against his.

When he trailed his mouth down my neck, his stubble brushing against my soft spot, I tensed. What the hell was he doing, and why was I letting it happen? I'd vowed to myself that I wouldn't fall into one of his annoying little tricks, but here I was.

"Damon, please, stop," I mumbled, pushing lightly on his chest even though every part of my body seemed to move on its own. I forced myself to shove him again, not able to have him kiss me any longer. "Damon! No."

Once he finally pulled away, he stared at me with blazing gold eyes. "You are my mate, Mae. Why do you keep thinking you're not?"

"Alexandra said—"

"Don't listen to what she says," Damon murmured against my lips, fingers tangled in my hair to pull me closer.

When he crashed his lips onto mine once more, I pushed him back. "But—"

"Mae, just shut up and enjoy this. *Enjoy me*," he said almost desperately.

As his lips brushed against mine, a jolt of electricity shot throughout my body. I despised my body's carnal desire for him, but I pressed my lips harder against him, relishing this moment with him because I didn't know how much more pain I could take.

"Damon, we need to talk," I said after he rested his forehead against mine, his minty breath making my lips tingle. I stood back and crossed my arms over my chest to block myself off from him because I couldn't fucking control myself. One minute, I hated him, and the next, I craved everything about him. This torture needed to end.

He sighed, gave me a quick peck, and sat on the bed, his green irises almost fighting with his golden ones. "Whenever we talk, we always end up fighting. I just want to enjoy time with you." He reached out for my hand, his rough fingers brushing against my knuckles.

"Then, let's do something that you like, and we can talk at the same time. That way, we both win," I said, feeling the jealousy boil up inside me yet again.

"I'd like doing you," Damon said, smirking slightly.

I averted my gaze, cheeks flaming, and walked to the door. "Let's go for a run," I said because he liked to run.

At least, he always ran with Alexandra. Maybe he would want to do it with me too. Hopefully, it would calm both of us down and clear our minds.

"You run?" he asked, peeling off his food-stained shirt and walking out of the bedroom with me.

"No," I said, passing the dining room and ignoring everyone

inside, especially Alexandra. I pulled open the back door and stepped out into the summer morning, the hot sun beating down on us. "But you do."

After leading me toward a path, he started jogging by my side. I tried my best to keep up with his fast jogging pace, short, ragged breaths escaping my lips every few meters. I didn't know how the hell this man ran for fun. Beads of sweat dripped down the sides of my face as I pushed my body harder through the dense woods, my feet constantly pounding against the uneven surface, causing my legs to burn.

Well, there went running and talking. I could barely run and breathe.

Deciding to slow down, Damon slowed too and arched a brow. "I thought you said that you ran?"

"I ... just because I said *let's run* ... I suck at running ... oh damn, this is hard," I panted, slowing to a complete stop under some pine trees and placing my hands on my knees.

"How are we supposed to talk and run if you can't even breathe while running?"

"You're the one who needs to do the talking," I said, standing up and walking next to him.

"What do you want me to talk about?" he asked.

I gave him a sideways glare. He knew what we needed to talk about; he was just stalling.

"Alexandra?" he asked, rolling his gold eyes. "Mae, I said it before, and I'll say it again. You don't have to worry about her. She's just a friend and one of my best warrior wolves."

"She told me that she was your mate," I said.

"The Moon Goddess has paired me up with you. She has made *you* my mate, not her."

"I don't like her, Damon. She's rude to me."

"I'll talk to her today. She won't bother you anymore, I promise."

After staring at him for another moment, I looked away at the dappled light under the leafy canopy of trees. We continued on the path, which looped around his entire pack, and then went back to the pack house, greeting some warrior wolves on their morning run. I didn't know if he was telling the truth or not, but something inside me stupidly told me to trust him to keep her in her place.

He was her alpha, and wolves always listened to their alpha or else there were consequences.

"How was your meeting with Richard?" I asked, remembering that he'd mentioned pups being kidnapped lately. I really hoped that it wasn't true, but last night, even Luca had said that it was happening to packs in Witver.

"A pup was taken from his pack." Damon opened the pack house door for me to enter. "He has warned me of rogues. He caught scent of them around the edges of the land."

I wiped the sweat from my forehead. "He thinks a rogue did it?"

"Who else would take pups from their packs? Rogues aren't good people, Mae."

Furrowing my eyebrows, I frowned. When Luca had come to Aaisha and me, looking for a place to stay, he'd told us that he was a rogue, but he wasn't bad. Not a single bit. For the past three years I'd known him, he had been the gentlest, most vulnerable person around. If anything, he had strengthened, supported, and stood up for me time and time again.

"Not all rogues are terrible," I said.

"They're dangerous. They don't care about who or what they kill. Stay away from them." Suddenly, he stopped in his tracks, caught my wrist, and stared down at me, darkness pricking at the edges of his gold eyes. "I can't let anything happen to you, Mae. Don't involve yourself with them."

Deciding not to push it, I nodded and glanced at my dirty shoes. If he found out that I lived with a rogue—a *male* rogue—he would freaking flip out and lose his shit. And I couldn't deal with any more drama now—at least, not until Alexandra was sorted out.

"How do you become a rogue?" I asked.

"There are different ways," he said, walking up the stairs to his room. "Sometimes, the pack kicks them out. Sometimes, they don't agree with the alpha and just leave. It depends on a lot of factors really."

Nodding, I excused myself to shower while Damon talked to Alexandra about harassing me. My entire body was sweaty from that two-minute run, and I didn't want Damon to argue about rogues anymore. I just needed some answers because Luca didn't speak much about his old pack.

When I finished showering, I pulled my towel high enough up my chest to cover that growing red mark, slipped into his empty room, and then tugged on his shirt and some shorts, my gaze drifting across his dresser as I tried so desperately to tie the strings around my waist tight enough so the shorts wouldn't fall down.

Scattered across the stand were four picture frames—one of Damon and his mother hugging near some illuminating moon-flowers; one of a group of malnourished young boys, tarnished so much that I could only make out the faces of Damon and Samuel in ripped clothes and dirty faces; one empty frame that had a sticky note with the words, *Picture with Mae when I finally get one*; and one of a couple.

Picking up the last frame, I studied the picture of the tall werewolf man with a human woman. She stood on her toes to kiss his cheek, big smiles on both their faces. And the male closely resembled Damon.

"It's done, Kitten," Damon said, walking back into the room.

I jumped up in surprise and clutched the frame a little tighter. "What's done?"

"Alexandra won't bother you anymore." He glanced down at the frame in my hand, his golden eyes turning green, and pulled it away from me, lips turned into a frown. And suddenly, he seemed more distant than he had all day.

"Who are they?" I asked.

Damon inhaled sharply and then pressed his lips together, a knot forming between his eyebrows. I stayed quiet and waited for him to continue. He relaxed for a moment, taking in a breath before his eyes glazed over like they did when he talked through his mind-link. The muscle in his jaw sharpened, and he rushed to the door.

"Stay here. I'll be back."

"What's wrong? Did something happen?" I asked, following him.

He stopped suddenly. "I said, stay here."

Once he shut the bedroom door and stormed down the hall, I peeked my head out and looked around for any sign of a warrior. When the coast was clear, I scurried out of the bedroom and walked to the back door, not wanting to be left alone. I hated being alone.

From the doorway, I saw Damon hurrying to the training area, so I decided to follow. I sped up a little, jogging down the moonflower path, and finally reached the opening to the training area to see a group of people huddled around a platform.

After they parted for Damon, I ran up to it and stood on my toes to watch what was happening. Was it wrong to snoop? Yes. But if Damon really wanted me to lead with him, I didn't want to be kept out of things. I wanted to know what was going on and how Damon would react to it.

A warrior wolf pressed his foot against a young male wolf's head, pressing him against the mat, while a middle-aged woman stared, wide-eyed, at the situation, her eyebrows furrowed. Another warrior wolf gripped her tightly around her arms.

Damon growled down at the man, "What is going on here?"

A menacing snarl rumbled from the wolf's throat.

Swiftly seizing the boy by his throat, Damon lifted him into the air and dug his claws into his neck. The wolf glared down at Damon like his threatening golden eyes didn't bother him, his feet dangling in the air.

"Who do you think you are, growling at your alpha?!" Damon roared.

"You are not my alpha," the teen said through gritted teeth.

"Get me silver," Damon demanded of one of his warriors.

A loud thud echoed through the forest as Damon threw the boy to the ground, his bones cracking at the sheer force. Grabbing a fistful of the teen's hair, Damon pushed the boy onto his knees, snapped a silver collar around his neck, and chained him to the ground. Skin scorching almost immediately, the boy yelped in pain.

"Please! Let him go!" the woman screamed with tears flowing down her face.

"I gave him a chance, and he disobeyed me once already. Disobey me again, and this is what will happen to you too," Damon threatened the woman, seizing some silver ropes from the warrior wolf.

My heart raced in my chest. If Damon used the silver rope, it would tear the poor kid's back to shreds. But Damon wouldn't actually do that; he was just using it to look ruthless, right? I had to be right.

Deafening silence penetrated the crowd. Damon stalked closer to the teen, the silver burning his palm. As my body shook in fear, the boy held unwavering eye contact with Damon. And I silently prayed to the Moon Goddess that he would look down, bow his head, and submit to his alpha.

"Don't test me," Damon said through gritted teeth.

"I will never submit to you. You are not my alpha."

"Your alpha was weak," Damon growled. "That's why he's not here anymore. That's why I took over his lands with such ease. That's why you will submit to me now." He stalked around the prisoner and roughly gripped his shirt, tearing off the fabric and throwing it to the side. *"Now!"*

When the teen refused to move, Damon whipped the rope, the loud crack echoing through the woods. I winced back in pain and slapped a hand over my mouth to hold back a cry at the sight of my supposed mate being so ... so cruel.

The whip wrapped around his abdomen like a boa constrictor would its prey, trapping the boy within its restraints. Blood sprayed through the air, splattering over the woman, her shrill screams penetrating the silence.

I shriveled back in fear, parting my lips to scream too, but my voice seemed to leave me. Pangs of horror jabbed through my chest, stabbing me repeatedly in the heart.

My eyes were fixed on Damon. How could he do this to such a young boy? How could he ... hurt his own pack member?

While blood seeped from the silver around his torso, the teen didn't flinch. My eyes flickered around the crowd, as I hoped to find someone who would stop Damon. He grabbed another silver rope from his warrior; however, everyone stared on in silence. And from across the crowd, I saw Alexandra watching and smirking.

"Submit!" Damon growled.

Despite the open wounds on his back and the restrictive silver around his body, the teen straightened his spine as best as he could and braced himself for another rope to be hurled at him, imprisoning him. "Not my alpha."

Damon jerked the ropes once more, letting the silver sink into the teen's broken flesh. This time, the teen fell forward with blood dripping out of his mouth. Though quickly, he regained his balance and sat back up, daring Damon to continue.

Hands trembling, I stepped back from the crowd and listened in terror. How could Damon do this? Was this how he acted all the time? Was he this reckless and careless about other people? Would he do this to me if I ever got out of hand?

CHAPTER 16

MAE

Before I could run in there and break Damon away from that boy myself, Samuel grabbed my arm and pulled me out of the training area, his eye still black from the other day when Damon smashed it in. "Mae, you shouldn't be here."

Over the cracking of the ropes and the searing of skin, I sobbed for that boy who I knew nothing about. "Samuel! We have to stop this. Please, help me stop this!"

I tried to pull away, wanting to run to Damon to try to stop him, but Samuel held me back and continued down the moonflower path.

When he finally pushed me into the pack house, my knees gave out, and I collapsed. Samuel wrapped his arms around my body right before I landed on the ground and held me up, stroking my back with his hand.

"How could you just let that happen? How could he do that?" I sobbed into his shirt, staining the cloth with my tears. "Why is he like this?! Samuel! Why? I don't understand how he could be so ruthless and uncaring!"

"Alphas do not like being challenged, especially after they've found their mates."

"Does that give him the right to almost kill the boy in front of everyone?"

Samuel grimaced. "He was using him as an example."

I glared up at him. "Using him as an example? That's no excuse."

"That doesn't mean that I agree with his actions," Samuel clarified. "I'm just telling you why he did it. The teen who Damon whipped has been acting out of line for a while. Ever since we took over their pack in a war a few years ago, this has been happening—not only with him, but with other wolves from that pack too.

"The war was messy, but when we defeated them, Alpha Damon gave the remaining wolves a choice. They could either become rogues or stay in the pack with their families and have protection from us. The ones who stayed agreed to be obedient, but as you can see ... that's not exactly what's happening."

"Why was there a war?" I asked, tears streaming down my face still.

My stomach clenched as the thought of Dad drifted through my mind. He had warned me that wolves were capable of terrible, heartless things, and I had ignored him because I wanted to believe that Damon would never do that.

"Damon wanted his lands back, so our pack could survive under better living conditions," Samuel said.

Thinking back to the picture of those malnourished boys, I frowned. Was that what all of the pack had looked like before Damon became alpha? Had his pack gone hungry and turned into savages?

"Did he lose the lands?" I asked.

After placing his hand on the back of my head, he pulled me

into his chest. "His father did. When we were growing up, Damon's father wasn't a good alpha. He chose his wants and needs over the needs of his family and pack. He had women other than his mate, he gambled, and he let other packs walk all over us. They stole our lands, our food, our women.

When Damon's father was killed, Damon promised our pack that he'd get everything back that his father had lost. Some of the elders wanted to challenge him for his position because they thought he would fall into the same path as his father, but they gave him a chance, and he has kept his promise. Our lives have prospered with him as our alpha, but he's had to use force to keep this pack in line, especially when he started. He thinks that if he doesn't, other alphas will think he is like his father—weak and easily taken advantage of."

I inhaled sharply and stared down at my feet through teary eyes. Still …

"Again, I'm not saying that it is right, but I'm just telling you why he does what he does."

"So, he just starts wars with wolves who have taken things from his father?" I asked, trying to make sense of this all.

"Usually, it never comes to war, but last time, there was something else involved that caused Damon to declare war and take another alpha's pack."

"What was that?"

He nervously chewed the inside of his lip. "Alexandra."

That fucking piece of shit was literally the cause of every single problem, wasn't she? She slithered her way into every situation that involved Damon and decided to make everyone's lives miserable, huh?

"Do you want me to bring you home?" Samuel asked when I didn't respond.

Deciding that I didn't want to see Samuel dead tonight, I shook my head. "Thanks for the offer, but I don't want you to get killed because of me. I'll walk."

Ignoring me, Samuel pulled me out the front door and to his car. "He won't kill me."

"Samuel, I don't think this is a good idea."

He motioned for me to sit and glanced over my shoulder toward the forest where Damon was, his ear lifted slightly. "Mae, it'll be fine. Yesterday, Damon's wolf was just reacting how any wolf would react if he saw his mate with another wolf."

Closing my eyes, I sat in the car and prayed that Samuel was right. I didn't want to find out that Damon had killed Samuel for being in the same car as me or something crazy like that. I just needed a few days without this Damon drama to try to figure out these stupid feelings I kept having for him. They were kind of getting on my nerves now.

Twenty-five minutes later, I sat in Hot Shots Tea Room with a steamy cup of coffee on the table and my thoughts all over the place. I needed something to get my mind off Damon, and the pub by our apartment was closed until noon. A coffee that would most likely burn my mouth should do the job.

Sinking into the cream cushioned seat, I put the edge of the cup to my lips and sipped it down, not caring that my gums burned. I had peace for once today, and I had to enjoy it while it lasted because, lately, I—

"Mae!" Brett called from across the shop.

After cursing to myself, I sat up taller and gave him my best forced smile. "Hey, Brett."

He sat across from me with his coffee mug, almost immediately dropping his beaming grin. "What's wrong? You look like you've been crying." He posted his forearms on the edge of the table and leaned forward, brushing a stray piece of hair out of my face. "And don't tell me that you haven't been. I've known you for years. I know when something's bothering you."

"Everything's fine," I lied, not wanting to involve him in my drama.

He narrowed his eyes at me. "Is it that wolf that you've been hanging out with?"

"Brett, please. I don't want to talk about him right now." I rubbed the creases in my forehead and swore that I'd kill him if he brought Damon up again. I had come here to relax in peace, not to talk about Damon and his ruthless ways.

Brett sat back and sipped his white mug. "I don't like to see you upset, Mae. Do you want me to talk to him?" he asked.

Though Brett had good intentions, him talking to Damon was not something that would end well for either of them, so I shook my head.

"Well"—he blew out a breath—"let's get your mind off things and go out for a real lunch. Just as friends. I want to see you happy. We'll hang out like we used to, just to take your mind off of everything."

I hated that my only options were to hang out with Brett, go scream at Damon for what he had done, or sulk alone at home, lost in my own hurtful thoughts.

So, I flared my nostrils and gave a slight nod of my head. "Just as friends. Nothing more."

"I know I said that I'd take you out as just friends, but you're fucking gorgeous," Brett said under Oasis's neon lights.

Oasis was a well-known restaurant on the outskirts of Witver, where both young werewolves and humans hung out. With his opinions toward wolves, I was surprised he'd brought me here out of all places.

I shifted uncomfortably on a teal stool at the dining bar and decided to focus on the pop music playing from the jukebox instead of Brett's compliments. A petite lady in a lime-green uniform and a white apron wrapped around her waist approached us, her brown hair covering her ears but the tops of them jutted out just slightly.

Hoping Brett wouldn't freak out that we had a wolf waitress, like his father had, I held my breath and smiled at her, my heart racing. With so many people, I had felt like I had been walking on eggshells lately.

"Hello, darlings. What kind of milkshakes can I get for you today?"

"I'll do chocolate," Brett said.

"Vanilla," I said.

"Can we get a side of fries too?" Brett asked.

With a curt nod, she scribbled our orders on a small notepad, stuffed it in her pocket, and smiled. "Comin' right up!"

Once she left for the kitchen, Brett grabbed my hand from across the table. "So, how've you been? We haven't really hung out in a while."

"Good, I guess," I said, not really wanting to give it much thought. I'd believed Brett wanted to take me out to *not* talk about what had been happening in my life recently and to take my mind off things, not ... ask me about them.

He raised an eyebrow. "You guess? Come on. Tell me what's really been bothering you."

The waitress placed our milkshakes between us. "Anything else I can get for you?"

Brett shook his head yet kept his gaze on me. When she walked to a nearby table, he brushed his thumb lightly against my chin. "Mae, I've seen through your lies since we were children. Tell me what's bothering you."

I wrapped my lips around my straw, taking a sip of the vanilla shake, and then sighed. "I've just had a lot going on recently. I haven't had much time to think about it all. I don't really want to talk about it."

Instead of listening to a word I'd said, Brett leaned back. "Like Aaisha getting marked by a brute?"

"How do you know about that?"

"I came over this morning to see if you wanted to hang out. Aaisha opened the door, and I saw the bite mark on her neck. Not to get you down, but you do know that there's a good chance that she won't survive the shift?"

"Yes, and I'm scared for her." I chewed on the inside of my lip.

I hoped she would make it. But what if she didn't? What was I going to do? I couldn't live my life without her. She was the one who had convinced me to move out of Dad's house, and she'd stood by my side time after time when he argued with me about wolves. I considered her to be closer to me than Dad was.

After a few moments, Brett's hands balled up into fists. "I hate seeing you like this!"

I jumped at his sudden outburst, my eyes widening. "Like what?"

"Like you're about to cry, like you've been dealing with too much. You know this could've all been avoided if you had just listened to your dad's advice and not associated with those beasts."

The waitress glanced over at us and raised a brow.

I turned away from her gaze, my heart racing. Why did everyone I know have to make a huge scene everywhere I went? I should've said no to Brett when he asked me to come out.

"Wolves are in our society and are treated by the government as equals. We have to associate with them whether you like it or not," I snapped at him, nostrils flaring. "And if you actually tried getting to know some of them, you'd realize that they're just like you and me."

"I just ..." Brett said, shaking his head. "I don't understand you. When we were teenagers, hanging out only with humans, you never had all these problems. Now, all of a sudden, you're drowning in them. Why do you like them so much? What is so fascinating about them that you'd rather hang out with them instead of me?"

"I don't know." I shrugged, sipping my shake. "They're just cool, I guess."

"You must think they're more than *just cool*. You live with one, and you're basically dating one. What do they have that you like?"

Even though I wasn't sure what drew me toward the wolves, I knew Brett wouldn't leave me alone until I gave him a straight answer. I raked my mind for something clever, something that would piss him off. "They have this type of edginess to them. They're strong, powerful."

"They're pretty stupid compared to us humans, if you think about it."

"Being smart isn't everything," I barked back, my hands in fists.

"In what situation does strength and power outweigh intellect?"

"In bed." Slapping a hand over my mouth, I widened my eyes at him, my cheeks flushing. *Did I just … say that?*

I glanced around the diner, hoping nobody had heard me, trying to desperately avoid eye contact with him. A clatter rang from the diner door, and a flash of blond hair exited the café, reminding me of the wolf from Damon's cabin the other night.

Deciding that I was just seeing things, I turned back to Brett. He rubbed the back of his head with his hand and readjusted himself in his stool, staying quiet for the rest of our meal. And I thanked the Moon Goddess herself when Brett finally took me home for the night.

So much for relaxing. He'd made me an anxiety-induced mess.

"Brett, you don't have to come up with me," I said as he parked. I just wanted to get upstairs and away from everyone's drama as soon as humanly possible.

His stubbornness getting the best of him, he followed me to

the apartment door. "Mae, I'm walking you up," he said. "I just need to make sure you get in safe. I told your dad that I would take care of you tonight and show you how gentlemen act because, apparently, all you're familiar with is how poorly the brutes treat you."

Exhaling through my nose, I clenched my jaw. "You told my dad that we were going out?"

"Yes," he said, holding the door open and following me up the creaky stairs to my apartment.

"Okay, Brett. Well, I made it up safe. I don't know what I would have done without you," I said sarcastically, turning around to tell him good night.

Standing much closer to me than expected, he placed one of his hands on the door next to my head, eyes flickering down my body. I shifted uncomfortably and leaned back against the door to put as much space between us as possible. Wanting to get away from him, I stuck my hand in my purse and fished around for my keys.

"Mae"—he gazed at my lips—"I don't know how many times I have to say this, but … fuck, you're so beautiful." His fingers brushed against my jaw. "I've wanted you for so long … so fucking long. You have no idea."

I squeezed my eyes closed. "Brett, please don't," I whispered, fingers fumbling in my purse. Where the hell were my keys? Where had I put them? This pocketbook wasn't that big. Surely, they were in here.

"All I want to do is give you the love that you deserve." He moved closer to me and trapped me between both his arms, his warm breath on my neck. "It's all I've wanted since we were children."

"Brett, you said you wanted to be a gentleman. Please, be a gentleman and leave. Don't ruin it," I said, fingers trembling.

He pushed a stray piece of hair out of my face and tucked it behind my ear. "Mae, you let those beasts love you. Let me."

He grazed his lips against my cheek and moved his mouth left to meet mine. Before he could press them against me, I turned my head to the side.

He snatched my chin between his fingers, harshly pressing down on the skin, and forced my lips in his direction, a knot forming between his brows. "Why won't you let me love you? I've waited years to hold you, to touch you, to kiss you. But you always ignore me. I've had to distract myself with girl after girl to get you out of my mind, but it never works. I still fucking want you, and it destroys me every time I see you with one of those things."

I placed my hands on his chest and shoved him away, unable to take this any longer. He staggered back slightly, still gripping my chin, and smirked at me. Fucking smirked. He pushed himself back against me and forced his lips onto mine.

After mustering up all my strength, I kneed him square in the groin. He clutched his stomach, doubling over in pain onto the dirty landing, and I dumped the contents of my purse onto the floor.

Finally finding my keys, I tried aimlessly jamming them into the lock but failing each time. Brett lunged toward me, still clutching his stomach, and pressed me against the door, his fingers digging into my sides. I cast my elbow back, hitting him in the stomach.

"Tonight, I'm going to have you even if it's just a kiss," he said against me, hand circling around the front of my neck.

"Please, Brett. Stop!" I shouted, stomping on his toes.

"I can't wait to—"

I hurled my heel back, hitting him in the kneecap, causing him to stumble back. And just as I tried to jam the key into the hole again and failed, someone snatched Brett by the neck and threw him to the other side of the hall, a menacing growl rumbling behind me.

Damon was here, and he had saved me.

CHAPTER 17

MAE

*D*amon grabbed Brett by the neck again and violently shook him, every muscle in his body taut with fury. Brett clawed at Damon's hand, trying to pull it away from his esophagus, but Damon tightened his grip and pushed his claws into his neck.

Distraught, I glanced between Brett and Damon with tears in my eyes. If Damon hadn't shown up, Brett could have done more than just kiss me, and even my best fighting skills wouldn't have been able to protect me. No matter how much Luca had trained me, I lost all sense of thinking in a situation like that.

"Damon, let him go," I pleaded for Damon's sake, clutching onto his bicep and pulling him away.

If he lost control and killed Brett, he'd be thrown in jail, and his pack would be alpha-less. Everything that Samuel had told me Damon did for his pack would be gone, just like that.

"Please, don't kill him."

Brett reached out for me, but I gave him no ounce of sympathy. He deserved this. If he claimed to care about me and then touched me like he had, I could only imagine what he had done to women he didn't care about.

After bathing in Brett's pain for another moment, I jerked harder on Damon's arm. Scaring Brett would be enough for now. Later on, I could figure out how to deal with him and how to make it so he never did anything like that to anyone again.

To my surprise, Damon slackened his grip and let Brett fall to the ground with a thud. "Leave before I kill you and don't think for a minute that I won't."

Brett stumbled to his feet and hurried down the stairs, leaving a small trail of blood on the ground behind him. My lips trembled as I pushed the key into the door and walked into the empty apartment. Damon shut the door behind us and leaned against it, his chest heaving up and down as he crossed his huge arms over his chest.

"You left me," Damon said through gritted teeth. "You left me today to go out with that fucking asshole, Mae, and he almost raped you! I told you to stay in my bedroom and not to leave. Listen to me next time."

Reeling with anger, I turned on my heel toward him. "I left because you tortured a boy, Damon; not to go out with Brett. As much as you want to think you're some kind of god who could do no harm, *you* drove me to leave you today."

"I told you not to follow me out to the training area today because I knew you wouldn't like what you saw. If you had listened to me, you wouldn't—"

"No!" I shouted, stepping forward and glaring up into his furious golden eyes. "Don't you dare blame this on me. You need to learn how to control your wolf."

His jaw twitched, hands balling into fists. "I know how to run my own pack. I've been doing it for fucking years. You don't get to tell me what I need to do, like you know the difficulties of being a leader."

Crossing my arms, I shook my head, ignoring that stupid honeysuckle scent of his that always seemed to calm me for some outrageous reason. "You know, I'm beginning to think that it isn't your wolf losing control, but you, because being an alpha does not give you the right to be an asshole. It doesn't give you the right to kill people. And it certainly doesn't give you the permission to mark me, like you were going to the other day."

Damon stepped closer to me, canines extending. "You don't understand our culture, Mae. This is what we do. This is how we live and how we've always lived."

"I understand your culture. And I know many wolves who don't act feral like this."

"You say you understand, but you don't. We're not like humans. We kill. We fight. We're possessive. It's how we live. You can't expect me to change something so innate to me. I'm willing to do a lot for you, but you can't change who I am. You have to accept me the way I am. You're my mate."

Blowing out a breath, I deposited my purse on the living room table and paced around. "You claim that I don't know your culture, but then you expect me to fit right in without letting me adjust to it. You wanted me to bear your pups just after a couple of weeks of knowing you. You wanted to mark me when I didn't want to be marked. You're just expecting me to be okay with punishment and violence when I've never been close to it before." My voice broke, emotions from earlier rushing through me. "It scares me."

Though I'd thought I knew their culture because I lived with Luca, I really didn't know much. I assumed that because many humans rejected them, they would want to blend into our culture in order to feel accepted. And while many of the wolves tried to fit in, just as many embraced their true identities.

I failed to understand and accept their feral side because, truthfully, it terrified me. It was uncharted territory, another way of life that Dad had sheltered me from while growing up. I had tried so hard to understand them, but I had failed so deeply that even I couldn't see it.

After a few moments, Damon sighed. "This is just as hard for me as it is you. Being a werewolf is all I know, and I know being human is all you know. Ever since I found you, all of my emotions have been so much more intense. I'm more possessive and jealous. You just affect me too much ... I can't understand it. I didn't want you to ever see my wolf that violent. I wanted you to see the good in me before you saw my beast like that. I'm willing to try to be more open to you, if you promise to try to do the same."

Eyes fluttering closed, I blew out a deep breath. Damon had hurt me in the past, but part of that had been my fault. I didn't understand him and his duties, the way people looked up to him and the things he had grown up with. I so desperately wanted to stay with him, but his wolf scared me sometimes.

"Let me show you that I can stay in control of my beast, and if I can't"—he swallowed hard, his golden eyes dragging me closer and trapping me in—"then you can make your choice of staying with me or not."

He was offering me a space to face my fears and explore a mysterious yet fascinating world that nobody had really ever given me before, not even Luca.

I blew out a deep breath and gently rested my hands on his chest. "Damon, if we're going to do this, then you need to stop playing games with me. You need to let me live my life the way I want to live it. I will choose my friends, and you can't get angry over it. And most of all, you need to treat me how I deserve to be treated, and I'll do the same for you. I'm not wasting my time on your games with Alexandra anymore. You respect me or I'll find someone who will."

"As long as your friends don't include that fucking asshole who touched you tonight."

"Deal," I said.

Brett was a prick that I wanted nothing to do with. I'd be more than fine without him.

I furrowed my brows slightly and arched a brow. "Deal—as long as you tell me how you knew I went to lunch with him."

The corner of his mouth curled up. "Your waitress is a member of my pack."

"So, you were spying on me," I said, walking to my bedroom.

Damon lingered in the hallway and sniffed, as if he smelled something off. Then, he sighed and followed me to my room anyway. "No, I was trying to find you after you left. Samuel said that he dropped you off here, but nobody was home when I came to pick you back up. I needed to make sure that you were safe."

Shutting my door behind Damon, I pulled my vibrating phone out of my pocket.

Dad: How was your date with Brett?

After rolling my eyes, I tossed the phone on the bed and laid down next to Damon, not wanting to deal with Dad or even think about Brett for the rest of my life.

"Who was that?" Damon asked.

"My other mate," I said sarcastically, watching his eyes turn to gold again. "It's just my dad, asking me how the afternoon went with good ol' Brett, who can do nothing wrong, an angel in my dad's eyes." It was sickening how much Dad wanted me to get with him sometimes.

Damon lay next to me, wrapping his arm around my waist and nuzzling his head into my neck. After inhaling my scent, he relaxed beside me and trailed his fingers up the center of my body until they reached my cheek. "I'm sorry I haven't been the man you deserve."

My fingers grazed down his lips. He must've heard the conversation between Brett and me.

I leaned my forehead against his. "Brett's just jealous of you. Don't listen to what he says."

"But you feel the same way, don't you?"

While brushing my nose against his, I gazed into his eyes. "We're both trying to understand each other. We've made mistakes, but we're learning from them."

"I don't know if I will ever be able to be that man for you," he said quietly, as if he could already tell our future.

The ruthless alpha was finally opening the door to his heart for me, allowing me to look in on all the insecurities he had bottled up.

I gently cupped his face in my hands and brought my lips to his, an explosion of tingles erupting on my lips. He slid his fingers into my hair and pulled me closer to him, so our bodies pressed together on my bed.

The phone buzzed again.

Dad: So???

Damon eyed me curiously, his brow cocked up. He propped his elbow up on the bed and rested his head in his hand, watching me with intent. "Are you going to respond to him?"

I rubbed my hand across my face. The last time I'd talked to him, we'd fought. Hell, nearly every time I talked to him, we fought. I wanted to relax for once. Just once. This day had been filled with one bad event after another.

"Well, if you don't want to tell your dad about it, tell me about your night."

My nose wrinkled at the thought, and I shook my head and plastered the biggest fake smile on my face that I could muster. "Oh, Damon. It was amazing! Brett is *such a great guy*," I said, sarcasm heavy in my voice.

He rolled over to lie between my legs. "Kitten, don't tease me."

"And what if I like teasing you?" I murmured against his lips, toying at the edges of his dark brown hair.

A low, sensual growl rumbled from his throat. "I don't know if you'll like the consequences," he said, his lips claiming mine. He gently nibbled on my lip and slipped his tongue into my mouth.

I wrapped my arms around his neck and pulled him closer to

me, the mere touch of his skin against mine setting my body ablaze. He was a fire I never wanted to put out, one that grew wildly and hastily, claiming whole forests in moments, one that could never be tamed.

Lips traveling down my neck, he sucked on the nape, where he probably hoped to mark me one day, though I never knew if that day would actually ever come. Humans very rarely survived that shift.

"I heard you think werewolves are good in bed," he said.

"H-how did you ... where did you hear that?" I panted, trailing my fingers down his ripped back.

"Do you think I'll be good in bed, Kitten?"

"I-I don't know," I breathed out, holding back a moan.

He ground his hips against mine. "Do you want to find out?"

I laced my hands in his hair, pulling him ever closer to me.

"I'll take that as a ye—"

My phone blared Dad's obnoxious ringtone. I shut my eyes and sighed, grabbing the phone from the bed and wanting to hit Decline because he had to ruin every damn moment of my life. Yet I couldn't get myself to press the button. He was the only family that I had left.

"You should answer your dad, Kitten," Damon said, sitting up and leaning against the headboard.

"Don't want him thinking you're tormenting me?" I teased him.

He smirked. "I don't want him knowing that you're enjoying it."

Tingles erupted on my cheeks, heat spreading down my neck. I glanced away for a moment and hit the Answer button, not really wanting to do this, but knowing that I had to—for Dad's sake. Brett had probably told him that I was with Damon; that man didn't know how to keep his mouth shut.

"Hi, Dad," I said.

"Mae! How was your date?"

"It was okay," I said.

"Anything exciting happen?"

"Brett tried to kiss me."

"You sound sad about that. You didn't kiss him back?"

"No, Dad. I don't want him kissing me," I said.

"I thought you liked him though."

"I *did*. As a friend. And even if I did like him the way you think I do, he basically forced himself on me." My grip on the phone tightened as I thought back to earlier and the way Brett had just … come upon me without giving me any say in the matter.

"Oh, Mae, women usually shy away from a kiss on the first date. It's our job as men to make it happen," Dad said.

My phone nearly slipped from my ear, shock rushing through me.

"Mae, are you there?"

"Dad, you've said some pretty fucked up things before, but that has definitely got to be the shittiest of them all. I could have been raped tonight, and you'd probably still take Brett's side because you think he's the most amazing person, don't you? Let me tell you, he's an entitled asshole."

"I didn't mean it like that, sweetheart. I just—"

"You did mean it like that."

"I'm sorry if I offended you. Let's talk about this tomorrow night. I'll make dinner at my house."

"I already have plans to have dinner with Damon tomorrow night," I said quickly.

He paused and cursed under his breath, probably at the mention of Damon's name. "Then, you will come over for lunch, and I will talk to Brett about what he did. Good night, Mae."

He hung up without giving me any time to decline, leaving me paralyzed in anger that my own father hated wolves so much that he would rather me date someone who had wanted to sexually assault me tonight.

CHAPTER 18

MAE

I stabbed my fork into the bowl of pasta in front of me, my gaze fixed on the bowl and *not* on the man sitting at the other side of the table. If Damon hadn't convinced me to come tonight for dinner, I would've still been at home, relaxed and content. But after I'd hung up the phone, Damon had dived into his relationship with his father and how it had been broken from the start, that he wished things could've been different and that he didn't want that for me too, especially since my mom had died.

Dad parted his lips to speak, but I shook my head. "I don't want to talk about Brett."

"All I wanted to say was that I talked to him and he apologized for his behavior last night. It won't happen ever again."

Twisting the noodles around with my fork, I reminded myself that not only was I the only family he had left, but he was the only family that I did too. If I had to endure one hour a week with him, I could do that, right?

Dad sighed, setting his silverware down, and leaned back in his seat tensely. "Well, if you don't want to talk about Brett, let's talk about what's going on in your life. Why are you hanging out with Alpha Damon? I thought I told you—"

"I'm not talking about him with you either," I said, wondering when he would stop with this all. He sounded like a broken record. "We'll just get mad at each other, and I'm tired of fighting with everyone. I just need a day of peace."

"What do you want to talk about then?"

Nothing. I wanted to leave.

Instead of being as rude as I wanted to be, I gently grasped Mom's necklace on my chest. I needed answers as to why the hell this thing had broken and what was inside of it. "Dad, you said this necklace made Mom stronger during the blood moon. What's so special about the blood moon to humans? Why did this necklace make Mom stronger? I don't really understand how a necklace can do that."

For once, Dad actually smiled. "Well, honey, that's a complicated question. When your mother was alive, she told me that during the blood moon—the pink blood moon, to be exact—she became very weak, and she would go through all sorts of pain."

"Did you see her go through pain?" I said.

"Well, the pink blood moon only happened once while we were together, once every few years it comes, so I did see her go through it that time."

"What happened?" I asked, brows furrowed.

"She was in pain for hours, complaining about how hot she was, sweating and cramping."

"Did you find out the source of the pain?"

He beamed with happiness, eyes glossing over. "You. You were born that day."

"Oh," I said with a forced laugh.

For some reason, I felt crushed. Maybe I'd wanted her to have had this necklace for a totally different reason, like for her to feel power. But of course she would think the necklace made her stronger during the night she birthed me.

I wrapped my fingers around my necklace, holding it closer to me. "Do you have any pictures of Mom on the day I was born?"

He paused for a few moments, and then he pressed his lips together tightly and looked down at his pasta. "No, sweetie."

Between the way he couldn't keep eye contact with me to how he picked up his silverware and twirled his pasta around aimlessly, I could tell that he was hiding something. But why? Why would he hide a picture of Mom from me? He had always wanted me to get to know her through stories, and now ... he wouldn't show me a picture of her.

So, me being me, I decided to snoop around after dinner. After telling Dad that I needed to freshen up before he took me back home, I ran up to his bedroom and poked around. He must've had a picture somewhere that he didn't want me to see, something that he had been hiding for the past fifteen years.

But when I opened his closet to search through his clothes, his wallet, his drawers, I found nothing. I checked the bathroom, knocking over shampoo and messing up the towels in the closet, and still nothing.

I glanced around the room, brows furrowed. Where could it be?

A small silver frame poked out from under his mahogany dresser. I reached under and grabbed it. In the frame, a crease divided the picture in half with one half being folded under the other. The front half of the picture showed Dad with his arm around Mom's shoulders with a baby in her arms, who tugged at the necklace on her chest. I flipped the frame around, took off the back cover, and slipped out the photo.

On the other side, two muscular men stood next to Mom— one with overgrown facial hair, glowing eyes, and ears coming to a point like a wolf's and the other with dark brown skin and small white freckles all over his body.

And … they were all smiling.

Dad was smiling near a wolf, an actual werewolf.

"Mae!" Dad snapped from the doorway, snatching the picture out of my hand. "What the hell are you doing with this?!"

My eyes widened. "Nothing. I was just looking. Who's in the picture?"

He effortlessly crumpled the picture up, like it didn't matter to him anymore. "That's none of your business."

"Dad, please, tell me. I just want—"

"You just want to know who they are?!" He unraveled the wrinkled picture and shoved it into my face, pointing to the wolf. "He's the one who killed your mother."

"What?" I whispered, unable to believe it. "But you look like best friends."

After a few rageful moments, Dad relaxed his clenched jaw and slumped down on the bed. "We were. Well, she was good friends with them. I didn't see them that often, but when I did, they were nice people." He smoothed out the picture and gazed down at it, eyes drooping. "Then, one day, he turned on her. I found him standing over her dead body with blood dripping out of his mouth, down his neck, onto his hands. He had torn her up, Mae. He had torn her to pieces."

Heart clenching, I sat next to him and gently rubbed his back.

He covered his face with his hands, tears streaming down his wrinkled cheeks. "I-I couldn't even recognize her. Her face had claw marks all over it. There were huge pieces of her flesh lying around. Mae, I couldn't … I didn't know what to do," he said, voice cracking. "I just stood there in shock, not knowing what to do or what had happened. I let him claw at her some more. I can't believe I just let him do that. If I had been home that day, I wouldn't have lost the love of my life. He took away my soul mate, zapped the life right out of me."

Never before having heard this story, I rested my head on his shoulder. He had refused to tell me details about her death for years. And now ... this was it. Someone Mom had trusted killed her. But how could a wolf just turn that quickly on her? How could he have torn her up like that? Had he lost control, like Dad always warned me about?

Wiping his face with the back of his hand, he glanced over at me. "That is why I don't want you near those beasts, Mae. You don't know when they will turn. They'll kill you without a second thought."

"Dad, not all wolves are—"

"Yes, they are." He balled his hands into fists. "Your mother trusted that wolf. They were best friends for years, Mae. Don't think for a second that those wolves that you're hanging out with won't do the same to you. You never know their true intentions."

Glancing down at my lap, I frowned. Would Damon turn on me? He had lost control of his wolf before, nearly killing Samuel, who was his beta and good friend. What if he got angry with me? Would he kill me? He'd turned on me before when I tried to protect Samuel. I didn't want to end up like my mom; I didn't want to die in the hands of a wolf.

If Dad lost me too, it would kill him.

"Mae"—he took my hands—"will you please try to be more careful with who you choose as friends? If you're not willing to stop seeing the wolves, please, please try to see that they aren't good people. Know what you're getting yourself into."

After the ride home, I lay on my bed and clutched a pillow, lost in my thoughts about wolves, Mom, and my entire life I'd spent without her. A single tear streamed down my cheek at the thought of Damon losing all control and killing me, just as Mom's best friend had killed her.

I picked up the phone, my hand trembling, and dialed Damon's number.

"Kitten," he said after the first ring.

My breath caught in my throat at the sound of his voice. I placed a hand over my mouth to quiet my sobs. I didn't want to die like Mom; I loved wolves, but Damon ... Damon lost control too much. Almost every time I was with him, I feared for my life.

"Mae?"

"Damon, I, um ..."

"Are you all right?"

"Damon, I don't think we can see each other anymore," I said.

Before I could take it back, I shut the phone off and hid it under my pillow. The hurt in his voice would break me, if I'd let him respond, if I'd stayed on the phone for another moment.

Since Luca and Aaisha were out, training for her to survive the shift, I stripped my clothes, jogged through the empty apartment to the bathroom, and slipped into the shower to try to keep my mind off of Damon. I picked up the soap and ran it over my naked body, my fingers trembling and my heart aching at the thought of what I had just done.

It had been a hasty decision.

I dropped the bar of soap from my hand and bent at the stomach, resting my forehead against the wall as my body heaved back and forth. It was a *senseless* and hasty decision. I had talked endlessly about accepting wolves as equals and learning more about their lives, but Dad ... Dad had gotten into my head.

My raspy breaths turned into hiccups, a loud sob echoing throughout the bathroom. Tears streamed down my face, and I sank down, unable to hold myself up.

How could I have just let him go, all because of what my dad had said? I loved Damon.

My eyes widened. *I love him?*

No, I couldn't.

But the more I thought about him, the more my heart ached.

How could I love that man and his beast?

He couldn't control his wolf. He killed without a thought. He lied. And despite all of that, he was trying to be a better person for me. He'd opened my mind to a world of new possibilities. Since I'd met him, our connection with each other had only grown and intensified.

Just the thought of saying that to him broke me to pieces.

Ugly sobs escaped my scratchy throat, and I wrapped my arms around my naked body to try to hold myself together. I needed to apologize to him. I needed him back. Grasping the shower knob, I pulled myself to a standing position and turned it off.

Suddenly, someone tore the shower curtain back, and Damon stood before me with a taut chest, golden eyes, and canines that could sink into any part of my body. He growled as he threw me a towel and stormed out of the room.

I wrapped the towel around my body, not bothering to wash the soap off of me, and hurried after him. "Damon!"

He sat on my bed with both sad and rageful eyes. "You don't want me?" he asked, holding back his wolf that I could tell so desperately wanted to claim me right here, right now.

But I had asked him to control himself more around me, and … he was.

"Damon, I made a mistake. My dad had finally explained the details of my mother's death to me, and … I got scared. I didn't want to end up in the same position as her, but I've realized that what we have is worth more than my fears. I'm sorry. I called you without thinking anything through. It was stupid and senseless."

After a few moments, all the anger faded from his face. He looked down at his feet and … nodded. Damon nodded instead of exploding at me, like he usually did to me and to everyone else. "It's okay. I'm sorry about your mom. Your dad and you shouldn't have had to go through that kind of pain. I know how it feels to lose people that you love." He grasped my hands and pulled me closer to him. "And that's why I can't lose you too."

CHAPTER 19

DAMON

Mae hurled the ax at the target behind my secluded cabin, the toe of the bit impaling the wood. I stood back, arms crossed over my chest, and blew out a deep breath, just treasuring this moment with her because I knew that being with her wouldn't last forever. Last night, Mae had nearly broken it off with me, and I hadn't been able to get it out of my mind.

I loved her, but if I marked her, she wouldn't be able to survive the shift.

And I couldn't let her die. I couldn't.

"Long time, no see," Samuel said to Mae, walking up behind me.

Mae twirled around, silver-blonde hair swaying in the slight morning breeze, and smiled at him, her rosy cheeks rounding. "Good morning to you too. Didn't I just see you, like, two, three days ago?"

Samuel cracked a smile at my mate. "Long time for you not to see this amazing face."

She laughed, voice drifting through the air. "I don't think it's been long enough."

"Can you both stop fucking flirting?" I growled, rage burning inside me.

My time with Mae was just that. *My time.* I didn't know how much longer I had with her, how much longer that I could continue to keep up this lie—that we would be together forever—just to please her and my wolf. I had to be the one to think straight about this. Mae would die, would leave this earth forever, once I marked her.

She would have the same fate as my brother's mate.

"We're not flirting," Mae said, pulling her ax from the target.

"Leave," I said tensely to Samuel. When he scurried away, I stalked closer to her. "I can't fucking wrap my mind around you. You want me to control my wolf, but then you go and flirt with one of my best friends right in front of me. You are provoking my wolf, Mae. And if you keep it up, you're not going to enjoy the consequences."

"All I was doing was talking to Samuel," Mae said, pushing some hair behind her shoulder. "Why are you freaking out on me for it? You've been picking fight after fight this morning. What's your problem?"

My problem? I balled my hands into fists. My problem was that I could never have Mae, no matter how much I wanted her. The Moon Goddess had cursed me with a human mate, a mate she knew could never survive as a wolf. My pack had already lost my alpha brother to suicide … I couldn't fucking leave them without any leadership if Mae died too.

"Can you just—"

"Excuse me," a petite woman from my pack said, hurrying in my direction.

"What?" I growled, my wolf on edge.

"I'm sorry for bothering you, Alpha Damon," she said, bowing her head. Eyes red and teary, she glanced back up at me. "I will come back later."

Mae furrowed her brows, placed down her ax, and hurried to her, wrapping her arm around the woman's shoulders and rubbing her back. "No! We're finished talking for now." She narrowed her eyes at me. "What's wrong?"

"*She cares. She is a good mate*," my wolf said in the back of my mind.

I pressed my lips together and ignored my wolf, hating how good she had fallen into the role of luna. I didn't want her to enjoy it, and I didn't want my wolf to praise her either. I loved her and hated her at the same time.

"What is it that you wanted to talk about?" I asked, eyes hard.

"My-my …" A hiccup escaped her lips, and she gripped on to Mae. "They took my pup! My pup is gone! I don't know how it happened."

My heart stopped, chest tightening. *A pup from my pack had been taken?*

"Who took him?" I asked, pushing my shoulders back and slipping into the role of alpha with ease.

"I-I don't know. He has been missing since yesterday. I tried to find him before I came to you. I asked everyone in the pack if they had seen him, but nobody has. I don't know who, or when, or why they took him. I-I just want my baby back." She doubled over in pain, knees buckling, and covered her face with her hands.

Mae knelt next to her and gently stroked her back.

"I want my baby back. I don't know … what I'm going to do. Please, please, help me, Alpha. I will do anything for you. I just need him back."

"I'll do my best to help you. You must give me time. We will get your pup back," I said, contacting Samuel, Alexandra, and some higher-ranked wolves in my pack to meet in my office in five minutes.

If a pup from my pack had been taken, that meant the rogues were close.

And rogues meant ... that someone might try to take more pups or even my human mate.

"Thank you, Alpha," she cried. "Thank you so much."

Once she left, I turned to Mae. "Mae, we are not finished talking, but I need to work now. We will continue talking over dinner tonight. I'm going to take you out."

"Do you need my help?" she asked, brows furrowed.

Though she cared about the children and my packmates, these kidnappings involved too much danger. Rogues would tear a human like her apart, shred her to pieces, and leave her as a pile of blood and bones.

"No," I growled. "For now, go to my room and don't fucking leave it. And I mean it this time. Rogues are about, and they won't think twice about killing you."

I couldn't let anything happen to her. She was mine. Mine to protect. Mine to love.

CHAPTER 20

MAE

"Did you find any new information about the missing boy?" I asked, sitting across from Damon at Oasis.

After this morning, I hadn't seen him all day. I'd so desperately wanted to help out in any way that I could, but he'd refused each time.

Damon sighed through his nose. "We're assuming that the boy was taken by rogues. Alpha Richard caught the scent of rogues after the abduction of some of his pack's pups. We believe it's the same people, but we have no other damn leads on it."

He seemed way too on edge today, too snippy, too.

"I'm sorry that you have to deal with that. It's terrible, what's happening. No mother deserves to be put through that." I frowned and grasped his hand. "How is she holding up? I can talk and comfort her if you want."

"No," Damon said, pulling his hand out of mine. "Alexandra has been with her the whole day."

Alexandra? He'd asked Alexandra and not me? Why couldn't he have asked me?

My nostrils flared, but I pursed my lips and averted my gaze. "Oh."

"I just hope we find something soon," he said, grabbing his burger.

"Maybe it's an inside job and not rogues. How could rogues get into your borders without you knowing? It would make sense if the pup voluntarily went with someone he trusted and then was abducted by him or her."

He raised his eyebrows, and then he shook his head. "If that were the case, Alpha Richard and some of the other alphas wouldn't have smelled rogues."

Realizing that Damon didn't want to talk about it, I dropped the subject and pulled my vibrating phone from my pocket to see a text from Luca.

Luca: Grabbing food for Aaisha and me. Want anything?

I wiped my hands on my napkin and glanced up to see Damon glaring at me, eyes shifting between green and gold.

"Who's that?" he barked.

After pushing my phone back into my pocket, I turned back to him and smiled. "Just one of my friends. Do you want—" My gaze shifted behind Damon's towering figure to Luca, who walked into Oasis.

Brows furrowed together, he sniffed the air and scanned the room, eyes eventually landing on me. After giving me a soft smile, he looked at the back of Damon's head and suddenly started storming toward us.

"Who's the—" Damon started, glancing back.

Before he could finish his sentence, Luca pummeled his fist down on Damon's face, cracked his jaw, and thrust him to the floor. My eyes widened, and I scurried out of my seat to Luca. Damon shuffled to his feet, his eyes glowing gold and canines extended.

"Luca, what are you doing?" I shouted, wrapping my hand around his bicep to try to pull him away.

He shrugged me off, and I stumbled back into my seat, hitting with a thud, the seat legs scraping against the wooden floor.

Growling, Damon lunged at Luca, but Luca quickly sidestepped him and caused Damon to stumble forward just slightly. When Damon regained his balance, he leaped into the air and shifted, baring his sharp canines at Luca.

What the hell was happening?

Luca shifted and circled Damon—his brown wolf just a bit bigger than Damon's black one—lowering his head, as if ready to attack at any moment. Damon lunged forward and sank his teeth into Luca's flesh, blood gushing into Damon's mouth.

Thrashing around, Luca ripped his four claws right across Damon's face, a puddle of blood forming underneath the two wolves. The other wolves and humans quickly ran to the sides of the room, their tables and chairs being knocked over by the two beasts.

Pieces of flesh and fur soared through the air in all directions. I flinched away as some rained down near me, blood splattering on my face. Every second that passed felt like an eternity.

Why was this happening? What were they fighting for? How much blood had they lost already?

"Luca! Damon!" I screamed. "Stop! Please!"

Tears streamed down my cheeks. Blood continued to stain the floor.

I glanced at the other wolves in the restaurant, throwing my hands up. "Are any of you going to do anything?!" I asked, but they all ignored me.

I reached for my phone and dialed Samuel's number. "Samuel! They won't stop. They-they are going to kill each other. What do I do? Please, you have to help!"

"Calm down, Mae. Who is fight—"

"Don't tell me to calm down! My boyfriend and my roommate are about to kill each other! What do I do?"

"Mae, who is fighting?" he said calmly.

"Damon, and Luca, my roommate."

The two wolves continued to attack, claw, and bite each other in any way possible.

"Shit," Samuel said. "I'm on my way."

Throwing down the phone, I balled my hands into fists, feeling nothing but pain in my heart. Luca leaped over Damon, latching his teeth into his upper back. Damon kicked his hind legs forward, pushing him onto his back, and crushed him with his weight. Blood splattered onto the walls as Luca fell into the puddle of blood.

If I tried to get in the middle of it, I would get hurt, maybe even die, but I didn't want either of them to kill the other. So, I gripped the back of a chair, lifted it over my head, and threw it at the men. It crashed into them, causing Luca to unclamp his teeth, and then they both jumped back from each other.

Before I could stop myself, I moved between them, my heart thumping in my chest.

"Mae!" Samuel shouted from the other side of the room, sprinting over to me and fastening his hands around my arms to pull me away from the men.

And as soon as I was out of harm's way, they pounced at each other again.

"You can't get in between two alphas! Are you crazy?!" he shouted, holding me back.

Alphas? Luca was an alpha?

My stomach tightened. "Samuel! You have to do something! Please. Let me go! I need to stop this." I panicked, arms and legs flailing around.

"If I release you, promise me you won't try to get in the middle again. I'll handle it."

After I nodded, Samuel released me and looked around frantically. I didn't know how Samuel was going to stop two overly aggressive alphas, who both moved at incredible speeds. Yet he looked at my chest and yanked my necklace off of me. For a split second, he winced in pain, but he quickly hurled it at the wolves.

Both men shuddered away from the silver necklace and each other; the strength of the silver had seemingly intensified for some reason because they both shifted back to their human forms. Samuel stood between the two bloodied wolves, holding his hands against their chests.

"I should have killed you when I had the chance!" Damon growled at Luca, pushing against Samuel's hand.

"You should have! But you didn't because you're weak. You always have been, and you always will be," Luca snapped.

"I'm the fucking weak one?! I distinctly remember you being the weak one when I took over your pack and forced you out of your lands," Damon said.

My eyes widened. This explained everything—from Luca being a rogue to that teenage wolf who wouldn't recognize Damon as his alpha. This was it. This was what Damon and Luca had been hiding from me all this time.

"Let's get one fucking thing straight, Damon. *You* were not the one to defeat me. If Alexandra wasn't in your pack, you would be dead." Luca seethed at Damon, brown eyes a terrifying black.

"What does Alexandra have to do with any of this?" I said, stepping forward.

Why was she always the topic of everything?

"Nothing," Damon spoke harshly, not even looking in my direction, fists clenched by his sides and green eyes as sharp as emeralds. "Luca just can't accept the fact that I defeated him and that he is a weak piece of shit."

"Bullshit. Alexandra has everything to do with it," Luca said, stepping toward me. "And don't talk to Mae that way." He turned in my direction. "Alexandra was my mate."

"She's your mate?" I asked in complete shock.

"*Was*," Luca started. "Damon used her to—"

"More like she used you," Damon spat.

"Shut the hell up for once," Luca growled, glaring at Damon. "I was an alpha, Mae, before I met you and Aaisha. Damon wanted parts of his lands back that his scum father had given away. My pack was already living on the lands. Long story short, I met Alexandra and marked her, as she was my mate. She lived with me in the pack house for a year. She gathered information about *my* pack and gave it to him." Luca pointed to Damon. "Our secrets, our strengths, our weaknesses. After Damon destroyed my pack, after my family was killed, after she took everything from me, she left with him. She left me for him."

"Why would she leave you for him?" I asked, throat closing up.

Damon had told me that she was just one of his best warrior wolves and not to worry about her.

Luca balled his hands into fists, blood gushing from the open wound in his naked abdomen. "Mae, is Damon the wolf you've been going out with?" he asked, jaw twitching. When I nodded, he shoved Samuel out of the way and landed another fist on Damon's jaw, sending Damon to the ground.

Almost instantly, Damon shot back up and wrapped his hands around Luca's neck.

"You didn't fucking tell her?!" Luca said, grabbing him back.

Didn't tell me what?

"There is nothing to tell," Damon said through gritted teeth.

"I can't believe you did this to her!" Luca said, claws stabbing into Damon's neck.

"What didn't you tell me?" I yelled over the chaos.

Damon shoved Luca away from him, his eyes shifting between gold and green irises, and a guilty look was written all over his face, as if he had lied to me about something—something terribly horrid, something that would break me to pieces.

"Tell her, Damon," Luca taunted. "Tell her your big plan. She deserves to know what kind of wolf she's been dating."

I narrowed my eyes at Damon, who couldn't even look me in the eyes.

"Goddess, tell her! Before I do." When Damon still didn't respond, Luca growled, "What's so hard about it, Damon? Why can't you tell her that you plan to mate Alexandra, my mate?"

Wh-what was he talking about? I was Damon's mate. He had ... he had told me that he wanted me and not her.

Tears pricked at the corners of my eyes. "What?" I whispered, voice cracking.

"Mae, you're weak." Damon clenched his jaw, and then looked at me with emotionless green eyes, not an ounce of sympathy, regret, or denial in them. "You're human. You could not lead my pack with me. You'd be the weakest link. Having you as the luna of my pack would make us an easy target for enemy packs and rogues. I cannot have you as my mate."

I furiously shook my head at him. No. What he was saying couldn't be true. It couldn't be.

"Don't lie to me, Damon." Tears flowed down my cheeks. "You always do. Don't do it now."

Cutting eye contact with me, he flared his nostrils. "You're weak, Mae! What don't you understand about what I'm saying?! You can't handle my wolf. You can't handle our way of living. You had a breakdown the other day because I was punishing that wolf for his misbehavior. You got angry because I tried to protect you from danger when you couldn't do it yourself. You believe your dumbass father when he feeds you information about wolves, information that he has no fucking idea about. And you go on and believe him. You will never be strong, Mae. I need a strong luna."

I reached out for Damon, not wanting to believe his words. "Damon, stop. Please," I begged.

He pulled himself away and straightened his back. "Alexandra has been by my side. She has not defied me. The pack loves and respects her. They would not respect you as a luna. She will continue to be strong for me and for my pack. She is going to be my mate."

"You're an asshole!" I screamed at him.

He'd lied to me. He'd told me I had nothing to worry about, that she was nothing to him.

I lunged at him, but Samuel gripped my arms to hold me back. "You told me that you loved me!"

"Mae," Samuel said, but I ignored him.

I glared into the eyes of the man that I'd once loved, the eyes that I still loved. "Get off of me!" I shouted at Samuel, yanking myself out of his grip. I stalked up to Damon and pushed him back. "I hate you! I hate everything about you! You're a liar and a cheater! How could you lead me on like that?"

"I'm not leading you on. It is my wolf. My wolf wants you, but I never did. I don't know how he could want someone as weak as you, Mae. I've *never* liked you. It is all him," Damon said, just rubbing it in that someone would never love me like a wolf could love his mate.

My lips quivered, and my hands fell to my sides. None of this made any sense. Since the day I met him, he had been so keen on marking me or being a stupid possessive asshole.

Damon stared down at me with stupid green eyes. "Mae Cogan, I, Alpha Damon, reject—"

Unable to listen to him finish his rejection, I sprinted out of the diner and left him behind. Colorful streaks of red, gray, green, and blue clouded my teary gaze. I turned my attention away from the busy street and focused on the sidewalk below me, putting one foot in front of the other.

Tears rolled down my cheeks, lightly dipping onto my lips and creating a salty residue. Not even the loud traffic horns and bike bells could deafen the vile thoughts in my head of Damon...

loving Alexandra, the woman he'd told me not to worry about, the woman he'd lied to me about.

Lost in my thoughts, I accidentally knocked into someone, tripped over my feet, and landed on the pavement with a thud. Pain pierced through my scraped and now-bloody knees. A few people glanced over at me, their eyebrows furrowing, but they continued walking.

After wiping the tears from my cheeks with the back of my bloodied hand, I whipped my head around, wanting to mutter an apology to whoever I'd bumped into. But Alexandra towered over me with a smirk on her stupid face and an outstretched manicured hand.

"Oops. Sorry. Didn't mean to run into you. Let me help you up."

I wanted to wrap my hands around her neck and watch as the life drained out of her.

She'd caused me pain, so much heartbreak.

"Come on. You look too weak to get up yourself," she said, waving the hand in front of my blotchy face.

Weak. Weak. I am not weak.

I leaped up from my spot, only to collapse back onto the ground, pain shooting through my knees. Blood dripped down my shins, soaking the sides of my legs and the cement below me. Maybe I was weak.

Alexandra cackled and skipped down the street, brown ponytail bouncing. When she retreated into the diner, I screamed out in frustration, dug my nails into my already-bloody palms, and pulled myself up onto a bench.

Why was this happening to me? Why had I fallen for him?

I hated him. I hated the way he'd led me on, only to throw me aside. I hated the way he'd told me he loved me. I hated the way he'd made me feel like I was his. But most of all, I hated the way I had fallen for him. My dad had told me he would break my heart, and I'd let him. I'd let him break me. I just hadn't thought it would happen so soon. I'd thought I'd have time to enjoy life with him.

"Mae!" Luca called from behind me, jogging out of the diner with Samuel.

Not wanting to talk to anyone right now, I stood to my feet, wobbling slightly, and staggered to the street, where a bus pulled to the corner. I stumbled up the steps, paid my fare, and limped to a seat. I didn't know where I was going, but I didn't really care.

As the bus pulled back onto the street, Luca and Samuel slowed to a walk outside the window. I rested my forehead against the glass, my head bumping slightly against it as the bus hit a pothole. I didn't need Luca's or Samuel's pity; it would only make me feel weaker than I was.

I replayed Damon's words over and over again, hoping to catch just a sliver of denial in them to show he actually cared. Yet each time I repeated them, the once-soft petals of my heart turned brittle, and I was left empty.

CHAPTER 21

VALERIO

"It's a dollar fifty to ride the bus, buddy," the bus driver said to me.

I tossed a twenty dollar bill in his direction, told him to keep the extra as a tip, and strolled to the back of the empty bus, where Mae glared out the window. Instead of sitting in the seat across from her or a couple of seats back, I sat right beside her and stared ahead.

She hiccuped and looked over at me with furrowed brows, her teary eyes widening when she saw me. "You're the waiter from Tangled Orchard Winery. I've been seeing you everywhere. Are-are you stalking me?"

My orders were to watch Mae, not to engage with her. But after what had happened at Oasis, I needed to make sure that she was okay. She was mine to watch and to protect, and I couldn't stand to see her this upset.

"No," I said, finally glancing over into her piercing gray eyes.

"Yes, you are." She crossed her arms over her chest, pushing some long silver-blonde hair behind her shoulders. "If you aren't, then why do I keep seeing you everywhere?"

"Coincidence," I said, leaning back and crossing my legs at the ankles.

If I had let her see me once or twice, I might've even gotten away with that excuse.

"I don't think it's a coincidence," Mae said, sniffling.

Arching a brow at her, I gestured around the empty bus. "If I were stalking you, do you think I would make it this obvious? I wouldn't sit next to you on an empty bus. Come on. I'd be smarter than that."

"Then, why did you sit next to me?"

"Because you look like you needed someone to get your mind off things for a couple minutes," he said, and my lips turned into a frown. "Well, this is my stop." The bus pulled to the curb, and I stood and walked to the front of the bus, needing to get out of here before *she* found out that I'd engaged with Mae.

But before I hopped off, I glanced back and smiled at her. "You're stronger than you think you are, Mae."

CHAPTER 22

MAE

I stared through the glass window and watched that stalker wolf shift into a magnificent beast and sprint into the woods at lightning speed, his blond fur blowing in the wind.

Who was he? And how had he known my name? Dad had said it at the restaurant, but how'd he remember it?

"Last stop!" the bus driver called, eyeing me through the rearview mirror.

Groaning, I walked to the front of the bus and assured the driver that I hadn't gotten my blood all over the seats. Then, I retreated down the stairs and stepped off into the most run-down part of Witver, where graffiti covered the sidewalks and cracked windows covered all the bars.

I nervously walked back in the direction the bus had come from, not knowing how to get home from here, with tears streaming down my face and dried blood on my shins. When I passed a group of human men, they nudged each other and nodded at me. I shivered and wrapped my arms around my body, hoping to shield myself from them.

Hearing them turn around, I quickened my pace and continued forward as fast as I could without running, my heart racing. Why did I always put myself in these types of situations? What the hell was wrong with me?

Suddenly, someone seized my waist with callous palms. With the little dignity left inside of me, I tried ripping myself out of their grip, but I couldn't, my body falling limp. No matter what, I should've been able to fight back, but ... everything felt so weak after Damon ... had rejected me.

So empty.

So vacant and desolate.

I didn't want to fight anymore, but I didn't want them to take me. So, I weakly threw my elbow back to hit one in the stomach, yet they dragged me into the thick Witver Forest. In the distance, a wolf with dark golden eyes growled viciously at the men. The men stopped, their faces paling, and released me when a familiar wolf appeared, baring his canines.

Not even strong enough to hold myself up, I collapsed onto my hands and knees, splitting open my skin again. The familiar wolf approached me with his head low and his ears up, and then he suddenly shifted. Luca knelt next to me, wrapping his arms under my body and lifting me off the ground.

I curled into his bare chest, listening to the soothing sound of his heartbeat, and wept.

"I'm sorry, Mae. I'm so sorry."

"There's nothing to be sorry about," I whispered, burying my head into the crook of his neck and breathing in his natural scent.

"I'm sorry I couldn't protect you from him. You didn't deserve to go through something like this," Luca said, tucking some hair behind my ear.

"You didn't deserve to go through something like this either, but you did. You don't have to apologize for someone else," I said.

I wanted Damon to apologize to me, to tell me that he'd made a mistake, that this was all just a big joke, that he fucking loved me.

Luca exhaled sharply, staring down at me with big brown eyes. "Mae, this is just the beginning. It's going to be hard for you, just as it was hard for me. Even though you're not a wolf and you can't feel the rejection as intensely, it will take you a long time to get over this. The mate bond already started forming between you two. His rejection will affect you in ways you don't even think are possible."

I stared emptily at the giant oak trees we passed, unable to understand what had gone wrong. A lot of shit had happened, but ... Damon had continuously told me how much he wanted me and how much he couldn't lose me. Why would he push me away?

"What if I never get over him?" I whispered.

"You will, Mae." He walked into a clearing by our apartment. "I'm going to help you and support you every step of the way."

"But, I-I'm weak, Luca. I won't be able to—"

Luca abruptly placed me down and stared at me, gripping my chin in his hand and forcing me to gaze up at him. "You are not weak, Mae. Don't you *ever* think that. Do you understand me?"

I swallowed hard and chewed on my lip to stop it from quivering. "But ..."

"No. He's the weak one. A strong wolf would have accepted you. Damon wouldn't have let his wolf control him for all this time and up until the scene at the diner. He couldn't see your potential to be a strong luna; instead, he just saw what he wanted to see."

Instead of letting me argue anymore, Luca wrapped his arm around my shoulders, pulled me closer to him—even though he was still naked—and ushered me toward our apartment door through the grass.

After reaching the door, he patted my back to go into the house. "When we get up there, I'm going to put some clothes on and then give you a bath."

"I'm perfectly capable of doing that myself," I said with a soft smile, my heart still aching.

"I know, but I also know that you like to cry in the shower when you're all alone, and I'm not going to let that happen again," Luca said, brown eyes shimmering under the flickering hallway light. He pressed a finger to my lips. "And don't argue with me either. You need someone right now. You can't be alone."

Glancing down at my bloody legs, I nodded. After walking into the apartment, Luca retrieved some clothes from his room and ran the bath. Aaisha kicked the front door open, snapping it against the wall, and stomped into the room with her nostrils flared.

"Oh, someone is gonna get his ass beaten today!" she shouted, swaying a baseball bat around.

Richard trailed behind her, his brows furrowing, and reached for the bat, but Aaisha pulled it away from him.

"Where is that little piece of trash?! I'm gonna go beat his head in and then find that other bitch and beat her face until it's uglier than it already is."

She swung the bat around the room, putting all of her strength into each swing. Richard tried stopping her, dodging a couple of her swings, but ended up getting smacked hard right in the chest.

"I might have told her about what happened," Luca said, hands on his hips behind me.

Once she finished swinging the bat around in the air, she sprinted to the couch and began beating the cushion. After getting *most* of her anger out, she threw it down and turned to me. "I swear to the Moon Goddess, I will kill him for you."

I placed my hands on her shoulders, trying to calm her down.

"Mae, I'm being serious. You tell me when you want me to kill him, how you want me to kill him, who else you want me to kill, and I'll do—"

"Aaisha, I don't want you to kill anyone," I said, giving her the best smile that I could.

For a few moments, she studied my face, her nostrils still flared, and then she frowned and wrapped her arms around me. "I'm so sorry, Mae. You deserve so much more," she whispered. "You deserve to be cherished. You put up so much with your dad; you don't deserve to be treated like shit in front of everyone like that."

"Mae needs to get cleaned up," Luca said, hand on my back.

Aaisha smiled at me, stroking my cheek. "Fine, fine. But ya know, the offer is always on the table. If you want me to kill him, I will. We're besties until the very end, Mae. I'd kill that fucker for you and happily serve my time in jail."

Stifling a laugh, I waved her and Richard off and walked to the bathroom, where Luca was waiting with a warm bubble bath. I peeled off my clothes. Luca had already apparently seen me naked before, so I wasn't too bothered by undressing in front of him. I stepped into the water and sank down into it, my shoulders slumping forward.

Luca slid the bar of soap across my back, caressing it.

I pulled my knees to me, leaning forward and resting my chest against them, my eyes closing softly. "I've never seen Aaisha so … so …"

"Aggressive?" Luca asked, taking the word right out of my mouth. "Since she was marked, she has slowly become more wolf-like. She'll experience increases in aggression. Also, she's been spending a lot of time with Richard, and you know what they're probably doing." He winked at me, and I wrinkled my nose. "Not only is she gonna become more physically aggressive, but also sexually aggressive."

She and Richard were probably going at it nonstop.

"The full moon is only a couple more weeks away. Is she ready?" I asked.

He paused for a moment. "No. She's getting there, but she's not ready yet."

I nodded my head but stayed quiet, my heart aching. First, Damon's rejection, and now, Aaisha might die.

What had been happening to my life all of a sudden? Why was I becoming more miserable by the day?

I had no control of anything, and it made me feel helpless. I couldn't help my friends or myself.

After cleaning my back, Luca sat on the side of the tub and faced me, brown eyes wide. With the soap, he lightly washed around the scrapes on my knees, his fingers gliding against my skin. He sucked in a deep breath, chest rising and falling harshly, and washed the dirt off my palms, touching me so soothingly that it felt … good.

Right almost.

When he finished, he handed me a towel. I dried off, pulled on some clothes that Luca had left on the counter, and padded to my room to drift off to a place worse than reality—my worst nightmares about Damon.

"Mae Cogan, I reject you," he said, the words effortlessly rolling off of his lips.

From outside of the diner, I stared in at the horrid scene and at my fragile body trembling in front of Damon's huge beast. Tears streamed from my eyes, and I watched myself sprint out of the diner.

Moments later, I found myself walking back into the diner with a smile on my face.

"Mae Cogan, I reject you," Damon said again.

More tears fell from my eyes, and I ran out.

Over and over again, he rejected me.
"Mae Cogan, I reject you."
I couldn't take it anymore. I couldn't scream or tell myself to stop.
"Mae Cogan, I reject you."
No.
"Mae Cogan, I reject you."
No.
"Mae Cogan, I reject you."
No. No. No. Stop it.

CHAPTER 23

LUCA

"Stop it!" Mae sobbed, her voice piercing through the walls. "Stop, please!"

Recognizing the sound of rejection nightmares, I shot up in the bed, tugged on a pair of gray sweatpants, and jogged through the apartment toward her bedroom, my thoughts racing as she yelled louder and louder and louder. Shoving open her door, I hurried in and scooped her sleeping body up in my arms.

"Mae," I cooed, lying down and resting her on my chest, "it's just a nightmare."

Mae curled her fingers against my chest and rested her head on my shoulder, still twisting and turning. She buried her nose in the crook of my neck and whimpered against me. "Please, make it stop," she whispered.

I gently stroked her hair and held her close. "It's okay. I'm here for you."

Body relaxing slightly, she mumbled my name and wrapped her arm around my bare waist, as if she didn't want to let me go.

And I held her because I knew how it felt to have a villain chase you in your dreams, never wanting to pull their claws from your heart, killing you slowly until there was no hope left and you felt like you could never love again.

But Mae was proof that, even after rejection, I could love again.

One day, she'd be able to love too.

CHAPTER 24

DAMON

"You're a terrible mate," my wolf said to me.

I paced around my bedroom, unable to sleep without having any nightmares, and punched a hole right through the drywall. Every fucking time I closed my eyes, I saw Mae's teary eyes staring back at me.

"Our mate would've been a perfect luna. Alexandra won't be."

"Can you fucking stop?" I shouted into my empty room.

Gripping the bedsheets, I tore my claws right through them and ripped them right off the mattress. For weeks, I'd desperately tried to ignore the pull between us, tried to think of all the reasons we shouldn't be together, yet she had come back for more, always giving me a second chance. Always. No matter how much of a dick I had been to her.

With her, I didn't have to face my demons alone, didn't have any more nightmares of my father again, and actually smiled effortlessly. No more pretending. No more faking how broken I felt on the inside. But ... I couldn't let her get close.

"I won't stop until you get her back," my wolf said.

"You know I can't do that," I scolded, hating myself for it.

While I wanted to explain why I had done what I did to Mae, I couldn't let her in. If she knew about the monster Dad had been and how badly he had torn our pack apart or even about what *I* had done to help my pack prosper again, she would reject me. I had no doubts about it. She deserved so much more.

At least me rejecting her—or trying to—was on my terms.

Now, she was safe from the rogues, from the shift, and from me—a coldhearted brute.

CHAPTER 25

MAE

"Good morning," Luca murmured, his brown eyes a sea of honey under the sunlight.

I smiled up at him and drew circles on his abdomen with my finger. "Morning."

Between the memories of our time spent together and the nightmares of Damon, it had been one devastating week since Damon had rejected me. Each night, I'd wake up, breathless, in a fit of panic and ache only to have Luca comfort me until I sobbed myself back to sleep.

But last night ... last night, Luca had decided to sleep in my room from the beginning. And for the first time in a week, I hadn't had any dreams of those haunting green eyes. I actually woke up rested.

"You're in a good mood today," he said, golden skin glimmering in the sunlight.

"Thanks to you, I actually got some sleep last night," I said, poking his hard abdomen.

Luca had been the only thing holding me together this past week. I didn't understand how or why Alexandra had rejected him. Caring, honest, supportive, and strong, he'd be the perfect mate and probably a damn good alpha.

Not only had he helped me, but Aaisha too. The full moon was only one more week away, and he and Richard pushed Aaisha's body and mind to the absolute limit during every training session. Aaisha, the strongest woman I knew, broke down in tears almost every day because of it. But we all knew that it had to be done.

Luca wrapped his strong arms around me and pulled me into his bare chest. "You didn't have another nightmare?" he asked me, lightly scratching my back. When I shook my head, he grinned, gaze flickering to my lips for a fraction of a second. "I'm glad I could help."

The soft hum of his voice made my chest tighten. He was too precious sometimes.

I glanced down at him, my eyes drifting to his lips, and swallowed hard, heat warming my thighs. Knowing that I shouldn't and that it was far from right, I pulled away from him and sat crisscrossed on the bed beside him. He stretched his arms over his head and his legs further down the bed, the sheet covering his torso sliding down slightly.

"My eyes are up here," he said, pointing to his face.

My cheeks burned. "Yeah, but your abs are down there."

"That's not the only thing down there," he said, wiggling his eyebrows at me.

I wrinkled my nose at him and playfully slapped him on the chest. "Ew!"

Luca grabbed my hand from off of his chest and gently pushed me, so I fell back onto the bed. He sat up next to me, posting one of his hands on the bed behind him and smirking with those devilish lips. "Don't act like that."

"Like what?"

"Innocent."

Lips curling into a smile, I laughed and laughed and laughed, loving the light feeling inside me again. I hadn't felt this happy in so long, and I had forgotten how good it felt not to have to worry about cheating or lying or loving someone who couldn't love me back.

"What?" I said, brows furrowed together when he suddenly stopped and stared at me.

"I haven't heard your laugh in so long," he whispered, gently grasping my chin and drawing his thumb down my bottom lip. Streaks of amber appeared in his brown eyes, the sunlight filtering through them. "It's nice to see you happy again."

Sucking in a slight breath, he brushed his fingers against my cheek and pushed away a strand of my hair, and then he looked at my lips. He leaned down slowly, the distance between us lessening by the second. I closed my eyes, my chest tightening in anticipation, ready for him to finally—after three years—claim my lips.

When his lips lingered mere centimeters above mine, someone opened my bedroom door. We quickly pulled away from each other before anything happened, and I sat up, breathing hard and staring at the man standing behind the door.

"I-I'm sorry," Samuel said. "Aaisha let me in. I can come back another time."

Luca growled, "What are you doing here? She doesn't need to see anyone who reminds her of him."

"It's okay, Luca. He's my friend." I placed my hand on Luca's shoulder and stood up. "You can stay, Samuel."

After glancing between us for a few moments with raging amber eyes, Luca grabbed his shirt from the dresser and excused himself by saying that he had someone to meet with today. Though I didn't think he really did. He would probably head over to the gym and relieve the tension somehow.

"I wanted to see how you were doing," Samuel said, sitting on the bed.

I wrapped my arms around my knees and rested my cheek against them. "It's been bad, but I'm managing. Luca has been amazing, helping me out."

Samuel looked over at the slightly cracked door and smirked. "I could tell."

Playfully, I pushed him and laughed. "Not like that."

"Suuuuure, Mae," Samuel said. "Whatever you say." When he looked back over at me, he took my hand. "How about we go get breakfast or something? Aaisha said you haven't left the house since last week. And remember what I told you ... food makes women happy."

After rolling my eyes at how silly and stupid he was, I threw on some presentable clothes and jumped in Samuel's car. He pulled up to the same diner, Midnight Treasure Café, that Damon had taken me to what seemed like ages ago.

Soft acoustic music played over the light hum of the customers, and the scent of bitter coffee drifted through the diner. Older wolf couples ate breakfast with each other, smiling across the tables at their mates. And all I could do was frown and think about what *my* life could've been like with my mate.

"Haven't seen you in a while, Beta Samuel," the waitress said, pulling out a small notebook and a pen that read *Witver* across the side. "What can I get you two today?"

"We're going to order for each other," Samuel said, throwing me an evil grin. "She'll take two pancakes, two waffles, four sausage links, four pieces of bacon, a chocolate milk, and ... hmm ... a chocolate."

My eyes widened. "Uh ... he'll get water with a ... pancake."

"A single pancake?!" Samuel asked when she walked away. "That's all I'm worth?"

"I ordered you some water too," I said, chuckling to myself. "But *I guess* that you can share mine." I went to tug on Mom's necklace but realized that it wasn't there, only that disgusting red mark. Scratching it slightly, I leaned forward. "How's the pup investigation going? Did you find him yet?"

The grin dropped from his face, and he slouched back into his chair. "Honestly? We don't have a single trace of evidence or a clue on where those rogues ran off to. No pack in all of Witver Forest does."

"I hope something comes up soon," I said, my heart clenching at the thought of rogues just stealing pups for no reason.

They had to be up to something more than just kidnapping pups for the sake of kidnapping them. And they didn't have any idea where the rogues had gone off to, which almost confirmed my suspicion of it being an inside job.

"That pup was like a little brother to me," Samuel said, shaking his head. "He always used to stand outside and watch me train, even when it was pouring out. Sometimes, I'd even let him train with me. He was so strong for such a little kid." He leaned closer to me and tugged on a strand of my hair. "I'd always let him beat me, like I almost did with you."

"Sorry to let you down, Samuel, but you didn't let me beat you. That was all me."

The waitress reappeared at our table with plates of food, laying all but one down in front of me. I gazed over at Samuel, who had a single sad pancake in front of him and a glass of water.

"How is this tiny little thing going to satisfy my growling stomach?"

"You're gonna have to make it," I said, enjoying all the pancakes and waffles myself.

He reached over the table, grabbed half of everything he'd ordered for me, and smiled. "That's better."

An hour later, an old '60s song played over the stereo, and Samuel tossed his napkin over his empty plates and stood, holding out a hand for me. "Dance with me."

Arching my brow, I glanced around at the older couples, who

looked over at him with lightness in their eyes, whispering something to their mates. "Samuel, it's not even ten in the morning. Sit back down."

Not taking no for an answer, he grabbed my hands and pulled me off the booth. "It's never too early to be dancing."

He twirled me around and around and around until I whirled into his chest and nearly lost my balance, laughter bubbling in my stomach.

Some of the older couples who had been smiling at us stood and swayed with their mates, their howls filling the room. I glanced around at everyone who—despite all the discrimination and heartbreak, backlash and bitterness—danced along with a human with nothing but a smile.

"I told you that it's never too early to dance," Samuel said to me.

And though Damon might've never thought of us as equals or of me as strong, this was … solidarity that I wouldn't trade for the world. He might've broken my heart, but seeing wolves—even from his pack—be so kind and gracious around me made me feel too damn good.

After Samuel got every wolf on their feet, he led me to the door and out to his car, a crisp summer breeze chilling my skin. Above, the gray clouds spoke of rain and fog, but nothing could dampen my mood now. At least, I didn't think it could.

"Oh, before I forget, I brought you your necklace that I'd ripped off of you the other night."

My eyes widened. "You did?" I asked, my neck having felt so naked without it.

Standing next to his car, he reached down into his jean pocket and furrowed his brows. When he didn't find my necklace in that one, he reached into his right side and then his back pockets. "Fuck," he cursed, rubbing his forehead. "I think I forgot it at my house. I can drop you off back home and then bring it back to you later. I know you probably don't even want to go near our territory again."

Knowing that Dad was bound to invite me over for dinner sometime this week and that he'd *kill* me if I'd lost the only piece of Mom I had left, I shook my head. I really wanted my necklace back. A part of me had felt like it was missing this past week.

"No, let's go get it," I said, waving him off. "I'll just stay in the car."

Samuel narrowed his eyes at me.

"Nobody will even know that I'm there. And plus, Samuel, I'm over him," I said, partly lying.

I wasn't totally over Damon. Hell, I was barely over him, but I wanted my necklace back now, and I doubted I'd even see Damon. He was probably out with Alexandra, doing Goddess knew what with her.

"Okay," Samuel said after studying me for a few moments. "But you will stay in the car."

"Deal."

CHAPTER 26

DAMON

Samuel had missed the warrior wolves meeting this morning, hadn't trained with us at noon, and hadn't been seen on his run last night. It wasn't like him not to show up to anything, and I needed to find him. This pup problem was getting out of hand.

Storming through the woods toward his house, I stopped suddenly, listening to the light rumble of a car engine and noticing his car sitting in his driveway. What was going on? Had he been here the entire time and slept in or something?

Instead of heading to his house, I hurried to the car and ripped the door open. "Samuel, where have you been? I've been—"

My eyes widened, Mae's lilac scent drifting through my nose and awakening my wolf, who I'd held back for this entire week. Mae was here right now, right in front of me, staring at me with those wide gray eyes I had fallen in love with.

"*Need mate,*" my wolf said in my mind, clawing for control.

It had been a week of absolute torture without my precious mate.

It wasn't just him who needed her. I needed her too.

"*Need mate,*" my wolf growled at me again, pushing his way to the surface, completely taking hold of my human. He yanked her out of the car and wrapped his arms around her, head buried in her hair and inhaling her scent as much as he could.

After stiffening for a moment, Mae ... slumped her shoulders forward and relaxed into me, almost as if she had been lying to herself this entire week about not needing me, just as I had lied to myself about her. It was wrong, so fucking wrong, and I knew that. But my wolf didn't.

"*Mate loves us. We love mate,*" my wolf purred.

"*Yes, we do ... but ... but ... we can't. You know this,*" I said to him, trying to pull myself away from her. Though I couldn't move a single inch. It was as if my wolf had attached to her and refused to let go.

Although Mae made me a better version of myself in every way possible, although I loved her with every fiber of my being, I couldn't mate with her. I just couldn't. I couldn't deal with the pain and heartbreak of watching her go through that shift from human to wolf, couldn't feel her die, like my brother had with his mate.

"*Yes, we can. Mate is strong. She can survive the shift,*" my wolf said.

"*We thought that about our brother's mate, and she died,*" I said to him.

Suddenly, Mae pulled away from me and shook her head, eyes wide with fear. "What-what am I doing?" she whispered to herself, taking another step back and staring at the ground. "No, we—I can't. I can't."

The moment she took a third step away, a feeling of abandonment—the same feeling I'd embraced since childhood—shot through me. I fucking hated the feeling. And now that I'd pushed my mate away, I would never feel whole again.

"*Mate can't leave us. She's the only good thing in our life. We must mark her,*" my wolf demanded.

"No. We can't," I argued.

"*If you won't, then I will,*" he said, taking hold of my body and stalking closer and closer to Mae, canines extending from underneath my lips.

As I eyed Mae's pale neck, unbroken and unbruised and perfect for marking, Mae looked up at us with fear in her eyes. I snaked an arm around her small waist and pulled her in closer to me, breathing in lilacs.

Heart thumping so loud that I could hear it, Mae shoved me away.

"*Must mark mate,*" my wolf growled.

"*She doesn't want us to. Please, stop. She'll hate us more than she already does.*"

"*Must mark mate,*" he said, grabbing her wrists and yanking her forward toward us. He growled in her ear and drew his nose up the column of her neck. "Don't be afraid, Kitten. I'm just going to mark what is mine."

She shook her head, voice trembling. "I-I'm not yours."

"*Need to show mate that she is ours. Need to mark her,*" my wolf said to me.

"*No, you don't.*" I struggled with him inside of my mind, refusing to let him mark her. "*If you mark her without her consent, she will hate us.*"

Despite my strongest attempts to control my wolf, he pressed her against Samuel's car. "You are, you have, and you will always be mine."

"Please, Damon," she whispered. "Stop."

Suddenly, someone wrapped their arms around my shoulders and threw me to the cement.

Samuel stood over me with extended canines and blazing

golden eyes. "What the hell, Damon?! Get the fuck away from her. I thought you wanted to mate Alexandra. Mae is weak, remember?"

"*Never mate with Alexandra,*" my wolf growled in my mind.

"*Stop,*" I pleaded with him. "*We cannot mate with Mae. Don't you remember what happened last time? Do you really want to watch our mate die, like our brother did? Do you really want to listen to her screams of agony? Do you want to feel her pain?*"

"*If we don't mate with mate, I will leave you,*" my wolf said, giving me no other alternative.

I didn't want my wolf to leave me. We had been together for years, training to be a stronger alpha to our pack, slaying enemies together, understanding what it meant to lead instead of to rule, which Dad had taught us by being the shittiest ruler I had ever known.

But … I wouldn't be able to handle if Mae died.

Mae deserved so much more than someone as fucked up as me.

Taking control of my wolf and accepting my fate, I nodded my head and growled at Samuel. "Why did you bring her here, Samuel?" I asked, curling my lip in disgust at the necklace in his hand. "I don't want to see her ever again."

"*Don't do this,*" my wolf warned.

"Do you understand me, Samuel?" I continued, feeling nothing but pain shoot through me. All these lies and all this agony I caused Mae was just because I wanted to keep her alive. "I don't need someone like her ruining what I have with Alexandra."

Mae stepped into the car and slammed the door shut.

I squeezed my eyes closed.

"I can't believe you." Samuel shoved me. "She's hurting because of you."

"Go!" I growled, feeling myself about to lose control to my wolf again.

If Samuel stayed here with her any longer, my wolf would mark her, and then she would die during the full moon without any training.

Samuel snarled at me and slammed the driver's door closed. Then, he sped down the dirt path, leaving nothing but dust in his wake. Once they were out of sight, I clenched my jaw.

"Fuck. Fuck!" I stripped my clothes and tried shifting into my wolf, needing to run to clear my mind, but I couldn't shift.

My body failed to fall over onto all fours and transform into my beast. I tried calling out for him but was met with silence. Deafening silence.

Balling my hands into fists, I swung at the nearest tree to release all of my built-up anger. Over and over and over, I hit the tree until my knuckles bled, but they didn't heal quickly, like they normally did. Hell, I could usually knock a single tree down in one solid punch. Now … nothing.

What have I done?

My mate was no more. My wolf had left me.

The two most important people in my life were fucking gone … because of me.

After punching the tree one last time, I balled my hands into fists and walked back to the pack house. I wished I could take everything back. If I had been honest with Mae from the beginning, maybe we could have lived a life together without me marking her. But … maybe that wasn't a good idea either. One day, my wolf might've lost control and marked her without her consent.

Either way, I'd lost.

When I was halfway to the pack house, Alexandra's foul stench filled my nose. Before Mae, Alexandra's scent had been enjoyable, but now, it was nothing but repulsive.

"Hi, babe!" she said, wrapping her arms around me from behind. "What do you want for dinn—" She stopped short, sniffed my neck, and inhaled sharply. "Why do you smell like that bitch? I thought you finally got rid of her."

I tried growling at her, yet I couldn't. My wolf was gone.

"Alexandra, don't start with me," I said through gritted teeth.

"What happened to the man I had fallen in love with? What happened to that strong, feral animal inside of you? Now, you can't even growl. Did he leave you over that weak piece of sh—"

"Stop!" I shouted.

She stalked around me until she stood directly in front of me. "You know what? I'm sick and tired of you telling me what to do. I helped you defeat Luca. Now, it's your turn to give me what I want."

"Alexandra, I'm not mating with you. And no matter how much I want pups, I don't want them with you."

"Well, it looks like you don't have much of a say in that right now, huh? Your wolf is gone, and you're weak, Damon. *Weak*. But thankfully for you, I think I might know something that will help us both out."

Before I could stop her, Alexandra leaned closer to me, lengthened her canines, and sank them into my neck to mark me, the feeling fucking killing all hope I had left.

I pushed her away, clutching the wound on my neck. "What the fuck?!"

Licking the blood off her lips, she stepped back and smirked. I wrapped my hands around her neck, gripping her as tightly as I could, but without my wolf right by my side, she easily pushed me away and laughed.

"Don't be so angry, Damon. Think about it ... now, you can lead our pack and not have to worry about a measly human girl dying or weakening you in the process. You can be strong for them."

My fingers slowly loosened around her, my neck aching, Alexandra's emotions flowing through me. If I was beginning to feel Alexandra's feelings already, did that mean a small part of my wolf was still here? Would my wolf come back if I mated with Alexandra?

Alexandra *was* right. I loved Mae, but I needed to be strong for my pack too. They deserved it. They believed in me, even after Dad had fucked them all over, and they'd all sacrificed so much.

Out of all of my brothers, I was the only one who could be alpha and lead these people. I couldn't give up on them.

And Alexandra wasn't that bad, right? She was a strong warrior. She could lead my pack with me.

As I tried so desperately to convince myself that this was the right decision—because there wasn't any other decision left to make—a weak, strained, and dying voice whispered in the back of my mind, *"Wrong."*

And it was the last word I heard my wolf mutter.

CHAPTER 27

MAE

"Are you okay?" Samuel asked, parking in my driveway.

I held my trembling fingers still and swallowed hard, all the emotions from last week bursting through me. "Shouldn't you just assume that I'm not because I'm weak?" I snapped, knowing that he really didn't think that but unable to stop myself. I wanted to be angry with everyone but myself, but this was my fault.

"Mae, if I hadn't said that to him, you would be marked right now," Samuel said, one hand on the steering wheel, the other resting on the center console. "His wolf hasn't come out for a week. Once he recognized it was you, he must've snapped. He was more possessive than I had ever seen before. I didn't know what to do. Damon's wolf can do some really, really bad things."

After a deep breath, I nodded. "I know. I'm sorry. I'm just frustrated that I reacted that way toward him." I'd thought I would hit him, smack him, punch him for hurting me; instead, I'd fucking let him wrap me into a hug and almost mark me.

Samuel gave me my necklace, which was wrapped in a plastic bag so he didn't touch the silver. "If you need me, please call. I know it's hard. I can tell by the look on your face that you're trying to forget him. Rejection sucks."

Taking the necklace from him, I thanked him and walked to the apartment. All I wanted to do was to cry in Luca's arms and ask him why I had been so stupid. He had to know the feeling; he had asked me that question about himself thousands upon thousands of times before.

But when I entered the apartment, I heard a man's voice that I didn't recognize. I sat at the counter, waiting for the guy to leave so I could cry to Luca, and I might've overheard some stuff that I shouldn't have.

"Alpha Luca, this is the perfect opportunity. Damon hasn't shifted in a week. He's weak without her. Please, consider what I am telling you," the man said, urgency in his voice. "Our packmates hate being under his rule."

"I know you mean well, but I cannot do that. I will not do the same thing he did to me. I don't need him to be broken in order to defeat him," Luca spoke with authority. "If I want to take my pack back, I will do it when he has his wolf back. I'm not going to destroy him like he destroyed me."

The man stayed quiet for a few moments. "You have every right to do so, but I respect your decision. You're a good person, Alpha. I hope, one day, the time will come for us to be a pack again. Everyone misses you. You're the strongest wolf I've ever known."

Despite the tears racing down my cheeks, I smiled at the thought of Luca being so genuine. No matter what Damon had said about him the other day at the diner, I would always look up to Luca as someone who cared about the people he had led.

"The day will come. Just be patient and trust me," Luca said.

When they walked out into the living area, I wiped my tears away in hopes of being strong in front of someone. I had felt like the weakest damn person alive this past week, and I hated the feeling more than I hated how I'd reacted so naturally to Damon.

"Mae, I didn't think you'd be home so early," Luca said, eyeing my tearstained cheeks. "What's wrong? What happened to you?"

After Dane, a burly wolf who looked to have fought many battles over his life, excused himself, I wrapped my arms around Luca and pulled him closer to me, resting my head against his chest and listening to the steady rhythm of his heart. "I saw him today, Luca. Samuel was going to get me my necklace at his house ... and ... and he saw me. He almost marked me."

Luca tensed. "Why'd you go there, Mae, knowing you'd see him?"

"I didn't know he'd be there," I whispered.

He grasped my chin and forced me to look up at him. "Yes, you did. You wanted to see him," Luca said, sadness laced in his voice. "I know what it feels like to think you're absolutely helpless, to deny your feelings, to make excuses, just to see someone you love."

I fixed my gaze on the ground, hot tears welling in my eyes again.

"Be honest with yourself about your feelings. Face them; don't fight them," Luca said.

"If I didn't fight my feelings for Damon, I would be over there right now, begging him to take me back," I admitted, shaking my head. I would be at his feet with fat tears rolling down my face, pleading with him to love me for just one more moment, to touch me like he had, to mark me and claim me and finally make me his.

"You say that because you think you're weak. You need to face this and understand why you're feeling this way, and then you need to understand why he is no good for you. If you hide your emotions or try to block them out with this anger, the pain will stay with you, and you'll never get over him," he said.

After a few moments, I sighed. Luca smiled down at me,

strumming his fingers across my cheek, amber-brown eyes inviting me closer.

Laying my hand over his, I leaned into his touch and gently brushed my fingers across his stubble. "How do you do that?" I whispered.

"Do what?"

"Make me feel"—*butterflies*—"better?"

"I guess I learned from the best," he said, stepping closer to me, gaze drifting from my eyes to my lips. He leaned down slightly, so damn slightly. "You've taught me how to be strong for the past three years."

My hand glided to the back of his neck, and I drew him closer until our lips grazed against each other for a moment. And for the second time today, I wanted to kiss him so freaking badly. I realized just how much I wanted him, not Damon.

Luca grasped my hips and pulled me closer, his lips brushing against mine again.

"Luca, are we going to go train or what?" Aaisha shouted from her bedroom.

Cursing under his breath, Luca pulled away and instead rested his forehead against mine. I clasped my hands together, breathing ragged at the thought of him finally claiming my lips.

He tucked some hair behind my ear and smiled. "One day, I'm going to kiss you and not be interrupted."

Cheeks flaming, I pushed him away when Aaisha walked into the room, on her phone.

She glanced up, her black curls pulled back into two tight buns. "What's goin' on in here?"

I pressed my lips together. "Nothing!"

Luca placed his hands on my shoulders and gave it a tight squeeze. "Just comforting Mae."

"Mmhmm. Well, I don't want to die next week, so let's go train."

After glancing at me once more, Luca left the room to grab his gear.

Aaisha watched him and then leaned closer to me. "How was your date with Samuel?"

"It wasn't a date."

"Sure, it wasn't." She winked. "Don't worry; I can keep a secret."

"What secret?" Luca said, walking back into the room with his bag strap crossed over his taut chest, muscles rippling under his shirt.

"Mae is dating Samuel."

"Is that so?" Luca asked, leaning against the wall, brown eyes fixed hungrily on me.

"First of all, we aren't dating," I said to her. "Second, you're terrible at keeping secrets."

"Luca is our best friend. He doesn't count." She gazed at her buzzing phone. "We gotta go."

"You wanna come with us, Mae?" Luca asked, twirling his keys around his finger.

Grabbing my phone and wallet, I lingered by the door and wrapped a hand around his bicep. "Can you actually bring me to Hot Shots? I wanna relax for a bit by myself." *And maybe pull my hair out at the thought of Damon.*

Two minutes later, I waved Luca off and walked into Hot Shots Tea Room, wondering why I'd ever fallen for Damon. From the damn beginning, we were never good for each other, and I'd kept going back to him over and over. And I knew that if given the chance, I would probably do it again despite my better judgment.

If I had just let him mark me when he wanted to or tried to understand his culture more or wasn't so much of a pushover, maybe this wouldn't have happened. I had tried to change for him, to understand him and his culture better, but I should've tried harder. As a human, I would never find a love like a mate's love. Finding such a strong and honest connection with another human was rare. I could search for years.

After ordering a small jasmine tea, I walked to my favorite secluded corner of the shop to sit. I placed my tea down, knots suddenly squeezing my stomach. The pain tore its way up my body, slashing its claws into my chest and up my esophagus to the nape of my neck, excruciating tingles numbing the area. Legs wobbling, I grasped the seat and doubled over, the pain so much deeper than physical.

"Mae!" someone said faintly behind me.

Through clouded vision, I saw Dad and Brett sitting a few tables down with wide eyes.

"Mae, are you okay?" Dad asked, bushy brows furrowed.

After taking a deep breath, I pushed aside my agony and forced a smile on my face. They were the last people I wanted to see right now. I had come here to drink my tea alone, not to feel whatever this pain was and ... to argue with Dad and Brett about wolves.

"Yes," I said, biting back my discomfort and sitting beside Dad at his table. Placing a hand on my neck to ease the ache, I cursed under my breath and sipped my tea, letting the smooth taste slide down my throat.

Brett glanced at Dad and then me. "Mae, I wanted to apologize for the other night. I shouldn't have done what I did. It was wrong, and I ... I deeply regret it. I don't ever want you to be that afraid of me again."

I pursed my lips and glared down at the glass tabletop. I didn't forgive Brett and didn't think I ever would. He'd overstepped—big time.

Brett leaned forward and *almost* grabbed my hand. "I heard what happened with Alpha Damon."

At just the sound of his name, my neck burned. I slapped my

hand harder over it and narrowed my eyes. "What? How?" I asked, knowing that whoever had been at Oasis that night was either a wolf or a wolf ally, nobody who would ever associate with Brett.

"Word gets around," Brett said. "I just wanted to say that he's shit for letting you go."

I pressed my lips together to stop them from trembling. "Can we not talk about him?"

"What did I tell you about him, sweetheart?" Dad said.

"You told me he was going to break my heart. I know, Dad. And I knew that he was going to from the beginning, but I pursued him anyway," I said, going along with it so he wouldn't make a huge deal out of it. I didn't have the energy to fight with him any longer.

"Then, why did you do it?" he asked, eyes softening.

"You do crazy things for love."

Dad clenched his jaw. "You're just lucky you didn't get yourself killed. I hope you stay away from them from now on. Don't run back to him and end up like your mother. You don't know what that'll do to me."

I gave an empty laugh and stared into space as I sipped my tea. No matter how hard I tried, no matter how much they hurt me, I could never stay away from the Witver wolves. All of my friends had wolf blood inside of them now—all of them, except me.

"Mae!"

I glanced over my shoulder at Samuel, who hurried into the tea room, running a hand through his thick hair.

Dad's lips twitched, and he shoved his chair back and grabbed his coffee, letting it slosh over the edge and onto the table. "I can't believe you, Mae. You disappoint me."

"I've always disappointed you, Dad." I waved him and Brett off. "I'm used to it by now."

Samuel swiped a napkin across the spilled coffee and stared at them as they stormed out of the café and down the street, passing by the large glass windows. "What was that all abo—"

"I don't even want to talk about it," I interrupted.

Samuel shook his head. "Anyway, you're not going to like this, but I wanted to tell you first, before you found out from someone else." He paused. "After you left, Alexandra marked Damon."

"What …" I started, my word trailing off into nothingness and a shaky breath escaping my mouth. My neck burned hotter and hotter, my heart empty. I gazed through Samuel, feeling as if my world had been shattered.

I … I … she'd marked him? Why? Why now? Why not before? He couldn't … she … what …

This must've been why my stomach was in knots earlier, why I felt that excruciating pain in my chest.

"Mae, are-are you okay?" Samuel asked.

Nothing about this made sense. Nothing.

And although my lips trembled, I refused to let my tears fall. This was going to happen sooner or later. I'd expected it to be later. I'd expected it to take at least a couple of days for Damon to get over me, but I was wrong.

Why had I been so stupid? Why was he my weakness? And why couldn't I have seen his intentions from the beginning?

Balling my hands into fists, I stood and tossed my tea in the trash. I needed something—anything—to make me feel better. I hated feeling helpless. And for once, I wanted someone to want me, like I was the only person they'd ever craved. I longed for love, not pity.

So, after muttering good-bye to Samuel, I excused myself from the shop and found myself hurrying back home, praying that Luca had finished training already. It hadn't even been an hour yet, but … I needed him.

I shoved my key into the lock and pushed the door open, finding Luca sitting at the counter.

He stood when he saw me, hair wet and tousled from his

workout, veins swelling in his biceps. "I came back as soon as I heard about Alexan—"

Unable to stop myself, I grabbed his face and kissed him.

For a moment, he just stood still, and then he gripped my hips and pulled me closer, his soft lips moving effortlessly against mine. When he parted them, I slipped my tongue in his mouth, needing more.

"Mae, I think we should stop," he said between kisses, hands sliding up my body. "This ... isn't ... right."

I wrapped my arms around his neck, realizing that he wasn't going to stop me from loving him tonight. "I don't care," I murmured against him. "I just want to feel loved, Luca. Love me."

He wrapped his arms around my legs, picked me up, and placed me onto the counter, pushing himself against me. "Mae, you're going to regret this later," he said, fingers dancing up my body.

Not caring anymore, I slid my hands underneath his shirt. I might regret this later, but I wanted him to make me feel whole again. He was the only person who had gotten me to smile and to laugh this past week. I needed someone like him right now.

I squinted my eyes open until they adjusted to the early morning sunlight, small goose bumps darting across my naked flesh. Memories of last night rushed through my mind of Luca, an alpha, being so gentle with me, caressing every part of my body, not stopping until he was sure I had been satisfied.

When I glanced over to his side of the bed, I frowned at the emptiness. Our clothes were picked up off of the ground, mine folded neatly on the dresser. My chest tightened at the thought of Luca leaving me and regretting what we had done, like he did after sleeping with any girl.

After tugging on some clothes, I gazed at the dark circles

under my eyes and even darker circle on my chest. My lips trembled. Did *I* regret it? What was I supposed to feel like after sleeping with someone who wasn't my mate? Sad? Disgusted?

Fists forming by my sides, I dug my nails into my palms. If Damon knew what I had done with Luca, he would kill him. But he had probably done the same with Alexandra, his eyes taking her in, his fingers touching her skin, his lips worshipping every inch of her.

A stray tear raced down my cheek, but I pushed it away. I couldn't let it get to me. I couldn't let him get into my mind, not now, not after I had been with Luca. I laced my hands in my hair and pulled gently on it, trying to rid myself of the pain. Though my mind told me not to regret it, a part of my heart already regretted my impulsive decision to have sex with Luca because I'd wanted our first time to be special.

For three years, I had dreamed endlessly of it. And it'd never turned out like this.

"Mae, are you okay?" Luca asked, standing in the doorway.

Quickly, I wiped the tear from my cheek and turned around to face him, giving him my best smile.

He furrowed his eyebrows, his lips turning down into a frown, and grabbed my hand. "It's okay."

"What's okay?"

"To regret it."

"I don't regret it," I said, half-lying to him.

"Yes, you do." He sat on the bed and pulled me closer until I stood between his legs. He tilted his head, just slightly, and gazed up at me. "I know how it feels, Mae. I've experienced this before."

An unstoppable, broken sob escaped my throat. I wrapped my arms around his neck, my head falling against his, and broke down. "Why doesn't he love me, Luca? Why doesn't my mate love me?"

He rubbed soothing circles on my back, tightening his embrace. "You might never understand what he sees in her or why he did what he did. All you have to understand is that he hurt you, but you will get over him. I promise you that. You *will* get over him, Mae. It might not be today or tomorrow or even a year from now, but you will. The pain will fade, and you'll find someone much better than him."

"Do you regret it?" I whispered, staring down into his big brown eyes, though I didn't think I'd be able to handle another rejection.

"No, I don't regret it."

After every night Luca had spent with someone who wasn't his mate, he would break down because he felt bad. Why wasn't he regretting it now? Was he lying to me, just so I wouldn't get hurt? If that were the case, I needed him to just be honest with me. I'd rather have the truth than to be led on, like Damon had.

"Luca, tell me the truth."

He cupped my face in his hands and gently caressed my cheek with his thumb. "I'm not lying to you. I-I don't know how to explain it. I thought I was going to regret it yesterday, before it actually happened, but I don't."

"But what about the connection with your mate?" I said.

"The bond has been weakening," he said, tucking some hair behind my ear. "I noticed it yesterday when I found out that Alexandra had marked Damon. I thought I was going to be angry with her for doing this to me, but I didn't feel anything at all." He smiled. "It's blissful, not to be weighed down by someone who doesn't want me anymore."

My chest tightened. After three tortuous years, Luca was finally happy.

And while everything seemed to be crashing down on me, I was happy for him too.

CHAPTER 28

MAE

"Mae, I swear to the Moon Goddess, I'm gonna kill Luca and Richard if they don't stop tryna assert their dominance when training me. They're killin' me. I'm 'bout to bop them in their heads with my bat," Aaisha said, breathing heavily over the phone later that day.

"Well, the full moon is in four days," I said. "Luca told me that wolves become more aggressive—alpha wolves, like Luca and Richard, especially."

"Yeah, but this is all damn day—from the moment Luca wakes me up to the moment I fall asleep. I barely get any rest, only when he bothers you at night. He hasn't been bothering you too much, has he? Because I'm ready to beat his ass if you want me to."

My lips curled into a smile as I thought back to last night. "No, Luca isn't a bother." *Especially when he sleeps next to me.*

The nightmares had disappeared, but the feeling of snuggling close to him and listening to his deep breathing actually soothed me at night.

"Good. And I swear, if that damn guy makes me do one more sprint today, I'll knock him out cold. Oh, you know, if he doesn't come home tonight, he's sleeping on the gym floor," she said.

"Aaisha, come on! Last sprint of the day," Luca yelled behind her.

"That man. I'm 'bout to beat his—"

The line went dead, and I smiled. From all the aggression to the growling, Aaisha was turning more wolfish by the day. Between Luca and Aaisha, I was surprised all the food in the fridge hadn't been eaten yet.

I opened the refrigerator door, ready to dive into the hamburger I'd saved from lunch, only to find the fridge bare. I'd spoken too soon. My stomach growled, and I slammed the door shut, my knuckles turning white around the handle. A human girl had to eat too, ya know.

While I threw on some sweatpants to pick up takeout, someone banged on the front door so loudly that I thought that the door would come off the hinges.

"Hang on!" I shouted, cursing myself out for not leaving to get food earlier.

Brett had mentioned briefly through text that he was going to stop over, and I wanted to be nowhere *near* the apartment when he did.

Stuffing my feet into shoes, I rushed to the front door to pull it open. "Wha—"

My breath caught in my throat as a beautiful pair of forest-green eyes, raging like a fire, stared down at me. Damon stormed into the apartment, every muscle in his body tense, that bright mark on his neck taunting me.

"What happened?!" he growled, canines extending far past his lips.

"Damon, what are you—"

He stalked closer to me and grabbed my jaw like he owned me. "Don't act innocent. What happened last night, Mae?" he snarled, claws digging into my flesh. "What did you do with him?"

"I-I don't know what you're talking about," I said, heart racing at his touch.

"Cut the bullshit!" he said, glaring down at me with green eyes.

His wolf wasn't the one angry. This was him. Damon.

I ached for him to touch me more but wanted him away. My mind was jumbled, the mate bond desperately pulling me closer to him but my consciousness knowing better.

"I know what you did with him. I could feel you doing it. You even have a hickey to prove it," Damon growled, eyes flickering down at the circular red mark on my chest that could easily be mistaken for a hickey. "Do you know how much that hurt me?"

"Oh, don't you dare ask me that." I shoved him back. "Do you know how much it hurt me when you led me on and then rejected me? Do you know how much it hurt when Alexandra marked you? Do you think it didn't hurt me, Damon?" I yanked down the neckline of his shirt to get a better view of the teeth marks Alexandra had left in his neck. "You're a disgusting hypocrite."

Grasping my wrist, Damon pulled me closer. "If you had let me reject you, we wouldn't be feeling this way. I had a chance to complete the goddamn rejection, but you were too weak to let me finish it. You had to just run out of the diner, crying."

Fury pumping through me, I crossed my arms and glared up at him. "You're a liar. Your wolf was all over me the other day. He still wants me, Damon. Even if you'd rejected me, he would feel everything ... every kiss ... every touch ... every time my heart beat a little faster for someone else. You not rejecting me has nothing to do with this."

"He wants you, but I don't," Damon said, jaw clenched hard.

"If I could've marked Alexandra, I would have, but he wouldn't let me."

I let out a lifeless laugh and walked away from him, pacing around the room. "I heard that he hasn't been out for a long time. Sucks, doesn't it, you asshole?"

Storming toward me, he pushed me against the wall near the kitchen and grasped my chin hard in his callous grip. "Don't you dare talk to me like that, like you know how it feels to be a wolf, to have a mate, and to have to reject her."

To have to reject me.

"Reject me then, Damon," I said, the words coming out hoarse. My heart pounded against my chest. Rejection was the last thing I wanted from him, but it would bring me peace. And if it would bring him peace too, then I wouldn't hold him back any longer. "Reject me! Do what you have wanted to do since you met me!"

Silence.

"Why don't you just do it, Damon?" I asked. Why wouldn't he fucking do it already?

He flared his nostrils, jutted jaw twitching and gaze traveling across my face, burning me in its wake.

"If you aren't going to reject me, then what's the real reason that you're here?" I asked, so damn tired of everything lately.

After staring me down for another moment, he leaned forward and kissed me hard. Tingles darted across my lips, slowly capturing every part of my body. I wanted to push him away so bad, but my body wouldn't let me.

When his hands released my wrists and trailed down the sides of my body, I let him. For once in his life, he didn't hold anything back. The love. The hate. The jealousy. The possessiveness. Our kiss held it all.

He wrapped his hands under my legs, picked me up, and walked us to the couch, not once breaking our kiss. This man was mine—mine to love, mine to devour. He could try to forget about me time and time again, but he couldn't stay away.

I wanted to wrap my arms around his shoulders and pull him closer. But I couldn't. I couldn't do this anymore. I couldn't put up with his lies, the endless drama, the constant push-and-pull, never feeling good enough, and never really knowing where he stood with Alexandra.

So, I pushed him away despite my body screaming at me not to. And when he didn't move, I shoved him harder. "Damon, stop."

"Come on, Kitten."

"No, Damon. I don't want you to touch me."

He pulled back slowly, burying his face into the crook of my neck, his canines grazing against it. "I know you've wanted me this last week as much as I've wanted you," he murmured against my ear. "Don't stop this. Just enjoy it. I've never gotten to be with you. Not once."

"What the fuck is goin' on?" Aaisha said from the doorway.

My eyes widened as Luca and Aaisha stood in the small foyer, Aaisha glaring at Damon in fury and Luca staring in horror. He parted his lips, a knot forming between his sweaty brows and his shoulders slouched over. I almost missed the slight quiver of his chin.

Broken.

He looked so broken.

My heart sank in my chest, yet I couldn't move. I couldn't speak. All I could do was watch my best friend try to stay strong after I'd betrayed him. We had given each other everything last night, and I'd let the man who had taken his mate kiss me.

I'd fucking let Damon kiss me.

"Aaisha, let's go. I'm sure these two want some privacy," Luca snarled.

Aaisha yanked herself out of Luca's grasp and placed her hands on her hips, glaring at Damon. "No! I ain't goin' anywhere until this guy has learned his lesson. He can't play with my girl's emotions!" she growled at him and then lunged at Damon.

He ducked out of the way, pulling me along with him and resting his hands on my hips.

Luca refused to look at me, yet I couldn't look anywhere else but at him. When he rushed out of the apartment, I went to follow, but Damon held me in place.

"Luca, no! Wait, please!"

"Get your hands off of her!" Aaisha hurled her fist at the side of Damon's face.

After Damon dodged it swiftly, I stepped between them and placed a hand on his chest, watching him instantly relax from my touch. I didn't need any more aggressive wolves just before the full moon.

"Are you serious, Mae?" Aaisha glared at me, cocking her head. "Are you really going to just let him come back into your life after what he did to you?"

"I—"

"We're mates. Of course she will let me back," Damon said.

My brows furrowed. "No, that's not how this mate thing works. I'm not a wolf, remember, Damon? You can't just expect me to take you back after you hurt me." I pulled my hand off of his chest. When he reached for my hand, I took a step away from him. "No. I'm weak, Damon. You said it yourself. You never want to see me again, so leave. Don't come back."

"You really want me to leave?" he asked, green eyes wide. "Because I will walk out of your life, and I won't come back—ever. I will fully mate Alexandra. She will be my luna and my future."

I wanted to be his future. I wanted to be the only woman he ever loved.

But I couldn't do this anymore. This fucking mate bond was making me go insane.

"Good." Aaisha stepped out from behind me. "You can have that little bitch."

Damon moved closer to me, tucking a strand of my silver-blonde hair behind my ear. "Is that what you want?"

My body shuddered, not me. I felt repulsed. He couldn't continue toying with my emotions. He didn't want to mate with me, but he didn't want to reject me. He loved me, but he'd called me weak.

How could I love someone who didn't value me?

He walked toward me with outstretched arms, his soothing honeysuckle scent drifting through my nose.

I stepped away from him and glared at the ground, jaw tight. "Leave, Damon," I whispered, ignoring the ache in my heart.

"You don't mean that."

"Yes, I do."

"Then, look me in the eyes and tell me, Mae. If you want me gone, make sure every single part of you wants me gone. Think with your heart for once."

Lifting my head, I gazed into his forest-green eyes. The walls he'd once guarded himself with lay in ruins, exposing abandonment, sorrow, and emptiness that he must've felt every day, but I couldn't keep up with this game.

"Leave," I said.

He blinked a few times, surprised, and then stormed out of the room.

Aaisha slammed the door after him and turned back to me. "Now, that's my girl!" She held up her hands for me to clap, but I brushed past her to the door. She placed her hands on her hips. "Oh, you'd better not be going to beg for his sorry ass back."

"No, I'm going to find Luca."

CHAPTER 29

LUCA

*P*ushing forth in the darkness, I ran for miles with the wind whipping my brown fur and the monstrous oak trees rustling above me. My heart thumped loudly, my breathing ragged. I pushed myself until I couldn't breathe, until I felt like I was suffocating.

After years of longing for Alexandra, I'd thought I'd finally found a woman who actually cared for me. Mae wasn't my mate, but I loved every smile, every laugh, every fucking moment I spent with her. Last night with her might've changed my life, but tonight had broken me.

I jogged to a stop and howled out, Damon's repulsive scent lingering this deep in Witver Forest.

Why was this happening to me again?

Mae knew how much Alexandra had hurt me and how torn apart she'd left me. I couldn't deal with another rejection; I couldn't fucking do it.

Was I unlovable? Had I been born to suffer through insurmountable pain?

Kicking up some dirt, I shifted into my human and trudged back to our apartment. I didn't have anywhere to go, and running away from the situation wouldn't do me any good. I was an alpha, and I needed to start acting like one again.

Maybe being an emotionless prick was what people wanted nowadays.

I balled my hands into fists and walked up the stairs, not smelling Mae anywhere. She'd probably left with that stupid fucking asshole who took every woman I loved away from me. It was a sick kind of payback for his father's appalling leadership.

Closing and snapping the lock on my bedroom door, I collapsed into my bed and stared up at the black ceiling. What the fuck was wrong with me? I didn't have a pack, a family, or even a mate to call my own. I had spent the last three years in this apartment with someone who I'd thought I'd get to call sweetheart one day.

Twenty minutes into wallowing in self-fucking-pity, someone knocked on my door. Mae's sweet lilac scent seeped into my room, her toes wiggling in the light from the living room. I sighed, not wanting to open it, but my wolf had another idea entirely.

He needed to feel loved again and thought that Mae could give that to him.

He was a lonely son of a bitch.

"What?" I growled, ripping open the door.

She gazed up at me with wide gray eyes. "Are you okay?"

I looked down at her dirty hands and arms, the leaf stuck in her hair, and then behind her. "I'm fine," I said, shutting the door in her face.

She knocked again, and I stupidly tore the door back open because she smelled so good, and my wolf couldn't seem to stay away.

"What?"

She placed her foot between the door and the frame. "You're definitely not fine, and I'm not going to stop bothering you until you are."

Tightening my grip on the knob, I shook my head at her, my throat closing up. "You knew how much he hurt me when he took Alexandra from me. How do you think it feels to watch him take you away too? How could you do that to me?"

It was selfish. I knew it was. Damon had rejected her a week ago. A mate bond didn't just disappear after a few days. It lingered for a long fucking time, years even. But it still didn't hurt me any less.

Chin quivering, she stepped closer to me. "You're afraid he's going to take me away from you?"

"You've been out with him all night, haven't you?" I asked.

"I've been out all night, looking for you. I ran through the woods for hours, trying to find you, Luca. I wouldn't go back to Damon. I knew it wasn't right when he kissed me. I'm sorry I hurt you by kissing him back, but you know how it is with the mate bond. You've said it before. You'd try anything to get her back even though you knew you were not supposed to be together."

As much as I wanted to hate Mae, I couldn't. She was right. If the roles had been reversed and Alexandra kissed me after just a few days following our breakup, I would've kissed her so fucking hard that it hurt me. I wouldn't have even had the strength to push her away, like Mae had with Damon.

"I still have a connection with him. I still love him, but…"

My chest tightened as I watched her speak, the moonlight flooding into the room from the curtains and bouncing off her eyes. "But what, Mae?"

"Nothing." She swallowed and glanced down at our feet. "Well, it's not nothing. It's just … I've liked you for so long. It sounds stupid, coming from me now, after I just kissed him, but I have never been so happy with someone before. I've never had someone stand by my side, no matter what."

Breath catching in the back of my throat, I swallowed hard. Mae liked me? Me? The alpha who had lost his pack, his family, his mate? The broken and beaten roommate who she had seen cry morning after morning, mourning the loss of a mate bond?

Unable to stop myself, I pulled her closer to me and rested my chin on her head. "I'm sorry I got mad," I whispered, blowing out a deep breath. "I don't want to lose you. You've saved me so many mornings. I lo—" I stopped myself, not knowing if it was too early for that.

She tensed. "What?"

"I love you, Mae."

Before I could take it all back, she swiftly pressed her lips to mine and breathed life back into my wolf, who hadn't truly loved for years. And in that moment, I knew both he and I would do anything to keep her by our side.

CHAPTER 30

MAE

"Shit …" I mumbled a few days later, fumbling with my keys and my tea from Hot Shots. When I kicked the front door open with my toe, the tea sloshed over the edge of the cup and burned my knuckles, the skin turning red—just like that damn mark on my neck. "Damn it."

Luca popped his head out of his room and hurried over to take the cup from me. After placing it on the counter, he took my burned hand. "Are you okay, Mae? This tea is still steaming. And your fingers are—"

"I'm good," I said. Clumsy Mae had spilled her tea on herself more than once, but today, it surprisingly didn't feel as bad and didn't hurt as much as it usually did. My hand would've gone numb by now.

Still, Luca ran lukewarm water in the kitchen sink and placed my hand under it.

I glanced up at him for a moment, my lips curling into a smirk. Luca loved me. How had I not seen that before? He treated me like a wolf should treat a mate. And I so wanted to tell him I loved him too, but first, I wanted to be sure, and I wanted to stop these lingering feelings I had for Damon.

While getting over Damon was difficult, I still had questions that I desperately wanted answers to. Why had he done it? He'd told me he *had* to reject me. Was there something else going on with him that he wasn't telling me about? Or was I just trying to make an excuse for him?

After about five minutes with my hand thrust under the water, Luca pulled it out, placed me on the counter next to the sink, and touched the burn with his fingers. "Are you sure you're okay? Last time this happened, your hand went numb for forty-five minutes."

Pulling my hand out of his, I brushed my fingers against his cheek. "Can definitely feel something still," I said, admiring the way his eyes flickered from brown to amber, his wolf slowly clawing to the forefront.

Luca curled his fingers around my belt loops and tugged me closer to him until my ass nearly hung off the counter. "I have something else you could feel too, if you're down for it."

Cheeks flushed, I slapped a hand over his mouth. Aaisha was here.

"Don't worry about her." Luca trailed his nose up mine, his minty breath on my lips. "I'm hungry, and something smells *delicious*."

I panted and pointed to the fridge. "There's food."

He kissed me and sucked my bottom lip between his teeth. "Not for food."

"What's taking you so long?" Aaisha asked, walking down the hallway toward the kitchen.

Luca quickly stepped away from me, resting one hand on the counter beside my thigh. If Aaisha found out about us, she'd make a huge deal out of it, and I didn't want that drama right now.

When she reached the kitchen with Richard trailing behind her, she lifted her nose to the air and sniffed in my direction. "Something smells …" She narrowed her eyes and raised an eyebrow, suspicious, but then she smacked her lips together. "Anyway, we're going out tonight for my last meal."

"You make it sound like this will be your last meal forever," I said, hopping off the counter.

She shuffled through the apartment and to the front door, hurling her purse over her shoulder, a knot forming between her brows. "Yeah … well, with this full moon tonight …" She trailed off, her voice just barely a whisper.

I frowned and glanced between her and Richard. Tonight, Aaisha would either complete her first shift or she would die and Richard would lose a mate. Luca and Richard had been training her for weeks, and she had become stronger, but that didn't mean she would survive.

Nobody knew until the time came.

Richard squeezed her shoulder and stared down at her with tired eyes and a strained smile, as if he was preparing himself for the worst.

But I refused to believe that this would be the last night with her. It couldn't be. What would I do without my best friend?

Twenty minutes later, we pulled up to Oasis—Aaisha's new favorite place and the place Damon had dumped me. Though I didn't want to face reality, if this really was Aaisha's last night, I didn't not want to go because some *loser* had nearly rejected me here.

Aaisha and Richard walked ahead of us, hand in hand, Aaisha proudly showing off her mark.

Luca told them to find us a table and then grabbed my arm to hold me back until they walked into the diner. "Are you going to be okay?"

"Why wouldn't I be?" I asked, lips curling into a smile. "Because of ... us?"

Luca glided his tongue across his teeth, sucked in a breath, and nodded to one of the many full-length glass windows of Oasis. Inside the diner, Damon, Alexandra, Samuel, and a few other warrior wolves sat with each other in a red-colored leather booth. Alexandra sat beside Damon, basically plastered to him with her chest rubbing against the side of his arm and her nasty hand on his thigh.

My eyes widened, and I swallowed hard. "I'll be fine," I whispered.

Damon looked out the window at me, his green eyes empty as he wrapped an arm around Alexandra and pulled her in closer to whisper into her ear, something that made her laugh. Pain shot through my heart, and I was unsure if it was the jealousy or the betrayal I felt from him this time.

When they pulled away from each other, Alexandra happened to glance out of the window and smirked at me, her lips in an evil snarl.

Luca stiffened and placed his hand on my lower back. "Mae, are you sure you're okay? We don't have to go in there if you don't—"

I linked my arm around his. "Let's go, Luca."

"Don't start anything with her," Luca said, walking beside me. "She's trying to get you angry. That's what she does to people she doesn't like."

"I won't do anything silly like that."

He raised an eyebrow at me and stopped. "I mean it, Mae. If you start something or say something to her, it'll only make you angry, and you'll be giving her what she wants. Don't let her win. She's not worth it."

"I'm not going to start anything with her," I reassured. "And don't worry; I'm definitely not going to say anything to her either!"

He narrowed his brown eyes at me. "Well, what are you going to do? Because it looks like you're about to do something to piss her off."

"This," I said, standing on my toes and pressing my lips against his.

Though I knew part of this was wrong, it felt good, being the one who caused the anger and sadness for once. But I didn't care how kissing Luca would hurt Damon—or if it hurt him at all. If he wasn't going to mate with me, he shouldn't have led me on from the beginning.

I was no longer going to be the miserable and angry reject. Now, I was Luca's girl.

"Are you going to kiss me back or …" I asked after a few moments.

"Mae, you're doing this for the wrong reason," he murmured against me, resting his forehead against mine.

"I'm doing this to claim what is mine, so Alexandra knows you're off-limits, and Damon knows that he doesn't get to fuck with me anymore because I have a man who has kicked his ass once and isn't afraid to kick his ass again."

A smile twitched on Luca's lips. "Are you sure that's the only reason?"

"Yes." I wrapped my hand around his collar and pulled him closer. "Now, kiss me."

Smiling against me, Luca grabbed my hips and pressed his lips to mine. The kiss was soft, gentle, and held so much love behind it that I couldn't stop myself from wrapping my arms around his shoulders.

"Hold the fudge up!" Aaisha shouted from inside Oasis. Sprawled across Damon and Alexandra's table, Aaisha stared, wide-eyed, through the glass window at us, her jaw nearly hitting the tabletop.

"Oh my gosh," I whispered into Luca's chest.

"Well, she was going to find out sooner or later," Luca said, taking my hand and leading me into Oasis.

"I was hoping for later."

When we stepped into the diner, Aaisha jumped up and met us at the door. "You guys … you guys are a …" A smile stretched across her face, and she threw her hands up in the air. "Yes! I've been waiting years for you guys to get together!" She jumped up and down and clapped her hands. "Oh my gosh, I knew it!" She looked at Richard and then pointed at us. "I told you! I knew they were hiding some—Wait!" She widened her eyes. "Did you guys do the n-a-s-t-y?"

"Aaisha," I snapped, not wanting everyone to overhear, but I couldn't hold back my smile.

Aaisha squeezed between us and looped her arms around my and Luca's arms. "YES! I'm so freaking excited!" She looked at me. "Was he good? Tell me. Tell me. Tell me. I live for this."

Alexandra growled slowly.

Aaisha looked over at her and rolled her brown eyes. "Oh, shut the hell up. I'm trying to enjoy the fact that my two best friends just banged! Maybe one day, you'll know what it feels like to be destroyed by a big di—"

"Aaisha, that's enough," I scolded.

After rolling her eyes again, she pushed me into our booth. "All right, but you'd better tell me all of those nasty details later," she said.

For the rest of the night, Aaisha wouldn't drop the topic of Luca and me and continued to glance between us, wiggling her brows at me. It got so bad that I excused myself from the table because my mind was reeling with way too many dirty thoughts about Luca that Aaisha had planted in my head.

"Damon, let me out. I need to freshen up," Alexandra said.

"Sit back down," Damon scolded, watching me pass them. "You're not going anywhere."

Thankful that Damon still had some sense left in him, I splashed some water on my face in the restroom, did my business, and willed myself to calm my hormones. I just couldn't stop thinking about Luca taking me to bed tonight and breaking his headboard. The closer we approached this full moon tonight, the more everyone was becoming aggressive, even me.

After drying off my hands, I walked back out into Oasis and bumped into someone. "I-I'm sorr—"

"Watch it, human!" a towering rogue-like wolf snapped, eyes smoldering with darkness. He looked me up and down and then smirked as if he liked what he saw.

Another rogue approached him from behind. "What do we have here?"

"Back off her, guys. She's cool," Brett said behind them.

The wolves glared down at him for a moment and then nodded. My eyebrows furrowed at the weird exchange. Brett might've hung around some she-wolves before, but he was a dick behind their backs. And I'd never, ever seen Brett with two male rogues.

"You know her, B?" the larger one asked, reaching out to tug on a strand of my hair, but I stepped away before he could.

"She's pretty," the other one said.

Brett smiled at me, his eyes ... glimmering. "I know."

I wrinkled my nose. Why was he hanging out with rogues? He hated werewolves.

"So, Mae, how's life without your mate been treating you?" Brett asked, rocking back on his heels.

Deafening silence fell over the once-boisterous diner, and everyone looked at me. If I wanted to prove that I was over Damon and Alexandra, I'd have to choose my words carefully. And with all these people staring at me and these thoughts racing through my mind, it was hard to think *clearly*, never mind carefully.

"It's been..."

Suddenly, someone wrapped their hands around my waist and pulled me back. "Leave," Luca ordered from behind me, his eyes an amber color. Then, he stood in front of me, guarding me from the wild beasts. "Leave now."

"I just want to talk to Mae." Brett threw his hands up. "There's no harm in that." He glanced over his shoulder at the rogues. "Can you give us some privacy?" he asked. When they actually turned away, Brett looked at Luca. "They're gone. All you have to do is ask nicely. Now, can I talk to Mae in private?"

Luca didn't move, but I wanted him to go sit back down. I needed to prove *to myself* that I wasn't weak, that I didn't need anyone to protect me from my feelings. All of my friends were now werewolves or soon-to-be werewolves; they were all strong. I wanted to show them my strength too. It was stupid, but ... sometimes, the strongest thing you could do was stand up to a bully and abuser.

"I can handle him, Luca," I said, urging him to go sit back down.

After Luca reluctantly left us, Brett smirked and inched closer to me. "Jeez, can't get any privacy here."

"What do you want, Brett?"

"Just to talk."

"If you want to talk, start by telling me why you're out with rogues. You hate wolves."

He nodded over to the two wolves sitting in the booth. "I do, but after my dad found out about what I did the other night when we went out, he kicked me out and told me that I needed to learn to respect women before I could come back. And the only decent place in Witver was with them."

"You're living with rogues now?" I asked, not believing his story.

When he stepped closer, I moved back, remembering the last time he had gotten this close to me. He had trapped me between him and my apartment door and promised to take me any way that he could.

"What are you doing?" I asked, watching him carefully.

"You're going to come begging for me one day," he whispered, leaning closer and grasping my hip.

"Take your hand off of me."

"You're going to want me more than you want those beasts," he said.

"Take your hand off of me—now."

"You're going to be begging me to touch you like this." He moved his hand around my hip and grabbed a handful of my ass.

Before I could stop myself, I slammed my fist into his pretty face and struck him in his nose. He stumbled back, tripping over a chair leg, and I pounced on him, ready to finally release all of the pent-up anger he had caused me.

He would finally get what he deserved.

CHAPTER 31

MAE

Pummeling fist after fist after fist, I hit Brett in his ugly face and rejoiced in the feeling. At some point, I might've liked him, but all that had gone out the window the moment he talked shit about wolves. I hated him more and more each day, and now, I could finally enjoy some damn peace.

Before I could hurl another fist at him, Luca gripped my waist and pulled me off Brett. "Mae! Calm down!" Luca said, tightening his grip around me.

I kicked and screamed and flailed my arms and legs all over the place, a growl ripping through my throat. Blood gushed from Brett's deformed nose, and he wiped it with the back of his hand and then stood.

"Let me go, Luca! Let me hurt him! He deserves it!"

"You'll be sorry, Mae," Brett said, stepping closer to me, but Luca shoved him back with one hand. "I'm telling you, one day, you're going to be crawling to me, begging for me to take you back."

Digging my nails into Luca's forearm, I broke the skin and seethed at Brett. "I don't know what kind of crazy, fucked up world you're living in, Brett, but I was never yours. *Never*! There is no taking you back if we were never a thing. You need to get that through that thick skull of yours."

Brett stepped back, trail of blood running down his chin and neck. "Have fun with your rejected mate over there," he said to Luca and then turned to me. "And your loser of a mate and his hot new girl."

"I will kill you, Brett, I swear! I can't wait for the freaking day."

"Sorry to say, but that day won't ever come." He smirked with sanguine teeth. "You're too *weak*."

Weak. I was fucking sick of people calling me weak. And I was so damn sick of him too.

"I am not weak!" I shouted, thrashing in Luca's tight hold. "Let me go! I'll kick his ass!"

"See you later, princess." Brett exited the diner with the wolves behind him, as if he were some psychotic leader and they were his little minions.

When they disappeared into the forest, I yanked myself out of Luca's grip and glared at him. Luca stared back, his amber eyes twice as hard and as furious as mine were.

"What the hell was that, Mae?"

My eyes widened, and I shoved my hands into his chest. "I should be asking you that question! Did you not expect me to defend myself after he grabbed my ass? Did you think I was too weak not to do anything about it?"

"You can't just go around hitting people, Mae."

"You did just the other week," I exclaimed. "In this same place!"

Luca growled at me, "You're acting like a—" He stopped and pursed his lips.

"Like a what?" I asked, waiting for him to fucking say something to me.

"I'm not talking to you about this right here." He pointed to the door. "Go outside. Now."

"No! You don't own me. I did nothing wrong."

"Now!" he said, posturing over me.

I tapped my shoe on the ground and crossed my arms, glaring up at him. I couldn't believe Luca. He had no right to talk to me like this. Brett had assaulted me, and Luca was angry with me? Me? I had defended myself, not letting a damn abuser walk all over me.

Growling at him, I turned my back to him and marched out of the diner.

Luca followed me out, shutting the door behind us and pulling me to the back of the parking lot so we were out of earshot of everyone. "Mae, what's gotten into you?"

"What do you mean?"

"You've been acting like a she-wolf during a full moon for the past few weeks."

"No, I haven't," I snapped. "I've just been dealing with idiots for the past few weeks."

"You've been on edge all week. You've been more sexually aroused than usual. You scarfed down dinner faster than I'd ever seen you eat before. You're always at the fridge or getting tea or wanting to eat. And you wanted to kill Brett. *Kill*, Mae. You said you wanted to kill him."

I crossed my arms over my chest, seeing nothing wrong. "I do."

He sighed and rubbed a hand over his chiseled face. "You're not listening to me."

"Did you ever stop to think that maybe I'm just sick and tired of everyone's bullshit?"

"Yes, actually, but this has been happening since a few days after you met Damon." He paused and then widened his eyes, a knot forming between his brows. "Did he mark you? Or bite you? Or anything?"

"No, Luca, he didn't. I don't know what you're trying to get at here, but—" I started.

"Wait," he said, pulling down the front of my shirt, enough to study the giant red glob of a mark on my chest. "Shit."

"What? What's wrong?" I asked, brows furrowed.

He cursed again and shook his head.

"What, Luca?!" When he still didn't answer me, I pulled the front of my shirt back up before he could touch it again. "Luca! Answer me! You're driving me insane."

"It's gotten bigger," he said, looping a finger around the hem of my shirt, snapping a picture of the mark on his phone and showing it to me.

A dark red complete circle lay on my chest. Maybe, if the edges weren't so perfectly smooth, I wouldn't think anything of it, but this … this was different. This wasn't normal. The mark had started out as just a sliver of a splotch.

"Do you think that this mark is linked to why I've been acting so wolf-like?" I asked in a breathy whisper, my heart now pounding inside my chest.

He lifted his gaze to mine. "I honestly don't know."

Hot tears welled up in my eyes. Why the hell did I feel like crying? I wasn't sure of anything anymore. I hated that this damn mark wouldn't go away. I hated Brett. I hated that I might lose Aaisha tonight. I hated Alexandra and Damon. I hated Dad too.

Burying my face in my hands, I stepped closer to Luca, needing him to comfort me. What could this be? Could it be wolf blood? My mother had had a werewolf friend. I didn't know why she would have a necklace full of werewolf blood, but that was the only explanation I could think of at the moment. My mind was too jumbled.

"What if it's wolf blood? Can't I turn into a werewolf like that?"

"It's not wolf blood," Luca assured, stroking my hair.

"How do you know that?" I whispered. "What if I'm going to turn into a werewolf tonight during the moon? If the blood seeped into my skin, it could have gone into my bloodstream."

And if wolf blood was coursing through my veins, my body would try to shift tonight.

What was even worse was that I wasn't prepared at all.

"Luca, could that happen?" I asked, tugging him into a hug.

He wrapped his arms around me and kissed my forehead. "I-I don't know if that could happen. We'll have to wait and see."

"Luca …" I whispered, resting my forehead on his chest and letting my tears fall, horrid thoughts racing through my mind. What if I died tonight? I wouldn't get to say bye to my dad. I wouldn't get to kill Brett. I wouldn't get to do a lot of things that I so desperately wanted out of life. "I-I don't want to die."

"You're not going to."

"But if this mark is werewolf blood and my body forces me to shift tonight, I won't make it … I'm too weak."

Luca pulled away and cupped my chin, forcing me to look up into his amber eyes. "I told you this before, and I'll tell you again. You are not weak, Mae. Stop thinking that. You can survive anything that life throws at you. Stop being scared and start being the strong woman I fell in love with."

Overhead, the light-blue sky faded away into a burning orange sunset, sun flares disappearing behind the dense, dark Witver Forest. The night was approaching quicker than I wanted. My stomach tightened, and I glanced up at Luca through teary eyes. If I died tonight, I wouldn't ever get to tell Luca that I loved him and really, truly mean it in *more than just a friend* type of way. I wanted to live to the day where I could look at him and not feel anything for Damon.

"We should go," he said, glancing back into the diner and nodding to Richard, who guided Aaisha out of the diner and toward us.

She hugged her arms around herself, her teeth chattering lightly, and walked up to us, uneasiness written all over her face because she might die tonight.

Wanting to be strong for her, I pushed away my fears. I didn't want her to worry about me during the hardest night of her life. If she wanted to survive, she needed to be strong for herself.

After Aaisha scooted into the car, Samuel shouted from behind us, "Wait up!" He jogged toward Luca and me, expression contorted into one of worry. "What's going on? I can tell something isn't right."

"Don't act like you actually care about her," Luca growled at him, canines extending. "Damon probably sent you over to find out what's happening, so he can mess with her again. And I'm not going to put up with it. He's hurt her enough."

Samuel crossed his arms over his chest. "I do care about her."

I stepped between the two men, looked at Samuel, and pulled down the front of my shirt to reveal my mark. "What's that?"

"Wolf blood," I said.

"We don't know that," Luca said.

"Fuck," Samuel breathed and shook his head. "Are you prepared for a shift?"

Luca gnawed on the inside of his cheek, his eyes flickering between amber and brown. "There is not going to be a shift."

"And if there is?" Samuel asked.

Silence lingered between us. If there were a shift, I would die. There was no doubt about it. I wasn't trained or prepared to change from a human into a monstrous beast. My body couldn't handle that kind of pain for hours upon hours.

A single tear slid down my cheek, which Samuel brushed away with his thumb. "You're strong, Mae. You have to believe that you're strong. Don't listen to whatever Damon told you. You can do this. If you do shift into a wolf tonight, you will survive."

After saying my good-byes to him, I looked over at Damon

for the briefest moment and then slid into the car next to Aaisha. Aaisha rested her head on my shoulder, lips pressed together.

Wrapping my arm around her shoulders, I pulled her in and gently stroked her back. Tears welled up in my eyes, but I refused to let them fall. I needed to be strong for Aaisha. She needed to survive for Richard, for her new pack, and most importantly, for herself.

Whatever happened tonight to me would happen.

When we arrived at Richard's pack house, warrior wolves greeted us at the car and led us to the backyard, where everyone gathered. Elder wolves smiled and waved at Aaisha while pups tugged on her shirt, trying to drag her in different directions, yet Richard urged her toward a circle of wolves who had prepared for Aaisha's shift.

Aaisha stopped before we reached the group and hugged me tightly. "I love you, Mae."

"I love you too, Aaisha," I whispered to her and swayed us from foot to foot. "Be strong. I know you can survive this."

Her chin quivered. "I-I can't. I'm going to die, and I don't want to."

"Aaisha, look at me." I grabbed her face, forced her to look me right in the eye, and pushed her tears away with my thumbs. I wanted to be strong for her, but what if her body really couldn't withstand the pain and pressure of transforming into a beast? Nonetheless, I gave her my best smile. "You're not going to die."

Richard looked up at the dark night sky and gently tugged on Aaisha's arm. "Aaisha, please, come with me. The full moon is close. We need to prepare you for what's to come."

As Richard pulled her away from me, Aaisha reached out until our fingertips no longer touched.

What if that was our last good-bye? What if that was the last time we touched? Would I ever see her smiling face ever again?

When she disappeared through the pack of wolves, my knees buckled, and I cried out, tears flowing from my eyes. Luca appeared in front of me, his face remaining emotionless but his eyes glossy. Unable to stand, I doubled over and rested my forehead on the ground, my stomach tight with knots. Luca sat beside me and pulled me onto his lap, rocking us back and forth.

"It'll be okay," he whispered.

But would it? Would it really be okay?

Ten minutes before midnight, Luca forced me to stand and pulled me to the front of the crowd to support Aaisha. She sat in the center of the wolves, only a white bra and underwear covering her body, with her knees to her chest and her lips pursed tightly.

I hugged Luca closer. What would happen? Would she survive? Would I survive?

I-I couldn't be here.

I needed to leave.

When she turned away from me, I jumped up and pushed through the crowd, sprinting up a small hill, unable to even stop myself. If Aaisha saw me in pain, she wouldn't focus on her own shift. She'd focus on getting me through it, and I so desperately needed her to survive. If anyone was getting through the night, it would be her. She had people who loved her in this pack, who'd be devastated if they lost a luna.

From here, I could see Aaisha, but she couldn't see me. I glared up at the moon and growled. Why did this have to be so painful for everyone? Why couldn't a shift be easy for a human? Sometimes, they didn't even mean to get bitten, and ... they could just die from it.

"Mae, why did you just leave?" Luca asked, racing up the hill.

"I don't want her to see me like—"

A horrid scream echoed through the forest. Aaisha doubled over and clutched her stomach, her shrilling sobs sending chills down my spine. For minutes, she rolled from side to side, trying to relieve the pressure, and then her first bone shattered to transform into a wolf.

"I can't! Mae! Help!" She sobbed, tears streaming down her face. "Help! Please!"

Legs buckling underneath her, she fell to the ground, posting her hands on the dirt. She cocked her head up in the air. For a moment, her nose lengthened, and her eyes flickered to gold, but then her human features returned.

"Help!" she howled. "It hurts."

My heart raced at the sight, and Luca tried to pull me away, but I wanted to see this. I needed to see Aaisha get through this. She was everything to me—everything. She kicked her leg back as it shifted into a wolf limb, her nose fully lengthening and altering into a snout.

"Help!" she screamed. "I can't ..."

She was half-wolf, half-human.

Another bone cracking split through the silence.

"Help!" She took her hands off the ground, trying to stand, but she doubled over and fell limp to the ground.

Her screams suddenly ceased, her body unmoving.

Richard stood over her and fell to his knees, howling out.

"No, no, no, no," I cried down at the crowd. "Get up, Aaisha! Get up right now!"

"Mae, you don't want to see it," Luca said, gripping my waist to hold me back from running down to her.

I yanked myself out of Luca's grip and sprinted down to the crowd, pushing my way around the wolves. I collapsed to my knees and pushed Richard out of the way.

"Aaisha, get up," I said, cradling her limp body in my arms. "Please, Aaisha, get up."

Aaisha couldn't be dead. She couldn't.

I held her to my chest, my body jerking back and forth from the sobs. She lay flaccid in my arms, her unruly black curls in every which direction. I pushed the hair from her face with trembling hands and wept at the sight of her paling, cold flesh.

Luca crouched behind me, rubbing small circles on my back, eventually wrapping his arms around my waist and trying to pull me off her. But I refused to let her go. I couldn't just leave Aaisha, my best friend, here, dead.

"Mae, she's gone," Luca said. "Please, let her go."

Not wanting to believe it, I held her closer to me and howled out. She wasn't gone. She couldn't be. She was too strong and too stubborn to let go, just like that. Aaisha still had to be in there somewhere, and I wouldn't stop until she ... woke up.

An excruciating pain split through my chest, and I screamed out in agony, my nails digging into Aaisha's flesh. The throbbing traveled down my torso and down my legs and arms, encompassing every part of my body and setting it aflame.

"Mae ..." Luca said, standing over me. He looked as if he was yelling, but I could only hear his voice in a whisper. "Mae, are you okay?"

The pain slithered up my neck and pierced me right through the center of my skull, my vision darkening for a second, small stars appearing. Aaisha twisted and turned in my head, her facial structure distorting into a swirl of features.

She shook wildly—or maybe that was just my arms shaking.

Unable to hold her steady, I released her from my grasp and leaned over her, posting my hands on the ground and gasping for any breath I could get, my esophagus closing up. I dug my nails into the dirt, trying to steady myself, fearing more pain would shoot through me at any moment.

The full moon. My shift. It was real, and it was here.

Something wriggled inside of my chest cavity, stabbing at the insides of my rib cage, thrashing against it and trying to break through the flesh and bone. Another pain riddled through me, my lips parting to scream, but I couldn't hear anything over the roaring thump of my heart.

My muscles strained, almost to the point where I thought they would burst through my skin. The ache spread rapidly from one single point in my chest to my whole body, coating me in a shell of agony, and the battering against my chest continued.

Whatever was inside of me wanted out, and it wouldn't stop until it did.

"Mae …" Luca said, his voice faint.

I looked up at him, trying to blink away the fogginess. He pointed down under me, his mouth moving sporadically and his brown eyes wide in worry. I furrowed my eyebrows and glanced down to Aaisha to see blood covering her beautiful brown face, trickling down the sides of her cheeks to her ears.

Where was the blood coming from? Why was this happening? How did I stop it?

I needed to stop it. I needed her to live. She would live. I just needed to stop the bleeding.

Anxiously, I wiped the blood from her face to try to find the open wound. But then blood dribbled onto my forearm from above. I pulled my arm away from her. If the blood wasn't coming from her, what was the source?

Another drop of blood dripped down the front of my white shirt. My eyes widened down at my nearly entire bloodstained shirt, and I pressed a hand to my mark, which was spewing blood. I let out a piercing scream, the first sound I could really truly hear in the past few moments.

"Luca! What's happening to me? What's happening?"

More tears streamed down my cheeks and neck, the salty liquid mixing with the iron. I doubled over, clasping my hand over my mark, yet the blood continued to ooze through the crevices between my fingers.

Luca sat next to me, wrapped his arms around my waist, and pulled me on top of him, pressing his large, callous hand over mine to try to stop the blood. He moved his lips again, as if he was speaking but I couldn't make sense of it.

I shook violently in his arms, my eyes fluttering closed. The pain was too much.

My best friend was dead. My life was completely ruined. And I wasn't shifting, but an unbelievable amount of blood was seeping out of my mark for no reason. This wasn't supposed to happen to me or to anyone tonight.

Slowly, my hearing became clearer, low howls replacing the silence. I opened my eyes, not seeing Aaisha's body anywhere, but a large brown wolf in Aaisha's place. I shook my head, unable to believe that this ... was her.

It couldn't be. She had just been dead.

She trotted over to me, stuck her tongue out, and licked the blood off of my hands. My heart tightened.

She was alive. Alive. My best friend wasn't dead, and she could finally be free and happy.

The pain in my chest slowly subsided, the edges of my vision darkening, and suddenly, I found myself suffocating in a world of darkness. But before I blacked out, I swore I saw a blond wolf staring at me from the woods.

CHAPTER 32

MAE

With bright light filtering through my closed eyelids, I fluttered my eyes open and squinted until I adjusted to the glaring hospital light. I pushed myself to a seated position and cursed at the pain, staring blankly at the cream-colored walls. An IV was jammed into my vein, monitors beeped steadily to my left, and Damon sat in a scarlet-cushioned chair beside my bed.

He sat back in the chair, his head resting on the wall, his eyes closed, a moonflower in his lap.

When the bed creaked, he blinked his eyes open and straightened his back. "Mae, you're awake, and you're okay." He smiled at me, his worried features softening. He handed me the moonflower. "I brought you this. It's supposed to help wolves heal, but, uh …" He scratched the back of his head. "I brought it for you. I know it won't do much to help you, but I-I …"

"Damon," I whispered, taking the stem between my fingers, "thank you."

"How are you feeling? Are you okay?" He pulled the chair closer to my bed and cupped my cheek. "Do you need anything? I can—"

"Where's Luca?" I whispered, memories of the full moon flooding through my mind. What had happened? Why had my mark bled? How had Aaisha survived? And why was Damon even here? I had passed out on Richard's property, not his.

"I leave for two hours to take care of business, and you come here," Luca said to Damon through gritted teeth, walking through the door with Samuel.

Damon stared at me for one more moment, trailing his fingers across my cheek, and then stood. Luca growled, canines lengthening, and I was just way too done with all this drama. I'd just woken up from Goddess knew what.

"Luca, please don't. He's fine here. He wasn't doing anything to hurt me."

"I know you probably hate me, Mae," Damon said. "But I-I couldn't help coming here. I needed to see you. I needed to make sure you were okay. I could feel you hurting last night, and then Samuel told me about your mark and that you might shift. I wanted to tell you that I'm sorry. I can't lose you whether you're mine or not. I'd die if you did."

Though I didn't want to believe him because he had already lied so much to me, I couldn't help but hear the agony in his voice. He was telling me the truth. If I had died, it would have broken him to pieces.

But then I saw the glistening mark Alexandra had left on his neck, and I tore my gaze away.

Luca approached me with dark circles under his tired eyes and sat on the side of my bed, tucking some hair behind my ear. "You have questions, don't you?"

"What the hell happened?" I whispered, trying to make sense of it all.

"When Aaisha stopped breathing, your mark started bleeding,

pouring all over her face and body. Richard's pack doctor is doing some tests on the blood from your mark. He couldn't draw any blood from it directly, but he took some of the blood that was on your hand."

"Why couldn't he take blood directly from it?" I asked. "Since it was an open wound, it probably just scabbed over. He can just rip the scab off and—"

"First, that's disgusting." Samuel wrinkled his nose. "Please don't ever rip your scabs off. Not even I do that, and I'm a guy. Second, it doesn't look like it was ever an open wound. There's no scab, and the skin where the mark sits is hard, not soft, like skin."

I placed my fingers on my chest and rubbed them against my smooth yet hard flesh.

No scab. No open wound. No soreness. How was that even possible?

"And how did Aaisha live?" I asked them.

In unison, they shrugged.

I sat up taller and rolled my eyes. "Oh gosh, you guys are useless. Is she okay at least?"

"You bet I am!" Aaisha said, busting through the door with Richard by her side, eyes flickering to a yellow color for a moment. She looked at Damon, disgusted, and then turned to me. "How are you doing, girl? I was hoping that you'd wake up soon."

A man in a white doctor's coat walked in behind them with a manila folder in his hand and a stethoscope around his neck. The doctor smiled warmly at me. "I'm going to have to ask you all to leave. I have to give Mae the results of her blood work."

"No," Damon said.

"I'm staying," Luca said.

"Yeah, I didn't almost die just to get kicked out of my best friend's hospital room," Aaisha said.

"It's okay. I don't mind if they know," I said, giving him my full attention. Maybe I could finally understand what the hell this thing was because it wasn't werewolf blood—that was for sure—but it did have some regenerative properties, like wolf blood does.

After nodding curtly, he opened the folder. "I examined your blood for any trace of werewolf blood, and it came back negative, as expected. There was, however, some substance that I've never seen before. I called a few doctors from other packs and even ones at human hospitals, and nobody has ever heard or seen it before in patients. It's not written about in any types of literature either."

"So, what does that mean?" I asked, brows furrowed.

"I'm honestly not sure at the moment. We can run more tests and study the substance, but I don't have anything beyond that for you."

"But this mark and my blood saved Aaisha, didn't it?"

"Correct." He paused and shut the door behind him for privacy. "It seems that just a single drop of your blood can revive a werewolf's dead cells very rapidly, though it does nothing to human cells."

After staring at him for a few moments, I lay back in the bed, folded my hands in my lap, and closed my eyes. The past few weeks had been filled with pain and sorrow. I wanted it to be over. I wanted to be normal again. I didn't want this new power that nobody understood.

"Other than that, everything is fine with you. Your vitals are good. Your iron levels are good. Blood pressure is right where it should be. You can leave whenever you feel like it," he said.

When I didn't respond to him or open my eyes, I heard Samuel shuffle around. "Is she okay?"

Tears flowed down my cheeks. "Leave, please!" I said. "I want to be alone."

Three of the five people cleared out of the room and trotted down the halls, but both Damon and Luca decided to stay.

"She said, leave," Damon growled at Luca from one side of the bed.

"That means you too," Luca snapped.

I opened my eyes and blew out a deep breath. "Damon, thank you for the flower, and I appreciate your visit, but I need you to leave and go back to your luna." I glanced at his mark and gritted my teeth. "Don't keep her waiting."

Damon flared his nostrils and walked out without saying another word.

Luca closed the door behind him and stared back at me, frowning. "Do you want me to leave too?"

Extending out my arm, I reached for him, wanting to be with him and only him right now. When he sat on the bed, I crawled into his lap and frowned. "What's happening to me, Luca? I'm a freak—a disgusting, weird freak."

"Mae, you're not a freak."

"Yes, I am! I have this damn mark on my chest that decides to bleed out of nowhere. The mark can also apparently bring wolves back to life. And then—best part yet—nobody knows what the hell is wrong with me!" I said.

Luca smiled down at me, a chuckle escaping his lips.

"Don't laugh at me!"

He scooped me up into his arms and set me on the floor. "I think I know how to make you feel like less of a freak." He tugged me toward the hospital door. "Come on."

An hour later, I stood in Sara's Tattoo Parlor and shook my head down at Luca, who sat in a reclined black leather chair. Sara leaned over his bare chest, pressing the needle against his flesh and giving him an immense sanguine circle tattoo.

"I can't believe you," I said, unable to hold back a grin.

Luca held his hand out for me. "Will you hold my hand? It hurts."

"You don't even look like you're in pain," I said but placed my hand in his anyway.

"Just needed an excuse to hold your hand," he said, intertwining his fingers with mine.

Tingles shot up my arm, an electricity that I had only felt with Damon rushing through me. Something about this and about him felt too right and too good to be true, and I loved that for the first time, I felt needed.

"All right, you're all done," Sara said, pushing back her black swivel chair. "Why don't you look in the mirror?"

After Luca walked to the mirror, I stood behind him, on my toes, and gazed at his sculpted chest that now had a tattoo the shape of a circle directly in the center. A small bead of blood ran down his sternum, and he wiped it away with his finger.

"I told you I'd get one, so you didn't have to feel like a weirdo. You didn't believe me?" He turned to Sara and smiled. "Thanks, Sara. I really appreciate it."

Sara bowed her head. "Anything for you, Alpha. You know it was more difficult than I'd thought it would be. I had to make sure to get the details in it," Sara said, referring to the smaller patches of dark red that were inside of the lighter-red circle. She took a step back and smiled. "You know what?"

"Hmm?" Luca hummed, looking back in the mirror at the mark on his chest.

"It kinda looks like a moon if you think about it—a blood moon!"

My face paled. *A blood moon? That was what this was?*

Luca grabbed my hand and pulled me to the exit of the parlor. "Thanks again, Sara! I'll see you soon." He ushered me into his car. "Blood moon. Didn't you say that your dad told you that the necklace made your mom stronger during the blood moon?" When I nodded, he skirted out of the lot and hurried toward the suburbs of Witver, where Dad lived. "Then, we're going to try to find out if he knows anything else about it that he didn't tell you."

"Luca, I don't think this is a good idea," I said as he turned onto Dad's street. "My dad doesn't know that I'm living with a werewolf. He thinks that you're just some human, and ... this is a no-wolf neighborhood."

"You didn't tell him about me?" he asked, brows furrowed.

I shrugged my shoulders. If I'd told him that a wolf wanted to live with Aaisha and me three years ago, he'd have basically moved me back in with him without giving me much of a say. Dad already hated the *monsters* like Luca even though Luca wasn't anything like those rogues that Brett now hung around.

Dad walked out the front door, eyes narrowed at the car and cell phone in hand, probably to call the police to complain that this was a human-only neighborhood, blah, blah, blah. I jumped out of the car to greet a seething Dad.

"Get him off my property."

"Dad, please, we need to talk," I pleaded, placing my hands on his shoulders.

He pointed at Luca. "*He* does not need to talk to me."

"Yes, he does."

Dad stared at me with wide eyes. "He didn't get you pregnant, did he?"

My cheeks flushed. "No, Dad, he didn't."

"Well, he's not stepping a foot inside my house."

"It's okay, Mae," Luca said. "Show him your chest."

As soon as I pulled down my shirt to show Dad the mark, Dad lunged at Luca with gritted teeth. "Did you give my daughter a hickey, you animal? I swear to—"

Luca side-stepped, making Dad stumble forward.

I stood in front of Luca with my hands on my hips and glared at Dad. "This isn't from Luca, Dad. This is from Mom's necklace. Whatever was in there leaked out and seeped into my skin."

For a moment, he softened his features at the sound of her

name. "Did you break your mother's necklace? That was the only thing I had left of her!"

Luca nudged me out of the way and grabbed Dad by the collar, his claws tearing his shirt. "Don't you dare fucking yell at your daughter," he growled, canines extending. "It's not her fault. She almost died last night because of that mark, and you have the audacity to yell at her for it. You know more about the necklace than you're letting on, don't you?"

A bead of sweat rolled down Dad's neck as he dangled inches off of the ground. "Let me down, you filthy fucking animal. I swear I'll call the police on you." He chucked his phone at me. "Mae, call them. Call them now."

I picked the phone off the green grass and handed it to Luca, who crushed it in his free hand.

Luca let the pieces fall to the ground and glared back at Dad, slamming him against the house. "What do you know?"

After another moment, Dad grumbled to himself. "Let me down, and I'll tell you."

"You'll tell us now."

I rested my hand on Luca's bicep. "Luca, let him down."

Once Luca placed Dad down, Dad smoothed out what was left of his torn shirt and crossed his arms, refusing to look at either of us. "I don't know as much about it as you think I do. Your mother had the same mark since the day I met her. Whenever I asked her questions about it, she would make up some excuse. She always hid something big from me. It was as if she was leading some sort of double life or something." He closed his eyes and cursed. "Listen, Mae, for years, I've been trying to find out the meaning behind the mark, even after her death. And I've come up with nothing, but I think that it has to do with werewolves."

"What about them?" I asked.

"I don't know, but like I said before, she was hiding something from me. Before we got married, she hid the fact that she was friends with werewolves. I think that those secrets might have something to do with it. That's the only possible thing I can think of," he said, staring at the white sidewalk.

"Great. Thanks for the help, Dad. Another person who doesn't know what's wrong with me," I said. It wasn't his fault, but I wanted and *needed* answers. I couldn't go on, not knowing what had almost killed me last night or why it had.

"I'm sorry that I couldn't be of more help, Mae," Dad said.

I closed my eyes. "It's okay, Dad. Would it be too much to ask to take that picture you have of Mom from the day I was born? Maybe I can ask around to see if anyone knows who those people are in the picture."

Dad glanced at Luca, lips curled into a snarl.

I stepped between them again and grabbed his hands. "Please, Dad. We might even be able to find the wolf who killed her, if he's still out there and alive."

After a moment of contemplation, Dad retreated in the house to retrieve the picture. When he came back out and handed me the photo, I smoothed the picture out and frowned at all four figures—Mom, Dad, wolf, and … a handsome black man with bright white freckles. Whoever these people were had to know about this mark.

"There is one thing that I forgot to tell you about the mark," Dad said. "It changes shape."

"Changes shape?"

Luca glanced at my neck and carefully moved the silver out of the way with his claw to examine it. "It's … a sliver smaller than yesterday, almost as if it's changing with … the shape of the moon."

My breath caught in my throat, brows furrowed as I glanced back down at the picture, an uneasy feeling bubbling in the pit of my stomach. "Dad, was Mom a werewolf?"

"No," Dad said, scowling in disgust. "She had an affection for werewolves, but she was certainly not one of them."

"No distant relative with wolf blood?" Luca asked.

While there was no hiding the fact that someone was a wolf—the ears and canines were an instant giveaway—she could have a very distant relative who was a wolf, someone deep in our family tree.

"If she had even the faintest sign of wolf blood, wouldn't she and Mae both be wolves too?"

I let out a sigh. Richard's pack doctor confirmed that my blood didn't have traces of werewolf in it, which meant that Mom wasn't a wolf either. But then how did that explain me? What was I?

CHAPTER 33

LUCA

"We'll figure it out," I said to Mae, holding our apartment door open for her.

Mae walked into the house and leaned against Aaisha's door-frame, staring into the empty room. Since Aaisha had shifted last night, she had moved in with Richard today, their bond stronger than ever right now. And part of me was jealous about it. I couldn't wait until Mae felt that way about me.

I slipped an arm around her shoulders. "Never thought this would happen. I'd thought we'd be stuck with her forever."

"I thought we'd all end up living here together until we died." She giggled and looked up at me, her gray eyes glimmering more than usual today. "I never thought this apartment could be this quiet."

"It doesn't have to be quiet…" I said, leaning down to capture her lower lip between my teeth. "You know, having the apartment all to ourselves means we can do this"—I gently pressed Mae against the door, sucking on her bottom lip—"more often."

"Nuh-uh! You still can't do that out in the open!" Aaisha said, walking in from behind.

Jumping back, Mae hit her head against the doorframe and groaned softly to herself.

Aaisha dangled a pair of hot-pink keys in front of us. "I still got the keys to this place, so don't you guys think you can go about and do those sexy things out in the open. Especially not in my room!"

I cradled Mae's head and pulled her out into the hallway, a sheepish smile on my face.

Aaisha wrapped her arms around Mae's torso and yanked her away from me. "Richard asked if you could come over for a meeting about the missing pups with the alphas in the area tonight, so you can't do anything sexy with Mae right now"—she narrowed her eyes at me and then leaned closer—"even though I'm super excited about you both!"

"But I'm a rogue," I said, pity washing through me. "Not an alpha anymore."

She raised an eyebrow at me. "You still have alpha blood. Just because you're a rogue doesn't mean you're not an alpha anymore, and Richard really needs all the help he can get. More pups were taken last night."

Last night? During the full moon? Everyone worshipped the Moon Goddess under the full moon, even rogues. Whoever had been taking these pups must not give two shits about the Moon Goddess or divine laws.

"Let's go now then," I said, wanting to find those pups—not only for Aaisha, but for myself too. I finally had someone who believed in me and someone to live for. I wanted to get my pack back as quickly as I could, and this was the first step.

Aaisha pulled Mae to the front door, and they swung their arms, smiling so hard. "Girl, we gotta talk about everything that's happened finally! I want allll the damn deets you've been keeping from me. Don't leave any out."

∼

An hour later, I sat across from Damon in Richard's meeting room with my hands clenched into fists under the table. I hadn't made eye contact with him at all tonight, and I planned to keep it that way. Something about that cocky fucking smirk on his face made me want to just bash his head in again.

Alphas and betas mulled over the thought of rogues taking these pups, tossing around idea after idea on where to even start. While my ex-beta had been feeding me this information on the side for weeks now, I hadn't gotten the chance to speak to anyone yet.

Because I wasn't an alpha with a pack anymore, nobody really gave my opinion much weight. So, I sat here and listened to stupid plan after fucking ridiculous plan, wondering when someone would actually come up with something good.

And when nobody had anything, I excused myself to get a drink and maybe to see Mae to calm my nerves. She and Aaisha had said they'd be in the meeting, but they never showed. They were probably gossiping in the kitchen or …

"Luca has been amazing, but …" Mae started just behind the kitchen door.

I stopped in my tracks, chest tightening. *But?*

"But what?" Aaisha asked. "He ain't giving you that good-good?"

"It's not that," Mae said. "I just don't know how to feel about everything. I never thought Damon would apologize to me, but today, he did and … I want to hate him, Aaisha. I want to fucking hate him with everything because I … I love Luca …"

Mae … loves me? My lips curled up slightly. *She loves me.*

"But you don't hate Damon," Aaisha said. "Do you love him?"

Silence.

Silence.

More silence.

"Mae, he—"

"No, Aaisha," Mae finally whispered, "I don't love Damon."

"Girl, I know you're in a sticky situation. The mate bond is strong as hell. I'll try to support you as best as I can through this," Aaisha said. "But you know, Luca understands this, and he loves you too. I have seen it on his face every morning for the past three years."

Sighing softly to myself, I decided to stop eavesdropping and return back to the meeting room. I slouched down in the chair, not knowing if I should feel fucking happy that Mae loved me or if I should hate that Mae still liked that asshole.

A few moments later, Aaisha kicked the door open and marched into the room with Mae in tow. "Do you guys have a plan yet? No? Didn't think so," Aaisha said, not bothering to listen to any alpha speak. "Well, you're in luck because Mae and I have been talking, and we do!"

"Aaisha," Mae whisper-yelled. "No, we don't!"

Aaisha smirked. "Well, I do. Just needed all the alphas to let out their testosterone on each other first before I said anything."

Some alphas eyed them curiously while others leaned back in their seats and rubbed their foreheads at Aaisha's over-the-top attitude.

Aaisha walked around the table until she reached Richard and stared everyone down. "First of all, we both think it's freakin' crazy how five pups could be taken so easily last night. Second, my gurl, Mae, over there knows one of your suspects—Brett."

Mae's eyes widened. "Brett?"

"You know those rogues that Brett was hanging around with yesterday?" Aaisha asked her. "Richard said that he faintly smelled the scent of pups on them, so he was planning on trying to find them, but he doesn't know where to find him."

"Sit down," one of the pissed off alphas said, standing. "You don't know anything."

Aaisha straight-up smacked him upside the head. "Don't

know anything? I don't know who the fuck you're talking to, but it's certainly not to someone working her ass off to put herself through eight years of college. Sit your ass back down and let me finish." Aaisha turned back to us. "As I was saying before someone rudely interrupted me, Mae can talk to Brett and finish kicking his ass too."

"No," I said, shaking my head.

"That's not happening," Damon growled. "Brett is too dangerous to just talk to. He'll hurt her easily."

Mae narrowed her eyes at Damon, jaw clenched. "Even after I save someone's life, you still think I'm weak, don't you, Damon? I'm too weak, too stupid, and I don't have the right connections. Is that what it is?"

"I hate to say this," I interjected, "but Damon has a point. Brett is stronger than you, and those rogues that he's with are a lot stronger than him. And I'm not saying that you're weak, Mae—please don't take it that way—but Brett's just stronger than you, and we can't chance it."

Crossing her arms, Mae pressed her lips together and stared at me with sorrowful eyes. Damon had fucked her up so much that she thought she had to prove that she wasn't weak to everyone, even after I had told her countless times that she was strong.

"My dad already invited me to Brett's new home tomorrow. I'll be going with him, and I'll be safe. You guys don't need to hold my hand with everything that involves me," Mae said. "Because I'm not going to lie around while pups are being taken from their homes, mothers, and packs. These families are broken without their children. And I know what it feels like for a part of a family to be missing; I know how broken and hopeless it makes them because my dad and I experienced it nearly every day when I was growing up. I'll do whatever it takes to get those pups back in one piece. And tomorrow, when I go with my father, I'll get as much information out of Brett as I can."

She stared right at me. "This is the only way. We all know it."

CHAPTER 34

DAMON

"Mae, wait up," I called after the meeting at Richard's. Arm looped around Luca's, she stopped and glanced over her shoulder at me. Luca whispered something to her, probably trying to take her away from me, but Mae shook her head and gestured for him to go to the car without her.

"What is it, Damon?" she asked, pushing some silver-blonde hair behind her shoulder.

"Can we talk? Really talk. No yelling or accusing," I asked, wanting nothing more than to grab her hand.

Every part of me still ached to be with her, and I so desperately wanted her back. I hadn't rejected her because she was weak or because she couldn't lead my pack, but because I didn't want her to die during the shift. I had told her that she was weak to convince both her and myself of it. But I had thought that she had been strong the moment I saw her yell at her father at the winery.

Now that a human had survived it, Mae might be able to too.

And, fuck, I'd kill for her to be able to shift with ease and become my luna.

"Mae, I made a mistake," I whispered.

She held her hand in front of her face to block the sun and squinted. "You did."

"I shouldn't have said those things to you. You deserve more than someone who treats you like that. Last night, during the full moon, I could feel your pain, every single ounce of it. I thought you were dying, or I thought Luca had bitten you and you were shifting. I thought I'd never see you again. It was like I was being torn apart." I folded my hands in front of me and glanced down at them. "Mae, you don't have to forgive me for what I said, and you don't have to take me back. I just want you back in my life. I will do anything for you."

After pausing for a moment, Mae sighed. "I forgive you."

My eyes widened. "You-you do?"

"Yes, you were doing what was best for your pack. I can't be as strong as Alexandra. She is good for you, Damon," Mae said, really fucking rubbing it in that I'd ever told her Alexandra was stronger than she could ever be.

It was a lie.

A straight-up fucking lie.

Alexandra was a tight-lipped snake.

"I want you, Mae," I repeated. "Even if it's just as a friend."

"Don't expect me to be in any type of relationship while she is in your life too."

"My wolf hasn't been the same since she marked me. I haven't seen him. I haven't run with him. He only wants you, Mae," I whispered, feeling a tug at my heart.

"Then, leave her, and I'll be back in your life," Mae said.

"As my mate and my pack's luna?"

I wanted her so damn badly. And I knew part of her wanted me too.

Mae crossed her arms. "As your friend."

"I need a luna," I said desperately.

Someone needed to lead my pack because I couldn't do it alone. When I had taken this pack from Dad, I hadn't thought it'd be so fucking hard and lonely. I needed someone strong by my side to help guide the pups, to show them how life was supposed to be, not the way I had grown up.

"And I need a man who will accept me just the way I am," Mae said strongly.

My heart broke. I'd never meant to make her feel so bad about herself.

"I'm sorry that you don't think I can be that man for you right now," I whispered, tucking a strand of her hair behind her ear. "But don't think I will ever stop trying to be. You can have Luca. You can love Luca. You can marry and mate with Luca. But you'll always be my mate, and deep down, you'll always love me."

CHAPTER 35

MAE

"And we're back with *Witver Without Wolves*," the radio announcer said over Dad's Mercedes-Benz speakers as we drove through the woods toward Brett's new place. "We've come to bring you shocking news about the wolves who live in our forest. From various sources, we've heard that the first human in years has shifted into a wolf without dying under the full moon. The wolves believe this is a huge success in their evil schemes, but I say this is all the more reason to—"

For once, Dad turned the radio station down to speak to me with a beaming smile. "I'm so happy that you want to come with me to see Brett today. I told Dr. Braxon that he was being too harsh on him and that Brett apologized, but"—Dad shrugged—"you know how it is sometimes between parents and kids."

My heart warmed slightly at the thought of Dad being excited to hang out with me. Usually, he just wanted to fight about wolves, but today, he seemed so upbeat. If he was like this all the time, I wouldn't mind eating dinner with him or going out to watch a movie or doing other fun things as a family.

And even if he was annoying sometimes, he wanted the best for me.

"And you dressed nice too," Dad exclaimed, looking down at my conservative sundress with roses.

I hadn't wanted to dress provocatively today because I didn't want Brett getting any ideas. I was going strictly for information.

Dad gently tapped my shoulder. "I'd tell you that you look beautiful, but you always do."

"Thanks, Dad," I said, legs bouncing slightly.

Dad continued on the tree-shaded road, not stopping once to ask why Brett had moved so deep into the woods. I guessed that he didn't know Brett now lived with two rogues who might be kidnapping children. And ... I didn't know if I should tell him or not.

Deciding to keep my mouth shut because we were having a good time this morning, I pulled out my phone to see about a hundred messages from Luca telling me to be safe and to call him if anything seemed *funny* with Brett today.

After ten more minutes, Dad pulled into a long dirt driveway lined with moonflowers. He parked behind Brett's car, and knots formed in my stomach. This was really happening. I was really out in the middle of nowhere, about to suck as much information out of Brett about his friends that I could.

When Brett answered the front door, he slipped his arms around my waist and hugged me tight to him, his muscles tauter than usual. "I knew you'd be back," he whispered, rough hands sliding against my skin. "I told you so."

Dad said hello to him and stepped into the house, glancing around at how enormous yet empty it seemed. There must've been fifteen bedrooms upstairs and even more downstairs, and this place kind of smelled a bit ... musty.

Sitting on the couch next to Dad, I inched as close to him as possible. I didn't want Brett anywhere near me after what he had done both the other night and at the apartment. And Dad would protect me. Brett never, ever made any advances on me in front of him.

When they fell into an easy conversation about Brett's parents, I took my first real gaze at Brett today and paled. Not even two days ago, I'd broken his nose at Oasis, and now, it was already healed. No black eyes either. Only wolves could heal that quickly.

Brett wasn't a werewolf. He couldn't be. He-he couldn't.

Definitely not because his ears were perfectly round still. Yet so were Aaisha's.

Maybe humans who were turned by werewolves didn't develop pointy ears and could easily blend in with the rest of the human race. But Brett ... he couldn't be a beast. He hated them as much as Dad hated them.

I dug my nails into my palm, my heart thumping.

"Mae?" Brett called, waving a hand in front of my face. "Are you okay?"

Not wanting him to know that I *might* know, I smiled. "Yeah, I'm fine. How are those ... friends of yours that I met the other night?" I asked, wanting to change the subject quickly so nobody asked questions.

"They're good. Why the interest?"

I shrugged. "Um ... you know, I thought one of them was pretty cute—that's all."

Brett pressed his lips together and blew an angry breath through his nose, like me just saying that I thought someone else was cute pissed him the fuck off. But I didn't know if I should get him pissed off enough for him to break and show his true self or if I should shut my damn mouth.

Suddenly, someone screamed in one of the downstairs rooms, and then a wolf growled. My heart raced faster than it had before, thoughts dashing through my mind. We all stood from the couch, Brett standing faster than Dad and me.

"Don't worry. That's probably just my friend," Brett said, urging us to sit and walking backward toward the hallway as another scream echoed through the corridor. "Stay here. I'll go see if he's okay."

When he disappeared, Dad looked at me with furrowed brows. "Mae, that sounded like a little girl," he said, thin, wrinkled lips in a tight line. "Something's not right. We have to go help Brett. Someone's in danger."

Rubbing my sweaty palms together, I followed Dad out of the room and through the empty and bland hallways toward the shrieks.

"Down the stairs, Dad," I said as we met the end of the upstairs hallway without finding her.

As we descended the stairs, the screams turned into desperate cries. I landed on the downstairs cement, the cold sending shivers up my spine. The cries became louder.

This was bad. This was really, really bad.

"You check over here," Dad said, jogging to the other end of the hallway. "I'll check down here."

Opening doors near me, I gazed into room after room after room and found nothing. I looked down the hallway at Dad, who had only opened one door and stared with horror into it.

"Mae ... Mae ..." Dad whispered, jaw slack and cheeks pale. "Mae, run! Run now!"

Instead of jogging back up the stairs, I ran toward him. "Dad, wh—"

An overwhelming scent of iron suffocated me, blood seeping out of the room and leaking through my shoes. The drapes and cement were splattered with gelatinous clots of gore. Small bodies lay lifeless in a puddle, their sunken skin an ashen color.

In the corner of the room, Brett held a small pup up by the scruff of his neck, his nails—no, claws—digging into the boy's flesh. My whole body went numb in fear. Brett and these rogues were the ones taking these pups and killing them.

"Brett!" I screamed and then slapped a hand over my mouth as soon as his name left my lips.

Suddenly, Brett whipped in my direction, canines extended from under his lips and eyes black as obsidian.

Brett was a monstrous, blood-hungry beast.

I stumbled back into Dad, who clamped his hands around my arms and threw me to the ground when Brett stalked angrily toward us. Brett charged at Dad and swiped his claws across his neck, killing him instantly. Blood squirted out of the artery in his neck, spraying all over his shirt, and then his lifeless carcass smacked against the ground.

With tears streaming down my face, I crawled through the puddle of blood to Dad's body and tightened my hands around his throat to try to stop the bleeding as his lifeless brown eyes stared up at me.

"No!" I screamed. "No, no. Please, Dad. Please, this can't be happening."

Brett grabbed a fistful of my hair, lifted me off of the ground, and flung me into the room. I smacked against the concrete floor, the blood from the puddle splattering all over the walls and the small pup Brett had been choking.

As Brett stalked toward us, I scrambled in front of the boy, holding my hand up and hoping he'd stop. "Please, Brett ... please."

He wrapped his hand around my neck and effortlessly lifted me into the air. I dug into his hand, trying to pull it away so I could breathe, but his grip tightened.

"Brett, wh-what—please, stop!"

Sniffing the air, he turned to the door. The rogue I'd bumped into at the restaurant barged in and glared down at two pups I hadn't noticed in the corner of the room, who were huddled together, tightly wrapping their arms around one another.

"Ron," Brett said to the rogue, who had blood smeared across his hands, "leave."

As if the rogue hadn't heard him, he sauntered into the room, grabbed my waist, and touched me. I flailed my arms and legs around, trying to escape Brett's grip, but he held me tighter.

"LEAVE," Brett growled, yanking me away. "She's *mine*."

Ron growled back at Brett, and then he stormed to the side of the room and grabbed one of the children, his hand closing tightly around her arm. When he dragged her to the door, she screamed and reached out for me to help her.

"No! NO!" I shouted through the tears. "Put her down! Please, take me!"

With a grunt, Ron threw the pup over his shoulder, walked out of the door, and then slammed it on us. The two pups left in the room whimpered and crawled toward each other, crying and sniffling.

"Shut the fuck up," Brett said to them, pushing me up against the wall harder.

"Brett, please, stop!"

"I told you you'd be begging for me," he murmured against my ear, drawing his tongue from the base of my neck up to my jaw and biting harshly like the psychopath he was.

"Stop it," I pleaded as he slipped his hand under my dress and grabbed between my legs. "Please, Brett, please! I'll do anything you want."

"I want you, Mae. I've *always* wanted you." He kissed me on the mouth. "But you've never wanted me. You've always wanted those beasts!" He choked me harder. "So, I turned into one during the full moon, so I could be one of them for you." He stared at me with blazing golden eyes. "Do you want me now, my love? Do you like my beast?"

I spat on him and shook my head. I would never like him or his beast. Never.

Without a second thought, he hurled me onto the cement and

unbuckled the button on his jeans. I rolled onto my back and kicked my feet against the cement to try to get away, the puddle of blood making it difficult. He caught me by the ankle and dragged me to him, forcing himself between my legs.

"That's too bad because I want you. And today, I'm finally going to have you."

"Brett, stop. Please." I pressed my knees together as hard as I could, but he jerked them apart. I turned my head away, not wanting to watch, and stared at the two pups in the corner of the room. "Brett, I'll let you do anything you want to me, just please bring me someplace else. I can't—I don't want the children to see."

He kissed down my neck. He didn't care about what I wanted or about the children. He wanted my body, and that was it. So, one last time, I desperately tried to close my legs, but he pried them open and gripped my chin to force me to look up at him.

"Oh, Mae, I want them to watch every second of me having you."

CHAPTER 36

VALERIO

*P*aws hitting the ground hard, I sprinted toward the sound of Mae's screams to an abandoned pack house just outside Witver Forest. I had left her in her father's care for a moment, a mere moment, to give the Queen a status report. And now, she was shrieking.

Mae had been safe for the past twenty years. I couldn't let anything happen to her now. It was my duty to protect her and to keep her alive. Too many people wanted her dead, and she didn't even know it yet.

I shifted, slipped in through a back door, and followed Mae's voice down to the cellar, the stench of blood perforating my entire body and making it difficult to breathe. Small yips and hiccups echoed through the narrow cement corridor. Pups.

Mae had uncovered a Challenger hideout.

"*My Queen,*" I said through my mind-link. "*Mae has uncovered a Challenger hideout. Please send Protectors here to help me. I'm not sure how many children are here, but by the stench, it must be at least twenty."*

After waiting for five minutes without a response, I tried again. *"My Queen, we—"*

"Valerio, there are no Protectors coming to help you. You must leave immediately and come back here."

"But Mae—"

"Valerio," she snapped. *"Back here now."*

Unable to leave the woman I had to protect in danger, I continued through the hallway until I reached the last door, peeking in every room to find any abandoned, tortured, or blood-drained pups.

"Brett, stop it," Mae sobbed on the other side of the door. "Please..."

Just as I was about to slip into the room, I saw a rogue walk down the stairs and disappear into one of the many empty rooms with a small pup.

"Fuck," I breathed out, running a hand through my hair. Who should I go after first? Which—

"Valerio, I said to come back now. Don't make me repeat myself," the Queen said.

"I'm not leaving Mae and a bunch of pups here with the Challengers," I said, lips pursed.

"NOW!"

Ignoring her demand, I stepped over Mae's father and quietly twisted the knob to open the door just slightly, so I could examine the situation before I barged into the room. If the Queen wasn't sending anyone to help me, then I would have to do it myself.

"Tell me that you love me, Mae," a male said from inside of the room, kissing Mae's neck.

Someone wrapped their hand around my neck from behind, choking me harshly, and the world darkened for a moment. When I could finally see again, I found myself standing inside one of the rooms of the Protectors' home, not back in that cellar with Mae.

With blazing silver eyes, the Queen glared down at me and crossed her arms over her chest. "When I say come back, you come back. Don't you dare defy me again, Valerio, or I'll take you off your assignment."

"I wasn't going to let Mae and innocent pups die," I said through gritted teeth.

She shook her head and stalked closer to me. "You're Mae's life mate. I've made a damn bond between you two, yet you don't act like it! You need to be strong, Valerio. And I needed you back here for that exact reason."

"How was I not being strong enough for you? I was going to save her."

"This is how you are strong for her," the Queen said, thrusting her fingers against my temples and taking control of my mind.

I gasped for breath, the room around me blurring. I blinked a few times, trying to readjust my vision, yet her fingers just pressed harder against my temples.

When I regained my sight, I was no longer in the Protectors' home but back in the dirty cellar. Brett was staring down at me and kissing my neck. My eyes darted around, looking for Mae inside of the bloodied room, but she wasn't here. And then I realized that the Queen had made me Mae in this vision and placed me inside of her body, so I could feel every ounce of pain.

"Brett, it-it hurts! Stop, please," I found myself saying.

He forcefully pushed his cracked lips onto mine, his callous and bloody fingers digging into my sides. I tried closing my eyes, but I couldn't get rid of the nightmare the Queen had placed upon me.

Not again. This was happening all over. I couldn't see this. I-I couldn't. Mom's rape had scarred me. I couldn't watch the one woman I was supposed to protect get taken ruthlessly too. I couldn't feel it this time. Why was the Queen making this happen all over again?

Brett grabbed me by the throat and squeezed hard, thrusting into me.

All I wanted to do was rip myself out of Mae's body and tear Brett to shreds. I flailed my arms and legs around, trying to get myself out of the Queen's hold but couldn't. She had me stuck in a trance that I couldn't pull myself out of.

"Queen, please. I won't defy you again. Let me save Mae. Please. She'll be broken after this," I said through the mind-link to her, yet she didn't answer.

I tried to scoot away, tried pushing my hands and heels in the river of blood beneath me, yet every time I made it an inch away, he would wrap his hand around my ankle, drag me closer, and shove himself into me again.

Glancing around the room, I spotted a small boy hugging another pup.

They couldn't see this. It would fuck them up. It'd fucked me up.

Brett grinned down at my pain.

Disgust.

Helpless.

Hopeless.

That was all I felt. What else *could* I feel?

Nothing. I could feel nothing.

In a moment, Brett faded from my view. I collapsed onto the wooden floor and stared up at the Queen's silver eyes, my mind desperately trying to untangle reality from the nightmare she'd just put me through.

Why had she made me go through that? And why the fuck would she make Mae, a lost girl who didn't know anything about her real parents, go through that?

I wrapped my arms around myself, pulling my knees to my chest in hopes of diminishing the feeling of a man between my legs. It was as if the feeling of Brett's hands on Mae's body were burned into my skin forever.

A stray tear slid down my cheek as I thought back to Mom's rape. But before the Queen could see how weak that moment had made me, I pushed the tear away, took a deep breath, and bowed my head to her.

"Next time I say to do something, you do it, Valerio. Do you understand me?"

"Yes, my Queen," I said, barely above a whisper.

"I will not stand here and let *your* weakness get in the way of Mae's safety. You will do anything you need to do in order to make Mae strong. When the time comes, Mae will be the only person to pull this species out of endangerment. She can't have weakness, and neither can you."

"Yes, my Queen."

"And, Valerio, I expect you to keep your mouth shut about this encounter."

"Yes, my Queen. I'll keep it quiet…"

But Mae would always remember what had happened to her and would never be the same again.

CHAPTER 37

MAE

When Brett rolled off me, I pressed my legs together to try to ease the burn between them and curled my arms around my knees with tears streaming down my face. I wanted to cry forever, but I didn't want to make a sound and anger him again. He would do it again—and worse next time.

Brett grinned and closed his eyes, chuckling to himself while I lay beside him, in fear that he would never let me or the children go.

Why had I been so stupid? Had I really thought coming to Brett's house was a good idea? Why couldn't I make any right decisions to save my life?

Dad was dead because of me.

On the bright side, I'd found the missing pups.

I waited and waited and waited for Brett to hop up and drag me to another room, bind my wrists with chains, and declare me his forever, but it never happened. Instead, he started snoring, as if raping me had taken too much out of him because I hadn't stopped putting up a fight once. I didn't want the pups to think that this was okay.

It was violating.

A pup whimpered from behind me, and I glanced over at them. We had to get out of here, but how could we? If we tried to escape and made it out of the room, the other rogues might catch us, were probably waiting for us, but if we stayed, there was no doubt that we would all die.

Posting my hand beside me, I sat up and winced. Already, I could feel my neck bruising from where Brett had choked me and the stinging between my legs. He had gone in dry and without a care in the world, just continued to force himself on me.

Cursing quietly, I clenched my jaw and knelt. I didn't even know if I'd be able to walk. Everything hurt too bad. But I needed to suck up my pain for the kids. They were more important than any pain I felt.

After holding a finger to my lips to tell them to be quiet, I glanced over at Brett. How would I stop Brett if he woke up? He had no control over his wolf. I needed something to suppress him, so I scanned the room for something silver and frowned. I guessed these rogues didn't need to keep silver in their torture rooms and holding cells because pups weren't able to shift or use their inner wolves to their fullest capacities yet.

Pain pierced through my chest, and I pressed my hand on top of it, my palm grazing against my necklace. My eyes widened. It was silver. I had something that might be able to do some harm to him.

Once I successfully clasped it around his neck without waking him, I stood, tiptoed over to the two children, and took them by the hand. We walked around Brett and opened the door, peeking out of the room and into an empty hall. Dad's body lay lifeless before us.

Biting back a cry, I reached into his pockets to try to find the keys to his car, but all his pockets were empty. We didn't have time to look around this monstrous house. We needed to get out of here. Now.

As we rushed down the hall, one of the pups tugged at my bloody dress.

"We can't leave without our friend!" she whispered to me. "She's here. They took her."

Stomach tightening, I pursed my lips. We *could* leave without her, but if she was alive now, she definitely wouldn't be when help came for her. So, we jogged back down the hallway and peeked inside all of the rooms. And when I opened the door to the last room on the right, one of the children screamed.

I smacked my hand over his mouth, my eyes widening at the sight. Inside the room, the dead pup lay upright in a machine that was slowly sucking the blood out of her, her eyes a lifeless white and her cheeks sunken in.

Not wanting to see any more, I shut the door and picked the two pups up, letting them cry into my neck. After sprinting down the hallway and not daring to look back, I slipped out a back door and ran into the forest, not sure where we were going but needing to get away from here fast.

Adrenaline pumped through my veins, beads of sweat dripped down my back, and the wind chilled my skin. I squinted my eyes, trying to see through the heavy fog that sat in the towering oak trees around us, hoping to find a landmark or street I could follow with the two pups.

I hoped someone would save us, but we were in the middle of an abandoned part of Witver Forest. Nobody was coming to help. We had to do this all on our own.

Running for what seemed like hours but was probably only minutes, I breathed heavily, a sharp pain stabbing me through my side from running too long with the two children on my hips.

"You can put us down, miss. We can run," the girl said.

After setting them down, I held their hands and sprinted

alongside them. Even though they hadn't shifted yet, they still could run much faster than I could. And part of me wanted to just let them run far away from here on their own, but ... I didn't know where the hell we were or which direction we faced.

When the sun set over the forest and darkness surrounded us, I urged them to slow to a jog, the dull light from the moon glistening against their faces.

"Do you know where we are?" I asked.

Maybe they could smell a pack nearby.

"It doesn't smell like anything really, just rogues," the boy said.

I swallowed hard. They were definitely out, looking for us. But how far away were they? Would we make it through the night, through the next hour? If they found us, they would torture and then slaughter us, and I couldn't let the pups die.

"Well, let me know if you smell a pack, and we will go there."

We continued to sprint for hours, the night too dark for me to navigate anywhere. My mind raced with thoughts about what would happen to us if I didn't get them home. Not only would Brett rape me over and over again, but the pups ... those rogues would do what they had done to that other young girl and drain out their blood.

"Miss, we're hungry and dizzy. We haven't eaten in two days. Can we stop for food?"

"Please, miss?" the girl pleaded with a pale face.

Glancing around, I hesitantly nodded. "Okay ... but we have to be quick."

We walked quietly through the woods, careful not to snap any twigs, and plopped down next to a berry bush. The pups pulled as many as they could off the branches and stuffed them into their mouths, hopefully filling themselves up for however long we had left.

The girl reached for my hand, pulled me onto the ground with her, and gave me some berries to eat too. "Miss, what's your name?"

"Mae," I said, giving her my best smile. "What are your names?"

"I'm Aarav!" the boy said.

"Tai!" the girl said.

"What pack are you from?" Aarav said.

"I'm not a werewolf," I said.

Their eyes widened.

"But you're so strong! How could you not be one?" Aarav asked.

"Yeah! You should be a luna! You're so caring!" Tai said, wrapping her arms around me and pulling me close.

Tears welled up in my eyes at the thought, the dream of what could've been.

"Yeah, our luna … she's"—Aarav glanced around the forest and then covered his mouth with his hand—"terrible."

"Yeah, Luna Alexandra would never try to come find us. She's mean," Tai said.

I pressed my lips together. Of course Alexandra wouldn't come to find them. Everything about her was fake.

"And ug!" Aarav said.

"Ug?" I asked.

"Ug-ly!" He snorted along with Tai, their giggles filling the air and eventually making me laugh too.

I clutched my stomach, a tear slipping down my cheek. And for the first time in a long time, it was a tear of glee. Who knew these two pups could make a bad situation into a decently pleasant one?

The pups grabbed each other's hands, laughing uncontrollably.

How could anyone do what Brett and the rogues had done to them? How could someone just drain the life out of the innocent? Why were they doing that to the children? Why not full-grown wolves? Did they think children were easy targets, easy ways to tear apart a pack?

"I have an idea!" Aarav said. He pulled the girl closer, covering his mouth with his hand and whispering into her ear.

A smile spread across Tai's face, and she nodded. "Yeah!" she squealed.

"When we get back home, we are going to kick Alexandra out and make you our luna!" Aarav declared, eating another berry.

"Yeah!" Tai said.

"Alpha Damon would love you because you're so strong. You can make our pack stronger!"

I smiled down at the pups. If they only knew that I could've been their luna, that Damon didn't think of me as strong despite his apology last night. To him, I wasn't strong enough to survive the shift and therefore not strong enough to lead his pack with him.

Not wanting to sulk anymore, I stood and grabbed their hands. "Well, if you want to make me your luna, we'd better go find your pack!"

They jumped up and sprinted ahead of me.

"We can't wait!" they said.

"I'm going to get there first!" Tai said, racing ahead of Aarav.

Trying to keep up with their increasing speed, I grasped my side and ran harder. Knots began forming in the pit of my stomach—and not the kind from running. The kind I got whenever something felt off.

And that was when I heard it.

A monstrous growl echoed throughout the woods.

The rogues were here.

"Run faster!" I said, my heart thumping hard.

The pups' little legs propelled them faster than before, and then they disappeared through the fog. I pumped my legs harder, branches scraping across my thighs, wind whipping my hair in all directions, pain shooting down my body from the center of my chest.

"Over here!" Tai said, looking back. "It's our pack."

"Don't stop running!" I shouted.

"But what about you?" Aarav asked, stopping.

"GO!"

They bolted away from me and farther into the woods as I stumbled to keep up. I looked over my shoulder to see a single wolf racing toward me, his hind legs thrusting over broken branches and a line of fur burned off around his neck from where my necklace must've been.

Brett.

He was quickly closing the distance between us. There was no way I'd outrun him.

When the children disappeared from my sight, I swallowed. I could stop running and distract Brett. It would give the children more time to escape. They had to return safely. Their pack and their alpha needed them.

Yet I continued on for a bit longer, my feet pushing me through the thinning woods until I saw Damon's cabin in the distance. Maybe he was there and could help me. I needed someone to kill Brett because I couldn't do it with my bare hands.

As I approached the cabin, I scanned the area for anything I could defend myself with—a knife, a rope, or ... *an ax.* Damon had left some out in his backyard, where he had taken me to throw axes. The metal part of the ax looked to be silver. Maybe, just maybe, I could use it to defend myself.

Pushing just a bit harder, I grabbed the ax. If Brett got closer to me, I doubted I'd be able to slash the ax hard enough into him before he launched his canines into my throat and killed me. I needed to throw it, and I had one shot. One shot. If I missed, I would die.

I dug my heels into the dirt to stop myself and turned around to face him. Brett was no longer a man, but a beast with terrifying golden eyes and bloody canines, which he'd drooled on me with earlier.

The ax trembled in my hand.

When he leaped toward me, I took a deep breath, cocked the ax back, and then lunged forward, releasing it. The silver impaled Brett right between the eyes and launched into his skull, stopping him immediately and causing him to fall limp to the ground with blood spewing from his wound.

I-I had just killed Brett.

I'd killed him.

I'd saved the pups.

Hands trembling, I stared at his carcass with wide eyes.

To my left, a pack of wolves emerged from Witver Forest and transformed into their humans, gazing at the sight in front of them. Damon and Luca were in front of the pack, their eyes flickering from me to Brett.

Tears ran down my cheeks.

I'd killed the man who had murdered my father.

I—

Something whizzed through the air from my right, and Damon and Luca both lunged forward, their relieved expressions turning into one of anguish. And suddenly, pain split through my head, and the edges of my vision darkened. The sky shifted diagonally across my sight, and I stumbled forward, fell to my knees, and let the blackness consume me for a second time this week.

"Alpha, you have to leave!" someone said to my left, yet I couldn't open my eyes.

"I'm not leaving until she wakes up!" Damon growled.

"Alpha, please," the man pleaded.

"Damon, come on. Let them work on her," Luca said.

Work on who? What was happening?

More growls rumbled through the room, followed by loud

clattering metal noises. I tried prying my eyes open again, but I couldn't. They were too heavy.

What was happening to me? Was this a dream?

"Damon, stop acting like this! You can't do anything for her now! Maybe if you hadn't told her that she was weak, we wouldn't be in this situation!" Luca growled.

"Me telling her she was weak has nothing to do with this!" Damon said.

"If you'd just accepted her from the beginning, she wouldn't have felt like she had to prove herself by going after Brett!" Luca said.

"Leave now!" the other man said.

A moment later, the door slammed.

"Give her anesthesia."

Earth-shattering sobs woke me from my deep sleep. Just the sound of them made my chest tighten.

Who was crying? Why couldn't I still open my eyes? What had happened to me in that forest?

"I'm so sorry," Damon said. "I should've been a better mate. I should've accepted you from the beginning." He grabbed my hand and intertwined our fingers. "I told you that you were weak when I was the weak one. I needed to reject you because I needed to prove to my pack that I wasn't going to be like my father, that I could be a good alpha, and that I wouldn't give up on them despite the circumstances. I wanted them to know that I'd do anything for them.

"But I also didn't want you to die during your first shift. If you died, I-I would break. I'd die with you, Mae. I'd rather see you happy with someone else than to never see your smile again. I wish ... I wish I had been stronger for you, for us. But I'm not as strong as I want to be."

My heart raced.

Damon had given up his own happiness for my life. He would rather see me happy than be happy himself. I didn't know if I wanted to slap him for doing that to himself or hug him for caring too much. I still loved him, but I wasn't sure if I was in love with him anymore.

Because I loved Luca.

"You probably hate me, but I'm sorry. I'm so sorry. This is my fault. I promise that I'll find out who shot you with that silver bullet, and I'll kill them. I'll do it for you."

Someone ... shot me?

A loud beep echoed throughout the room, and someone opened the door.

"Alpha, you have to leave. She's unstable."

He squeezed my hand one last time and pulled away. But I didn't want him to go. I didn't want to be alone again. It was so lonely here, wherever this dark place was.

"So, we've been talking, and he was like, 'I want pups!' I just looked at him, and I was like, 'nuh-uh, no! Ain't no pups coming out of this girl's vajayjay!' Ya know what I mean? But then we got into a fight and made up with some realllllly good sex!" Aaisha said to my left.

I desperately tried to open my eyes and smile at her, but I couldn't.

She grabbed my hand off of the bed and placed it on what felt like a paper towel. "What color do you want me to paint your nails? Red? I was thinking the same thing! Great minds think alike, ya know."

When she opened the nail polish, it reeked. She gently took my hand and brushed it onto my nails. Despite everything that had happened in the past few days, Aaisha was still Aaisha.

"I miss you, girl. It's not the same without you."

I missed her too. I wanted to wrap my arms around her. I wanted to open my eyes to tell her that I was still here. But ... I couldn't.

After finishing my in-hospital spa day, she curled up next to me and opened a container. "You want some chocolate cake? Hmm? No? I guess more for me!"

My heart warmed. I loved her. She was my best friend. I only wished I could see her crazy, loud, smiling face, but the darkness seeped into my mind again and consumed me.

More cries awoke me from my slumber, the darkness still as prominent as ever, yet this time, these weren't quiet cries but loud ones, cries that couldn't be bottled up anymore, cries of fear, despair, and sorrow.

The bed dipped next to me, and someone scooted closer, his arms wrapping around my waist and his touch igniting my skin. "Mae, please, come back. Please. I've been a mess without you. I miss your smile, your laughter, your happiness. I miss holding you when you're sad and letting you vent when you're angry. I miss you, Mae."

I missed Luca too. So fucking much.

"If you're listening, just please know that I love you. I know you still have feelings for Damon, but I love you. I've loved you since I met you. I'll love you whether you choose to be with him or not. You don't have to love me back, but-but ..." Something wet dripped onto my arm. "But I-I don't know what I was going to say, honestly. Just know that I love you."

Someone knocked on the door.

"Come in," Luca called.

"Hey, Luca. Would you mind if I came and sat with her for a

few minutes? I have a couple of little people who want to talk to her," Samuel said.

After placing a soft kiss on my cheek, Luca wrapped me into a hug and then left the bed, shuffling away and leaving me feeling empty.

"All right! Go get her!" Samuel said.

Quick footsteps padded across the floor, and then the bed dipped on either side of me, small bodies cuddling close to me.

"Hi, Mae!" Aarav said.

"Mae! Why don't you wake up? We know you're strong enough to," Tai said.

"Yeah, you're wicked strong! You even proved it!" Aarav continued.

The pups. The pups that I'd saved were here.

They talked with each other, rambling on about pup things for a while, and then skipped out of the room together, talking about who was going to get to Alpha Damon's pack house first.

Samuel shut the door behind them and sighed. "I was hoping that you put yourself in a coma because you were moody and tired of everyone's shit, so I decided to bring you food to make you feel better! I asked the doctor if I could put some of it down your feeding tube—because you got one of those now—but he said no. So, I came up with a better idea! I'll just eat the food for you."

He sat down in the chair next to me and ate. "How's life in there? To be honest, sometimes, when Alexandra is ordering me to do something, I get jealous of you because you don't have to see her face." He laughed and then gave a long-drawn-out sigh. "Anyway, love you. I hope you wake up soon."

"Oh, look at you," Alexandra said into my ear, a shudder running down my spine. "Poor thing. I actually feel kind of bad for you.

You don't have to hear Damon complain and whine all day about missing his mate."

Why was she even here? She didn't care about me in the slightest.

All I wanted to do was peel my eyes open and rip her throat out.

"It's a shame, what happened to you. Hopefully, they'll find your attacker …" She laughed and leaned closer, her stench of perfume overwhelming me, even when I was in this stupid coma thing. "Well, I'll see you later … or not."

She paused, and then I heard a pop, as if something had been pulled out of a socket. After a few moments, she walked away and shut the door behind herself. And I wanted to thank the Goddess that she had left, but … my throat suddenly closed up, my breathing becoming ragged.

I-I couldn't breathe.

What was happening?

I tried parting my lips, but I couldn't.

My throat was dry, scratchy, and tight. The beeping on my heart monitor—if that was what it was—quickened or slowed. I wasn't quite sure. All I knew was that the thing started beeping like crazy until someone opened my door.

"We need a doctor! She's unstable!" she shouted, voice becoming quieter as she hurried to find someone.

A few moments later, a man wrapped their arms under my body.

The doctor was here.

A mask was ripped off my face, and I finally opened my eyes for the first time in a long time. But it wasn't a doctor racing me out of the hospital room, but that familiar man with blond hair.

CHAPTER 38

MAE

"She's healed," a woman with a soothing, almost celestial voice said.

I gazed up at her, admiring her long silver hair and pale face as she looked between that blond wolf and another older wolf who stood next to him.

I lay in a hospital bed with an IV sticking in my arm that had a white liquid pumping into me. Another hospital.

Why was I here? And where was *here*?

"I had to do everything in my power to heal her," she said.

"Everything? Even—" the older wolf said.

She held up her hand, commanding him to stop speaking. "Yes. Even that."

The blond wolf glanced at me, noticed that I was awake, and stalked over. He pressed his lips into a thin line, the emotion disappearing from his face, and placed a mask over my nose and mouth.

I flailed on the bed. I didn't want to sleep again. I'd slept so much. I was missing so much. I couldn't handle another darkness. I needed light. I needed to breathe, to live.

∽

When I reopened my eyes, I sat on the couch in my apartment and blew out a deep breath.

Oh gosh. It was all a dream. One big, terrible fucking dream.

The mark, Damon, Aaisha turning into a wolf, killing Brett, getting shot, Dad dying.

A tear slipped down my cheek. "A dream... thank goodness."

After wiping away the tear, I walked over to Aaisha's room and peered into her open door to see her bed made, her laundry in her hamper, and her makeup spread out across her bed. She stood at the other side of the room in front of a mirror, smoothing out a cropped pink shirt.

Overcome with happiness, I skipped into her room to hug her. But when I wrapped my arms around her waist, she disappeared into thin air, and I stumbled into the mirror.

Wh-what was that? She was right here. Right in front of me. How did she just disappear?

Lifting my gaze, I looked into the mirror and froze. Smack-dab in the middle of my chest was the brightest red mark I'd ever seen, glimmering against my skin, like it always did. I guessed it was too good to be true.

This was my life.

Constantly stuck in a dreamlike state.

I stepped closer to the mirror and noticed a circular scar on each of my temples. My fingers trembled as I gently rubbed those wrinkled marks from what looked to be a bullet. If what Damon had said was true and I had been shot by a bullet in the brain, how was I still living?

Two distinct male laughs drifted into the room from the living room. I jogged to Aaisha's doorframe and gazed out to see

Damon and Luca sitting on the couch, laughing with each other. Their smiles faded into frowns when they saw me.

"What are *you* doing here?" Damon snapped.

"I-I live here," I whispered, confused about how Damon and Luca—two enemies—were in the same room without trying to rip each other's throats out.

Luca chuckled. "No, you don't. How many times do I have to tell you to leave?"

"Don't you know when to stop? He's already rejected you," Damon said.

My eyebrows furrowed. "But ... you ..."

"She just can't handle the rejection, I guess," Luca said. "She's too *weak*."

What was he talking about? Why was he calling me weak? Was this nightmare what people truly thought of me? Or was my mind just playing tricks on me? Was I seeing *my* worst fears?

"You're weak," Damon said.

My knees buckled, and suddenly, tears raced down my eyes. Why was this happening?

"Don't be a baby. Get up! Get out of my apartment!" Luca shouted.

"You're just a weak human, thinking you could mate with a werewolf. Who does that?" Damon said.

"You wouldn't even survive the shift."

"I hope some rogue bites you before the blood moon, so you die in agony when your body tries to shift."

I covered my ears, not wanting to hear any more, and sprinted to the door. After running out of the apartment, I slammed the door and slid down to the floor with my back against the wall. *Thank the Goddess that is over, and I can—*

Instead of being outside my apartment, I stood in the foyer of Dad's house. Twenty years younger with hair still brown and eyes so bright, Dad entered and strolled by me as if he hadn't seen me. I stood in shock because the last time I had seen him, he was nothing but a carcass lying in a puddle of his own blood.

He walked to the kitchen, and I followed. Blood was splattered all over the kitchen cabinets and floor, and a woman's body with gashes and chunks of flesh missing lay on the ground with a wolf standing over her.

"Mom," I whispered, staring down at her lifeless body. I turned to the wolf. "Stop! Please, stop!"

Yet the wolf with a large gash in his cheek didn't even gaze my way. I tried running to him to tear him off of her, but my feet led me in the opposite direction, and I found myself running out of the house.

This time, when I ran out of the house, I walked into Brett's torture room.

Brett grabbed the pup by the scruff of his neck, dragged him to the center of the room, and pushed him into the upright machine. Then, he turned toward me and tossed me a knife. "Drain him."

My eyes widened, yet I took the knife. Trembling in fear, I desperately tried to keep myself from moving toward the pup. I couldn't. Instead, I pressed the silver blade against the pup's neck artery and sliced him open, his pulse slowly fading as the blood drained out of him.

I squeezed my eyes shut. I needed to get out of here. Now.

After all of the gore seeped out of him, I let the knife clatter on the floor and squeezed my eyes closed.

When I reopened them, I was lying in the hospital room I had last woken up in, the bright lights blinding me. It was all just a dream—a nightmare. At least, that was what I hoped. But everything had felt so real; it was hard to tell what was reality and what was just fabricated by my consciousness.

The woman from earlier sat at my bedside, tears slipping from her silver eyes.

"Mom?" I whispered, suddenly recognizing her.

When her name left my dry lips, she stood abruptly and scurried out of the room. I yanked the IV out of my arm and sprinted after her down the long corridors decorated with maps of the stars and diagrams of the moon. A door shut to my left, and I shoved it open, knowing that I had trapped her in whatever kind of dream this was now. I had questions that only she knew the answers to.

Inside, a never-ending library of books, stacked all the way to the ceiling, with large red-cushioned chairs fit for a king, the blond wolf relaxed with a *romance* novel in his hand. No Mom.

When the wolf saw me, he placed the book down and cocked a brow. "How was your sleep?"

I narrowed my eyes at him. "Am I in hell?"

It was the only explanation.

Why else would I see and do the worst things in life? Why else would Luca, the man who had confessed his love for me, reject me and laugh about it? Why else would I watch my own mother's body be torn to pieces? And how could I see my mother if she was dead?

He placed the book on a side table and stood, stepping closer. I moved back.

How could I trust him if I couldn't even trust myself anymore?

"You could call it something like that," he said.

"Wh-what do you mean by that?"

"By the time you're finished here, you're going to think it's hell, but I promise, everything I do to you will make you stronger," he said to me, taking one final stride.

I placed my hands on his chest, pushing him away. What had he meant by that? What was he going to do to me?

In one swift movement, he grabbed my wrists, pushed the door open, and dragged me out of the room. I yanked, kicked, screamed, and shouted for him to stop, yet he pulled me down the corridor, opened a hidden door behind a painting of a goddess, and pushed me down stone steps and into a cellar.

My body hit the cement floor with a thud. I turned onto my butt and scooted away from the man, who grimaced and looked behind me. I twisted my head, my jaw slackening.

"Fuck ..." I breathed out.

A pack of abnormally large wolves—at least, that was what they looked like—were lined up against the far wall, teeth dripping with saliva and golden eyes fixed on me and only me. The blond wolf nodded at the others, giving them some sort of silent orders, and the wolves all lowered into a fighting stance.

"One little piece of advice, Mae," Blondie said. "Don't stop fighting."

And after those final words of wisdom, the wolves sprinted at me. I closed my eyes, hoping and praying that I wouldn't die here as the first impact sent me flying across the room. My back smacked against the cement wall, my head bouncing off of it. Darkness clouded my vision for a few moments, and I closed my eyes.

When I reopened them, I was lying on my back with three wolves on top of me. One monster overextended my right arm, the joint snapping back. Another wrapped his hands around my throat and squeezed until I couldn't breathe. I dug my fingers into his, trying to peel him off of me.

"S-s-stop," I cried.

The wolf's grasp slackened. "Valerio, wh—"

"Don't stop. She needs to learn," Blondie said.

Tears streamed down my face. Someone kicked my stomach, sending me onto my back. I clutched it and stared up into the sea of golden eyes, sharp claws, and terrorizing canines. I was going to die.

I was really going to die here.

"Let's go!" Valerio shouted into the library, his jaw taut but his blue eyes so ... remorseful. "Why are you still in here? I said a quick shower and then back to the cellar. You have training to complete before you get any breaks, Mae."

"Please, I've been fighting them for days." I stood up from the leather couch, my knees wobbling. "Please ... please let me rest for just a few moments."

"You rested last night. Now, come."

"No. I keep having nightmares. I didn't get any rest ... please ..." I slumped back down in the couch, my eyelids drooping. "They're too strong ... stronger than Damon ... Luca ..." My voice faded off to a whisper, talking more to myself than him.

Large purple bruises covered my body, new ones forming every day. My muscles ached from the sheer force they continuously put on me. I didn't know how long they'd trapped me here with no interaction with the outside world, no sunlight, no phases of the moon to track my days.

I couldn't handle it. I wanted it all to stop. What had I done to deserve this punishment?

"Up now!" Valerio roared, wrapping his hand around my wrist and dragging my bruised body all the way down to the cellar, where the pack of wolves waited to feast on my body for the umpteenth night in a row. "If I have to force you to, then I will."

Waiting anxiously for Valerio to give them orders, the wolves stood by the cement wall on all fours, saliva dripping off their teeth and onto the ground beneath them. Valerio pressed his lips together, walked to a cabinet built into the wall, and retrieved a chain from it. After forcing me onto my knees—I didn't have it in me to fight back—he bound me up tightly.

"You were five minutes late. You will be punished for each minute until you learn."

Punished? I was being punished enough.

He extended his serrated black claws inches from me, glided

them across my cheek very gently, and then grabbed a fistful of my hair, forcing me off my butt to a vertical kneel. I sucked in a breath and braced for the worst punishment of them all.

"Count, or we will restart from the beginning," Valerio said.

"Pl-please," I pleaded.

He dug his claws into my back, tearing my clothes and lacerating my flesh. I screamed out in pain as my skin was ripped out in grooves, trails of blood streaming down my back and around my rib cage, dripping on the cement floor.

"Count!" Valerio growled.

"One!"

Another slash. Blood splattered all over the ground.

"Two," I said through gritted teeth, the searing pain unbearable. "I-I'm sorry for whatever I did! Ple—No!" I screamed out as he hacked his claws into me again. My elbows gave out, and I tumbled to the ground at the sheer force. "Th-three," I whispered.

"Get up."

I placed my hands on the ground and pushed myself up with all the energy I had left. "Please … I'll submit to you … I'll do anything …"

When his claws dug into my skin for a fourth time, he pulled out a chunk of my flesh and flicked it down next to me in the puddle of blood.

"Fou …"

The room spun, darkness clouding the edges of my vision. One more. One freaking more.

After he slashed me one last time, I fell to the ground in the puddle of my gore, skin, and flesh, my lips barely moving. "Five."

"Mike, heal her," Valerio ordered.

A wolf approached me and knelt by my side. When his fingers grazed against my back, I flinched away and cried out for someone to help me.

Valerio crouched by my side, an almost-painful expression on his face, and shortened his claws. "He's just going to heal your wounds."

I whimpered as the man trailed his hands over my broken back, sending excruciating amounts of pain through my body. After the blood stopped dripping off my rib cage, Valerio picked me up in his arms and set me down on the bottom step.

Why would Valerio want to heal me after he hurt me? Was this all just some sick game?

He placed a glass of water to my lips and let me happily drink it down. "You will learn pain. You will learn fear. You will accept them both. And when you're finished with training, you will be numb to them. Do you understand?"

My head nodded even though I didn't understand why he was doing this. I just didn't want him to hurt me again.

Why was he making me fight these beasts? Why was I having nightmares? Why was I being punished?

"Good," Valerio said, glancing at my back and then down at the ground as if he couldn't look me in the eyes. "Stand up. It's time to train."

Though I wanted to protest, I didn't have the energy to endure another punishment like that. My body would forever be scarred by his claws, deep grooves always in my back, chunks of flesh never to return.

When training was over, I curled up into a ball on the cement cellar floor with tears racing down my cheeks. Valerio turned off the lights and shut the door, leaving me shivering on the bloody floor.

"You will sleep in my room tonight," Valerio said to me after I'd had another grueling day of being clawed and beaten by beasts.

Some of the wolves glanced over at him with nervous eyes

and tight lips, as if me sleeping anywhere, except the cellar, was forbidden.

I swallowed hard. "I thought I couldn't ..."

"You're not supposed to," Valerio said, scooping me up into his arms and bringing me up the stairs. He set me down in the corridor and took my hand to lead me to one of the many rooms in this palace. "But you need to shower and rest." He pushed open a large oak door that led into a grand bedroom with a king-size canopy bed, silk curtains, and a bathroom big enough to fit ten. "There are clothes for you in the bathroom. You can sleep on the couch tonight. It folds out into a bed."

Deciding not to test my luck, I shuffled to the bathroom and stripped off my clothes in the floor-length, silver-encrusted mirror. Dark circles lay under my eyes, dried blood and dirt covered my body, and my sanguine-colored mark was nearly a full circle again. Yet ... the muscles in my arms swelled, and for the first time ever, I could see my abs.

I turned around and winced at the deep scars on my back and those horrid grooves.

Valerio was right. In the most fucked up way, this place had made me stronger.

One day, I hoped to be strong enough that I could break down these heavy doors and flee from this place forever.

CHAPTER 39

VALERIO

"Let Mae rest," I pleaded with the Queen. "She has gone through enough painful torture these past few weeks. She doesn't need to be tormented in her dreams too. I know that you need her to be strong, but I don't think this is the way."

We walked down the corridor toward my bedroom, where Mae slept in my bed. I had moved her there to be more comfortable for the night. The Queen had forbidden me to bring her anywhere other than the cellar, but she needed the rest, and I was damn tired of torturing her every day.

If I'd had any say in the matter, I would've trained her differently.

But the Queen had powers that far surpassed my own. If I didn't do it, she'd force me.

Turning to me, the Queen swept her silver hair over her shoulder and stopped at my door. "If you stop her training now, will she be ready, Valerio?" she asked me, her silver eyes, as bright as the moon, penetrating through me.

"She will."

She folded her arms over her chest and stood taller, her skin shimmering more and more every night we approached the full moon. "She must. The pink blood moon is nearly a month away. She needs to survive the shift."

From inside the room, I heard Mae suck in a breath. And it wasn't like the breaths that she'd taken while sleeping in that dirty, old cellar. I knew those all too well, having stayed up every night to make sure she made it through her sleep. This was a sharp, panicked inhale.

"She has become a lot stronger since she's been here," I assured, hoping that she'd agree. "She's numbing to the pain. She willingly takes on our men in the training room. Her fears are slipping. She's gained insurmountable strength since starting training with the Protectors."

"If she isn't ready by the pink blood moon, then she and I will both die," the Queen said, narrowing her eyes at me. Her chosen Protector, the man who had trained me to be ruthless, stood behind her with pursed lips. "You understand what that means, right?"

I nodded. "I do."

"Make her fearless. Don't make her fear you," the Queen continued.

But I didn't understand how Mae couldn't fear me after everything this woman had forced me to do to her.

"She has strength beyond measure." The Queen pressed her lips together, as if it was hard to admit that anyone could potentially be more powerful than she was or than she once had been in her thousand-year lifetime.

Again, I heard another sharp breath come from inside my room and knew Mae was listening to every word of this. She was probably standing with her ear pressed to the door just a few feet away, taking in all this new knowledge about her life.

"Yes, Valerio," my trainer stated. "Remember that she is stronger than you. You'll be with her for the rest of her life, so don't get on her bad side." He glanced at the Queen and smiled. "Or she'll make sure that *you* get punished for it."

The Queen laughed, the celestial sound echoing through the grand halls.

Suddenly, from behind, Mae flung the door open, a look of recognition crossing her face when she looked at the Queen's guard, and charged at my trainer with intent to kill or severely hurt. "How can you live with yourself?" she screamed at him, not even taking a look at the Queen yet. "You killed my mother, you selfish bastard! You're the same man from the picture, the same man from my nightmares. She was your best friend!"

"Mae," the Queen said, her voice both delicate yet demanding. "Mae, look at me."

Against her will, Mae slowly tilted her head to meet the Queen's gaze and stared up at her. Mae loosened her grip on my trainer and turned to the Queen, all the emotion draining from her face. "Mom?"

CHAPTER 40

MAE

Mom.

My mother stood in front of me. Alive. Laughing. Fucking thriving.

She smiled softly at me with glowing silver eyes, the mark on her chest mirroring mine, except hers burned a bit brighter. I looked between all three of the individuals, nostrils flaring when I laid eyes upon who I thought was Mom's killer. Both he and my mother looked timeless and exactly like they had in Dad's picture.

Unable to even process this, I closed my eyes, shook my head, and turned on my heel. This was probably just another one of my nightmares. Any minute now, I'd wake up on Valerio's couch and wished that I had fucking died in my sleep.

"Mae, where are you going?" Mom called, her voice too soothing to be real.

"Back to bed because this is either another one of my nightmares, where this guy over here"—I pointed to the man beside her—"is about to kill you again, or I'm in hell. Either way, I don't want to deal with it. It's too early."

"Wait!" She hurried over to me and grasped my shoulder with her soft fingers. "Let's talk. There is probably much that you want to ask me and want to know."

"I love you, Mom, but I'm not talking to a dead person." I shook my head and stared emptily at the marble floor. "I already think I'm going a little crazy. That would just make me insane."

Before I could slip into Valerio's room, Mom sighed. "I never died, Mae. I faked my death."

She'd faked her death? I laughed. *No ... no, she hadn't. This is just a dream.* I didn't actually believe this, yet my chest tightened.

I reached for Valerio's doorknob, but the door suddenly slammed shut, as if a gush of wind had magically come into the hall.

After yanking on it a few unsuccessful times, I turned back to Mom. She looked angrily from the door to me.

"Talk to me, Mae, and then I'll grant you the rest and peace that you deserve. Valerio tells me that you've exceeded all expectations."

I cut my eyes to the man torturing me every day, and then I pressed my lips together and returned all my attention to her—my mother, who had supposedly left her daughter and her husband for a new life.

"What do you want to talk about?" I asked.

Mom turned on her heel, walked down the corridor, and beckoned for me to follow. I rolled my eyes and walked to a large door with a mural of the phases of the moon, painted in blood red. She took a seat at a long meeting table, and the two men sat next to her. When she motioned me to sit at the other end, I crossed my arms over my chest in refusal.

"What would you like to know?" she asked calmly, though her jaw twitched.

"How are you alive?" I asked.

"I faked my death," she said.

"Why? Why would you do that? Are you really that selfish that you faked your own death, so you could be with"—I pointed to the man beside her—"whatever the hell he is to you?!"

She shook her head and pursed her lips. "Mae, it's not what it seems."

"No! It's exactly how it seems. You know how much Dad loved, thought, and cared about you. And you couldn't even love him back? You had to fake your own death instead of owning up to your feelings and telling him the truth? Why would I ever want to talk to someone that self-serving?" I glared down at her, feeling adrenaline pump through me. "I always thought that your lover over there was the reason that Dad hated werewolves, but apparently, you're the reason too. I can't believe you—"

My mother stood abruptly and leaned over the table, fingertips paling. "That's enough," she declared in a strict tone. "Sit. Now."

Suddenly, my knees bent slightly, but I fought my own body and stayed standing. I was tired of people telling me what to do and of people leading my life for me. I couldn't let anyone else walk all over me. This was my life. I was in control.

"You sit down," I commanded.

For a moment, she bent as if she was about to sit but then straightened her back and stayed standing. "The only reason I left was to protect you."

I narrowed my eyes at her. "Protect me from what? You?"

Shaking her head, she took a breath and sat back down. "You were in danger while I was around. I couldn't let anyone hurt you."

"That didn't answer my question," I said. "What are you? Whenever Dad used to talk about you, he told me how amazing and generous you were. But you're nothing like that. A true 'queen,' as Valerio calls you, would *never* back away from danger. She would eliminate a threat, not hide from one."

THE MARKING

"You're talking about things you know nothing about, Mae. I was—I still am protecting you from people who fear the divine, from people who would do anything to take away our power," she said.

Divine? Power? What is she talking about?

Valerio nodded at her. "She deserves to know. Tell her."

"Mae, I'm not a queen," she said, pushing some silver hair behind her shoulder. "I am the Moon Goddess."

"The what?" I asked, making sure I'd heard her correctly.

"The Moon Goddess."

Unable to stop myself, I snorted right in front of everyone and clutched my stomach. *She isn't serious, is she? The Moon Goddess—really? Come on.*

In a moment, everyone would start laughing and tell me this was all a joke, and then I'd wake up from this goddamn nightmare.

When nobody cracked a smile, I dropped the laughter and pulled out the chair. "You're serious?"

She nodded and smiled at me. "Yes, I'm serious. And you are a demigoddess."

I raised my eyebrows and pointed to myself. "Me?" I whispered.

"Yes, Mae. You. Demigoddess and heir to the moon."

"No." I shook my head and laughed nervously. There was no way I could be a demigoddess. I was too weak. I was just human. "No. That can't be. You have it all wrong. I'm just a human. I'm no demigoddess. Good one, Mom."

"Stand," she commanded, walking to my side of the table.

I found myself standing to face her, my heart thumping against my rib cage.

"You are not weak, Mae," she said, as if reading my mind. "You are strong beyond your belief. You have the power to bring whole packs to their knees and bow in submission."

A moment later, she returned to her seat, and I stayed standing with way too many questions reeling around inside me.

"Why did you leave? Why did you fake your death? What were you protecting me from?" I asked, needing to know what Dad had died for.

"There's a clan who calls themselves the Challengers," Valerio started.

"After you were born, they emerged as a group that wanted to take away my power," Mom said. "They believed—and still believe—that I controlled everything about the lives of wolves, and in some way, shape, or form, they were hurt. Maybe a loved one was taken from them, maybe they were forced to be a rogue—something like that. You get it.

"They wanted revenge and to force me out of power, so they could live off of their free will. We tried to explain to them that I controlled some of their lives but not all of it. I don't make their decisions for them. They do have free will to some extent. But because they'd been hurt and they were in pain, they didn't want to believe that their own decisions had led them to be in the position that they were in."

I nodded, slowly taking this all in. Maybe that was why those rogues had taken those kids.

"A couple of years after you were born, they found a way to drain my power," Mom continued. "They took pups before they could shift for the first time and drained the life out of them. Each pup they drained would drain a little bit of my power.

"Pups are special to me because I place a substance in their blood that keeps their bodies from shifting until they are mature and able to shift. I use my power to give them this strength. When the pup finally shifts and becomes a werewolf, this substance is released, and I can absorb it back to use for future pups.

"When they drain the pups, the substance, their strength, and my energy do not get returned to me. And in order for me to survive and for the werewolf race to survive, more pups need to be born every so often. If I keep giving my energy to these non-shifted pups and they are drained, I will eventually die, and so will the species."

My lips parted, and I just stared at her, unable to believe this all.

Pups were dying because people were mad at someone they hadn't even met before?

"With me around, there was a high risk that the Challengers would find you and drain you, too, since you had an essence inside your blood that prevented you from shifting into a demigoddess until you were ready. I couldn't bear to see my only daughter die. If they found you and drained you, then much of my strength and power would be sapped from me as well because we are connected. Without our power, the werewolf species would die," she said.

Placing her hand on Valerio's shoulder, she continued, "When I left, I began training Valerio to protect you. He has been your guard ever since and has been there for you, even when you didn't see him. He's always with you, even when I can't be."

I swallowed hard and looked between Valerio and Mom, narrowing my eyes. "If you've always been with me, then where were you when I was running away from Brett? Where were you when I was shot through the head?"

Valerio clenched his teeth and looked at the mahogany table, guilt in his eyes. "I was there. I watched as it all happened to you. I wish that I could've stopped it, Mae. I sincerely apologize for it."

Mom gave him a tight smile, as if apologizing for mistakes was forbidden here. "I told him not to interfere in your life that much. He was to just watch over you and report to me if anything had happened. As for you getting shot, your blood and your mark kept you alive. If you didn't have it, you would have died immediately. You're a demigoddess, but that doesn't mean you are divine. You can die, and he was to make sure you didn't."

Everything finally started to make some sense—seeing Valerio all the time, the draining of the pups, why I felt so connected to wolves. But I had questions. Tons of them. Why was I here? Why was Valerio torturing me? What was this mark about? But most importantly ...

I balled my hands into fists and glared at Mom. "Did you have the power to stop me from getting raped?"

Silence.

Silence that broke my damn heart.

"Let's get you to bed, hon. You look tired," she said without answering my question.

"Wait," I demanded. "I want answers. What does the mark on my chest mean?"

"It means that during the pink blood moon, you will ascend as the new Moon Goddess."

My jaw slackened, brows rising. "Excuse me, what?"

"You will become the Moon Goddess, Mae."

"But how? Aren't you already the Moon Goddess? I can't be one too."

Mom clasped her hands together. "I told you that they were draining my power little by little. When you got shot in the head, your blood could only keep you alive for so long. Once your blood couldn't keep you alive any longer, Alpha Damon's doctors put you on life support. You were doing fine until someone took you off of it."

Fucking Alexandra. It had to have been her.

"At that moment, Valerio brought you back here, and I used the little power I had left to save you."

"Why?" I whispered.

For the first time tonight, she offered me a genuine smile. "Because you're my only daughter, and you're smart and strong. If a new Moon Goddess ascends, then she will have enough power to find all of the Challenger groups and destroy them while also keeping the werewolf species alive. The Challengers have weakened me, Mae, and now, only you can stop them."

But how was I supposed to lead packs of werewolves? For the majority of my life, Dad had refused to let me even be in contact with one. And now, I was supposed to be their Goddess? How would my friends take this news? When would I get to mourn Dad? What if I wasn't truly ready?

"And what if I don't accept this whole thing?" I asked. "What if I want to go back to being a human and forget about werewolves and Moon Goddesses?"

"It has already been done. I have given you the rest of my power, and you will ascend during the next pink blood moon whether you accept it or not." She grasped my hand and squeezed. "But I hope you accept it, Mae. You're their only hope."

CHAPTER 41

MAE

Valerio stood next to his bed and crossed his arms. "We need to train."

Sunlight burst through the curtains, the AC making me shiver. I pulled the blankets over my head and pleaded for five more minutes of rest. I hadn't had this much good sleep in weeks. But the more I begged, the harder Valerio tugged on the blankets.

"Why?" I grumbled to him, sitting up and leaning against his headboard.

"Out of bed," Valerio said. "Now."

After huffing and puffing, I pulled on some fresh clothes and walked with him down to the cellar. "Your shift from a demigoddess to a Goddess is much harder on the body than a shift from human to werewolf. Everything is stronger and more powerful. Your body needs to be ready."

Valerio didn't ask me if I wanted to accept my power; he just assumed. It would be best for me if I did though even if I didn't want the title. Since I was just a girl, I'd loved werewolves. I couldn't let the whole species die because of my stubbornness.

Instead of throwing me into the hungry pack of wolves today, Valerio placed a hand on my shoulder and stood beside me in the cellar. "These men and women are the Protectors. They've fought and trained all of their lives to receive the honor of protecting the Moon Goddess. She handpicked them to do so, and when you ascend, you will do the same. They're much stronger than your average wolf."

The Protectors.

Even though they had beaten the shit out of me for the past few weeks, I couldn't help the small smile that tugged at my lips. These were the best of the best, the strongest of the strong, the highest position one could receive as a wolf. And soon, I'd be leading them ... if I survived the shift.

"Protectors, in a few short weeks, Mae will be your new Goddess." Valerio smiled down at me, his blond hair glimmering under the cellar lights. "Well then, let's train. Harder today than we did yesterday. You have a goal now."

With something to fight for now, I lowered into a low stance and watched the wolves charge at me. Despite the constant kicks, punches, and cracks of my bones, I pushed through the pain. Everyone depended on me to survive the shift and to become a divine. Even Mom.

And so, for another week, we trained until I was numb to the pain. The punches didn't hurt anymore, and I fought back with ease. I had come to terms with my nightmares and with my fears better than I'd ever thought I could.

"Tomorrow night is the full moon," Valerio announced to the pack after training one night. "That means, we have one month until the pink blood moon. Due to tradition, a pack chosen by the current Moon Goddess will hold the Ascension Ceremony during the pink blood moon. We will be traveling to introduce Mae to their pack tomorrow and will be staying with them until the Ascension to prepare our security measures. Get some sleep. We leave early tomorrow."

Like I did every night now, I followed Valerio up to his room and tore off my bloody shirt once he shut the door.

"You will be introduced to their pack tomorrow as the new Moon Goddess. You will not have to speak. We're going to leave early to make sure that the transition of power and the Ascension go smoothly."

I nodded eagerly. This was the first time I would be leaving this place in a long time. Maybe I could convince Valerio to make a pit stop back at my apartment, so I could check in on Luca and Aaisha. I missed them more than anything.

"Will they ask me questions?" I asked.

"They won't ask any questions that you don't already know the answers to. I'm sure that they'll just want to introduce themselves to you," Valerio said with a smile, peeling off his sweaty T-shirt and tossing it in the hamper.

"I'll finally get to relax for a little before the Ascension."

He chuckled and shook his head. "You will still be training with us, but we're going to be training there. You can't get too comfortable because if someone challenges you for your position as Goddess, you will have to accept and fight to kill."

"Challenges me?" I asked, brows furrowed.

"Don't worry about it, Mae. Nobody has challenged a Moon Goddess in over seven hundred years. And if they do, you'll kill them. If you can keep up with the Protectors, then a challenge from a regular wolf will be nothing for you."

I walked to the bathroom to shower, my throat closing up at the thought of someone challenging me. With my luck, it was bound to happen.

Lingering by the bathroom door, I gnawed on the inside of my cheek. "So, I know you're my guard, but when I become the Moon Goddess, are you still going to be protecting me? I'll be stronger and more powerful than you, so I don't see the point of you watching over me all the time."

He cocked a brow, a smile twitching his lips. "Trying to get rid of me already?"

"No … well, maybe," I joked.

After sauntering over to me until he stood a foot away, he looked down upon me with those golden eyes. "Mae, I'm not to leave your side. I will be protecting and aiding you for eternity or until you die."

"Don't goddesses live for a long time? How will you live as long as I do if you're still just a werewolf?"

"Your mother has power to do some unbelievable things, Mae." Valerio stepped by me and toward the shower, as if he was going to steal my much-needed shower from me. "After I was assigned to guard you, she used her power to give me nearly eternal youth."

"Nearly?"

"Nearly, meaning that when you die, I die with you. She formed a life bond between us."

A life bond. So, we were bound together to death—literally. That must be why Mom and her Protector didn't look like they had aged since I was born and why they had such a deep connection.

"When I ascend, will I have that power as well? Can I make people live eternally?"

Valerio stuck his hand into the warm shower. "You will receive all of your mother's powers, and if you become more powerful than your mother was when she ascended, you will potentially receive other powers as well."

Before Valerio could steal my shower, I pushed him out of the way and back into his room, my hands flat against his muscular back. "Okay, okay. Those are all the questions I have at the moment. Get out of here. The water is getting cold."

Valerio chuckled and then walked to his nightstand. "Oh,

Mae?" He carefully pulled a chain from the drawer, the silver gently burning his skin. "I have something for you."

My eyes widened at the sight of Mom's necklace. When I'd put it around Brett's neck, I'd thought it would forever be lost, but now, it was lying right here in my hands. Examining it, I noticed that the container, where the red liquid once had been, now had an ashy substance in it.

"What's this?" I asked.

Valerio took the chain back and clasped it around my neck. "It's your father's ashes. I returned to the rogues' house to retrieve your necklace, and I thought it would be nice for you to have a little piece of your dad with you even though he passed away."

Chest tightening, I twirled around and wrapped my arms around Valerio's shoulders. "Thank you," I whispered, a stray tear rolling down my cheek. I tightly gripped on to him, not wanting to let go. "Thank you so much."

He stiffened but then hugged me back.

Even though I didn't want to accept Dad's death, having a little piece of him with me on my journey to becoming a divine made everything easier. I might not ever get to see him again, but he was here with me. He always would be.

Valerio pulled away and nodded to the bathroom. "You'd better hop in that shower ... before I do." He cracked a smile. "And get some sleep tonight, Mae. We leave early tomorrow."

"This is ... Damon's pack," I muttered in disbelief the next morning as Valerio pulled up to the pack house.

My stomach tightened at the thought of finally being back because the last time I had been here, I'd killed Brett with an ax and gotten shot right through the skull.

"He's holding the Ascension," Valerio said, opening my door

to a pathway of sparkling moonflowers and taking my hand. "Come. We're going to be late for the meeting. Everyone is thrilled to meet you."

Letting him lead me to the pack house, I glanced around at the surprisingly eerie woods. For as long as I had known Damon, this part of Witver Forest always had people or pups running through it. Either Damon was taking precautions with the Challengers or everyone was really waiting to meet me in the pack house.

Valerio paused in front of auditorium doors that I hadn't even known existed in the pack house. I guessed I'd never really learned much about Damon and his pack in the short time we were together. Maybe that could change.

"Does Damon know I'm here?" I asked, stopping him from entering.

This would be the first time I'd see him in nearly a month. How would I react to finally seeing him after all of this time? Would my body crave him? Would I still feel disgusted by him? What about Luca? When would I get to see him again?

"No, he doesn't." Valerio pressed his fingers between my shoulder blades and gently pushed through the doors, the howling wolves suddenly silencing as they looked in our direction.

I sucked in a breath and found myself scanning the room of lively faces until I saw *him*.

Arms crossed over his chest, dark bags under his eyes, a scruffy beard, Damon sniffed the air and immediately looked up at me, his eyes wide and flickering between green and gold. Before I could react to seeing him, he sprinted over to me and held out his hands, ready to wrap me in a hug, but Valerio stepped in front of me and pushed him forcefully to the ground.

Damon growled viciously at Valerio and jumped back up, canines extending. I wanted to tell Valerio to stand down, but he was doing his job, protecting me from someone who had hurt me in the past.

While Damon stood no chance against Valerio, he charged at him like a feral and furious animal. Valerio grabbed him by the collar and flung him against the wall, making some of the drywall crumble. Damon leaped up and stalked toward him again, a purple bruise forming on his jaw.

"You took her from me!" Damon seethed through gritted canines, almost as if he and Valerio had been in contact. "All this time, you knew where she was?! You don't know how worried I was about her! I thought she had died. She was unstable. She was—"

Valerio yanked Damon closer by the collar. "You rejected her. Get over it. She's not yours anymore," he said and then tossed him to the ground like he was nothing.

In a fury, Damon glared at me. "So, you're with him now?"

I parted my lips to retort, but Valerio shook his head. "Don't. He's not worth your time."

My throat closed for a moment. I wanted to tell Valerio that Damon had once brought me to my knees, that some part of my being still wanted him even if our pull had diminished quite significantly, but that would make me look weak. And I couldn't look weak in front of the wolves, not anymore.

"Sit," Valerio commanded Damon with an authoritative tone.

Damon tried to fight his body but started sitting. I raised my brows.

An alpha had sat after another wolf commanded him to? That was different. Usually, alphas never followed the commands of others. Valerio was much stronger than Damon, but I hadn't thought he held that much power over other wolves.

After a moment, Valerio guided me to the podium on the platform. I stood before the other wolves and stared out into the crowd as the back doors opened. Luca, Aaisha, and Richard walked in and took a seat in the back. My eyes widened in excitement, adrenaline pumping through me.

My friends had come. Valerio must've invited them.

With dark circles under his dull brown eyes, Luca took one glance up at the stage and rushed toward me with relief stretched across his face. However, Valerio stepped in front of me and held out his hand, stopping Luca from approaching us. Luca pushed against him, but Valerio shoved him back harder.

"Luca, go sit back down."

"Let me see her," Luca growled.

Valerio shook his head and gripped Luca's shirt. "You know I can't let you do that now. You can talk to her after she has been introduced. Don't make me embarrass you, too, like I did with Damon," Valerio said, as if Luca was a friend.

Maybe they knew each other.

Either way, I could not wait to jump into his arms later and tell him about all the damn torture my mother had put me through this past month. I wanted to know everything that had happened with him and Aaisha too. Seeing them again made me so freaking ecstatic.

"I thought you said I wouldn't be able to see my friends," I said, gently nudging him.

"I wanted to surprise you," he said with a smile. "To put it lightly, the past few weeks have been shit, and I know how much Aaisha and Luca mean to you. I thought it would be good after everything you've been through."

"Wow, actually being kind to me for once."

"When *haven't* I been nice to you?"

"Hmm, let's see. The time you watched me almost die, the time you manipulated my dreams, when you tortured me"—I took a deep breath, heaviness falling upon us—"when you watched Brett rape me …" A foul taste burned the back of my throat. This was the first time in weeks I thought about what had happened.

"Okay, okay. I get it. Your mother ..." He grimaced and looked down. "Forget it. Let's get back to the announcement. We have other things to discuss today."

Once everyone was seated, Valerio cleared his throat to address the room. "In one month, a new Moon Goddess will ascend. She has trained hard and is destined to protect us as a species against anything. She will be given the responsibility of deciding mates, allowing pups to come into our world, and keeping us from our own destruction. I present to you Mae Cogan, demigoddess and heir to the moon."

When Valerio stepped back, some people whispered, others gasped, and I found myself looking toward Damon for approval. All this time, I felt the need to prove myself to the man fated to be my mate. And hopefully, this would prove everything to him.

Anxiously waiting for some kind of response, I shifted from foot to foot.

"Yeah! That's my best friend!" Aaisha stood up with her hands in the air.

"Go, Mae!" Tai said. Tai and Aarav clapped their small hands together.

"Yeah! You should've been our luna though!" Aarav shouted, which earned him a glare to the back of his head from Alexandra, who looked pissed the fuck off that the attention was on me and not her for once.

Slowly, some people in the crowd started clapping, and before I knew it, the whole crowd stood and cheered for me. Though I wasn't fond of all the attention, I smiled.

Two months ago, I would've never known what kind of difference I could make in some wolves' lives. But now, I had the entire species to protect.

CHAPTER 42

MAE

"Mae!" Tai and Aarav squealed once the meeting was over, arms wrapped around each one of my legs.

I stood outside the cabin that Valerio and I would stay in during the weeks approaching the pink blood moon and ruffled their hair. "How are my two favorite pups doing?"

"Great!"

"Yeah! Where have you been? We wanted to hang out with you!"

"I've been busy with a couple of things," I said, poking Tai on the nose. "But I'm back now, so we can hang out allll the time. You tell me when, and I'll be there."

A woman with brown hair pulled into a tight sock bun approached us and pulled Aarav off me. "Thank you so much for finding my son and Tai. I couldn't appreciate it more. You have no idea how helpless I felt without Aarav and his best friend. I'm so happy that you're becoming our new Goddess. You will do wonderful things for us." She wrapped her free arm around me and pulled me into a hug. "Thank you," she whispered in my ear before trotting off with Aarav and Tai for lunch.

After watching them depart, I smiled at the Protectors guarding our new home and walked into the cabin. When I walked in, Luca's and Valerio's voices drifted through the cabin, Luca's scent lingering everywhere.

"You still have a choice, Luca. The Moon Goddess has requested that you join the Protectors. You're one of the strongest alphas out here. You've gotten over your mate. You can join us, if you would like, with no questions asked," Valerio said.

Mid-step, I froze and glanced into the back hallway. Mom had asked Luca to become a Protector? Did that mean that he'd always be training and living around us? Would he become one of—

"I'm thankful for the offer, but I can't accept it now. My pack members want to eventually come together again. I don't know if I could dump them like that and join you to be one of the Protectors of the Moon Goddess."

"Your pack would understand. Plus, they have Damon as a leader right now. As much as I hate to admit it, he is a good alpha," Valerio said.

Luca sighed. "I'll think about it, but I can't make any promises."

When they walked out into the living room, I jumped into Luca's arms. He pulled me to him and spun us around, his fingers igniting my skin in ways they hadn't before.

"Mae," he murmured into my ear, hot mouth on my neck.

He pulled back just enough to look into my eyes and smiled. I brushed my fingers across his cheek, feeling his stubble, and kissed his soft lips, my heart clenching. I was really back with him after all this time.

After a few heated moments, Valerio cleared his throat. Luca gazed over at him and smirked, picking me up bridal-style and walking down the hallway to my bedroom.

"Don't wait up for Mae. She'll be busy all night," Luca called to Valerio, kicking the door shut.

"What am I going to be busy with?" I asked once he tossed me onto the bed.

"*Me.*"

I raised my eyebrows at him in challenge, and before I knew it, he dug his fingers into my sides to tickle me. Laughter danced out of my throat. Against his fingers, I rolled over onto my stomach and crawled further up the bed, trying to escape. But he just crawled on top of me from behind and straddled my thighs, pushing me down and continuing.

"Luca! Pl-please ... oh my goodness ... st-stop ..." I said, giggling.

Leaning forward, he pressed his hips against my backside and snaked a hand around the front of my neck to pull me up gently. "You want me to stop?" he murmured against me, placing a kiss just below my ear.

I sucked in a deep breath, warmth suddenly gathering between my legs.

"Do you want me to stop?" he repeated.

"No," I whispered.

"Good, because I want to worship every inch of your body tonight."

"That was amazing," I whispered, pulling the blankets over my chest.

Luca turned onto his stomach and smiled at me, tucking some silver-blonde hair behind my ear. Despite everything I'd been through in the past few weeks, I felt safer in his arms than with anyone else I had been with, more than anyone else who could protect me. Luca was ... mine. And I wanted to finally tell him that I loved him because he deserved to know.

"Luca, I lo—"

Someone knocked on the door, and Valerio peeked his head into the room. "Your mother is here to see you."

Luca sat up and widened his eyes. "The Moon Goddess is here?"

I shooed Valerio out and watched Luca scramble to get dressed.

"How do I look?" he asked.

"Like you just had sex," I said, ruffling his hair.

He rushed to the bathroom, wetting his hair and parting it to the side, like he always did.

I rolled my eyes at him and grabbed his wrist. "Jeez, I wish you got this nervous about seeing me all the time."

"I do." He winked. "I just hide it better."

After wrapping my hand around his bicep, I dragged him to the door and out into the living room, where other Protectors, Valerio, and Mom stood.

"Mae," she said softly, grinning and turning to Luca, who bowed his head. "Luca, it's nice to finally meet you."

He smiled brightly at her and nodded.

"Valerio has talked to you about my offer," she said. "And you don't want to be a Protector of the Moon Goddess?"

"No, I don't... at least not right now," Luca said honestly.

This was an amazing opportunity for Luca. It wasn't every day that a wolf was offered a position to protect the Moon Goddess. Any wolf would jump at the chance. And it made me kind of sad because Luca knew that I would be Moon Goddess in a few short weeks. Who knew what that would entail? I would love to have him by my side at all times, so we could spend the rest of our lives together.

She nodded in dismissal to Luca who walked out of the room and turned to me. "So, how did it go today?"

"Good," I said.

She raised an eyebrow at Valerio, who left the room, leaving me alone with her. "I heard you saw Damon." She took a deep breath. "And I know, deep down, you still love him, but I made you Damon's mate to teach you a lesson, not so you could fall in love with him. I needed you to learn the feeling of rejection and to show you how much it affected a wolf's life, so you could be a better Moon Goddess than I was."

My lips turned into a frown. All her teachings were pretty shitty experiences in my most humble opinion—from the rape to the torture to *this*.

"Your father was my soul mate," she continued. "We weren't mated in a wolf sense, just human mates, but he was my weakness. I was warned to not fall under his charm because it would be my downfall, but I did. We were hopelessly in love, and then you were born. You were my downfall, and I'm not saying that as a bad thing, Mae. You're the best thing that has ever happened to me. I guess what I'm trying to say is that Damon is always going to be your weakness. Always. But you can't let him be. If you want to be a strong Moon Goddess, you can't let men or women get in your way. You choose your life. Don't let people choose it for you."

"You knew he would reject me?" I whispered.

When she didn't say anything, I felt my heart sink. "You used Damon because you knew he was broken. You knew that he felt like he needed to prove himself because of his father. You used his weaknesses against him and against me. How-how could you be that ... that terrible? Why would you ever do that to us?"

"You needed to know rejection, Mae," she said with a tight jaw, yet there wasn't a single ounce of regret on her face. "You still need to learn plenty of things about being a Moon Goddess, which I will teach you in the next few weeks. Your first lesson will be tonight. I hope—"

"Stop," I commanded. "Stop! Get out!"

This woman had caused nothing but pain to seemingly everyone. Me. Damon. Valerio too. I had seen the way he looked today when he mentioned her name. She'd let me deal with so much agony. I didn't want to feel it anymore. I couldn't believe how she could use someone like that. Damon was even more broken now because of her, and there wasn't much of a chance he'd piece himself back together.

"Don't you say a word. Please, leave me."

After another moment, she nodded and disappeared into thin air. I retired to my bedroom, my eyebrows furrowed, thinking about everything she'd done to me. She had made me stronger, but she had gone about it so wrong. She had hurt me more than helped me.

Why would a mother do that to her child? Why would she choose to give her child pain instead of showing her child the good from the bad?

Deciding that I wouldn't let it get to me anymore tonight, I sank into my bed and prayed that tomorrow would be better than all the shitty days I'd had before this.

"He will betray you," Mom *whispered, voice drifting through the bathroom, slithering around me and squeezing tight like a serpent.*

I stared at my reflection in the mirror, a sharp pain piercing through my back. I turned to my left and gazed at the knife impaled in my scarred flesh.

"Always keep your guard up," she whispered again.

Another knife launched into my back.

"Don't trust him," she whispered one more time.

A final knife jabbed into my skin.

I fell to the ground, blood trickling from my wounds.

Betrayal? Who was going to betray me?

"Get up!" Valerio shouted, tugging the blankets off me.

I grumbled to myself and wiped my eyes, sick and tired of all these dreams Mom fabricated in my head. Wasn't sleep supposed to rejuvenate the body, not make it an anxiety-induced mess?

"Today is your first day of training at Damon's pack," Valerio said, clapping his hands together. "Everyone is going to be there to watch you."

"Another reason not to train today," I mumbled, closing my eyes and not even caring about the blankets anymore. I was so damn tired; I would probably easily fall asleep in the AC.

He wrapped his callous hand around my wrist and dragged me to the front door. Training nonstop had drained me, both physically and mentally. I didn't want to see anyone today, especially Alexandra, who would definitely be there to watch my every move.

On our way down the moonflower path, Mom's words from my dream drifted through my mind. If Damon was my weakness, did that mean he would betray me? Knots formed in the pit of my stomach. Somebody was going to betray me, but I didn't know if it was him or not. She'd said it was a male, so it could be Luca, Damon, Samuel, Valerio, or Richard. Anyone relatively close to me, who I would trust with my life.

But if Mom trusted Valerio enough to create a life bond between us, it probably wouldn't be him. And I wouldn't exactly say I trusted Damon after what he had done to me, but I couldn't determine if he would betray me. Even if it was neither of them, why couldn't have Mom told me herself? Why did she have to speak in riddles?

We approached the training field, where Damon's warriors fought on raised platforms, their half-naked bodies drenched in sweat. I glanced over at Damon as he fought against Samuel, his muscles rippling under the humid summer sun, and then he eventually flipped Samuel onto the mat and pinned him.

When he stood up, he peered my way and smiled so genuinely.

My cheeks flushed, and I broke eye contact with him, refusing to let him see the effect he still had on me. I hadn't talked to him yet since I had returned, and I planned to keep it that way for as long as I could.

"Mae!" Valerio called, already warming up on a platform.

Knowing that I would get sweaty, I sucked in a breath and cautiously pulled off my shirt, all my scars on display for Damon's entire pack to see. The warriors on other mats slowed to a stop, everyone staring at us—especially me—some whispering.

I looked around the crowd, making eye contact with Samuel, who mouthed the words, *You're so strong*, to me.

I wanted to smile or laugh, but after last night, I needed to keep my guard up.

Valerio held out a hand for me. I placed my hand in his and hopped up onto the raised platform bed, my toes curling into the black mat. Before crouching down in the fighting stance I had seen the other Protectors do during practice, I caught sight of the one and only Alexandra storming toward the platform.

Lips pursed tightly, nostrils flaring, Alexandra pushed her way through the crowd and jumped onto the platform next to me, everything about her screaming *fury*. Damon jumped up onto the platform and grabbed her arms to pull her away, but she yanked out of his grip and glared at me.

"I'm here to challenge Mae for the spot of Moon Goddess."

CHAPTER 43

MAE

*P*eople gasped. Warriors ceased fighting. I stood in shock.

This would be the first challenge in centuries. And I was terrified that I wasn't ready.

"What?" Damon shouted, snatching her wrist again to pull her off the platform. "No! Alexandra, you aren't challenging Mae for her rightful spot. She's trained to be there. You can't take it from her."

She jerked her hand out of his grip and glared at me. "Watch me."

After shoving Damon away, she transformed into her brown wolf and bared small canines at me.

When Damon lunged to grab her once more, Valerio stopped him. "You can't, Damon."

"You're going to let this happen?" Damon exclaimed. "Mae isn't going to fight a wolf."

"She will," Valerio said, nodding to two guards, who then

approached Damon and linked their arms around him to hold him back.

Valerio turned back to me and set a hand on my shoulder. "You have trained for this. Don't bother trying to get her to submit to you. Kill her."

From across the mat, Alexandra glared at me with golden wolf eyes. I swallowed hard. I had known this was going to happen, but a part of me had hoped it wouldn't. Alexandra was always jealous of me, always hated me with her entire being.

And what if I'm not good enough? What if she defeats me?

"I-I thought you said that I *have* to kill her to win," I whispered.

He pressed his lips in a thin line. "You don't have to, but you will," he said, and then he walked between Alexandra and me to address the growing crowd of warrior wolves. "The heir to the Moon Goddess has been challenged. The victor of the fight will be announced when the other submits or is killed."

My stomach tightened. Alexandra always had one up on me but not this time.

As soon as Valerio stepped out of the way, Alexandra lunged at me, leaving me with no time to think or react. She clamped down on my thigh and sank her canines into my flesh as deep as they would go. When she ripped a chunk of muscle out of my body, I anticipated pain, but I felt nothing.

Valerio had numbed me to it through my training.

Spitting the flesh at my feet, she stared up at me with wide eyes, blood oozing out of her mouth. I stood tall, unfazed by her attack. She might've expected me to weaken, but I was stronger than she thought, stronger than anyone thought.

When she lunged again, I snatched her neck and pressed my thumbs against her arteries to cut off her circulation. She thrashed around in my hands, limbs flailing all over the place, but I held her steady and glared down at the woman who had made me unsure, who had preyed on my weaknesses.

After another few minutes, her wolf grew limp, and she shifted back into her human form, yanking at my wrists to breathe again.

I pulled her closer to me. "You're *weak*. You don't deserve to have the title of luna. All you want is power. You've never cared about Damon or Luca." I gripped her neck tighter until her cheeks flushed and she gasped for air. "You have to make everyone else's lives miserable, so you can be powerful."

She parted her lips, trying to speak but nothing came out. The tables had really turned for her. She feared me now. She knew she had made a mistake. She didn't want to die. And I was drinking in the position I had over her.

"Kill her," Valerio said, walking up beside me. "What are you waiting for?"

I took a deep breath, wanting to finish her more than anything, but something inside of me told me I shouldn't and that I should use Alexandra to reveal the man who would betray me in the near future. It was wrong, so wrong. Alexandra had been such a bitch and had ached to kill me for a long time.

But Mom's warning from my dreams continued to replay through my mind.

"He will betray you."

I stared at Alexandra's red face. "I can't kill her."

"Yes, you can."

"She's not mine to kill," I said, thinking back to Luca.

Alexandra had put him through hell. And sure, she might've put me through worse, but if Luca killed her, he would prove his trust and loyalty to me. After that, my list of suspects would be narrowed down by one.

It felt dirty to test Luca's loyalty, but I had to do it. I couldn't chance the wolf species.

"You want Luca to be a Protector like you?" I said, watching him nod. "Then, let him prove himself to us. He will be the one to kill her."

Valerio grimaced. "In a challenge, you must kill her, or she must submit, Mae."

"Then, as much as I hate saying this, she won't die today." I threw her to the ground. "Submit to me."

She rolled onto her stomach and looked up at me, gasping out for breath. Desperately, she tried forming words with her mouth through her coughs, but nothing came out. I reached for her neck, ready to choke her out again, but she bowed her head in submission.

"I submit! I submit!"

She placed her hands on the ground, trying to push herself up, but her knees buckled from underneath her, and she collapsed.

Feeling an overwhelming sense of pride and a need to embarrass her like she had done to me countless times, I grabbed her by the hair and dragged her to the edge of the platform. "You look too weak to get up. Let me help you."

Everyone stared at me with wide eyes as blood seeped down my leg from my open wound, leaving a scarlet trail behind me.

I pushed her off the platform and onto the ground, and then I looked around at the other warriors. "Does anyone else want to challenge me?"

Sucking in a collective breath, the wolves bowed their heads in submission to me. All, except Damon. Damon stared at me with the smallest, proudest smile on his face, and then he bowed his head, as if bowing to his mate was the greatest fucking thing he had ever done.

After washing all the blood off of me, I convinced Valerio to drive me to my apartment. Before I got out, Valerio grabbed my wrist.

"I know the real reason you didn't kill Alexandra and why you're here. You're going to ask Luca to kill Alexandra for you to prove his loyalty." He paused. "I saw the dream you had last night."

"How did you see it?" I asked, guilt washing over me.

"We have a life bond. I know all the information that you know. It's for your protection."

I grabbed the door handle and swallowed hard, looking up at our tiny apartment in the center of Witver Forest. My stomach twisted at the thought of doing this to Luca, but I didn't have much of a choice. Mom wouldn't tell me directly because she either didn't know or thought that this was another one of her good lessons.

"Asking him to kill her for you is a big decision. It's not something to be taken lightly. I hope you take that into consideration," Valerio said before I got out.

Shutting the door behind me, I walked up to the apartment, where Luca waited for me in a bundle of nerves. He opened the door, shirtless, before I could even knock and wrapped me up in a hug. I kicked the door shut with my heel and brought him to his bedroom. Collapsing onto his bed, I pulled him down with me, rolled onto my side, and brushed my fingers across his cheek. I rested on his chest and trailed my finger up and to his red moon tattoo.

This man wasn't even my mate, yet I had fallen in love with every part of him.

Every single part.

Drawing his fingers up and down my side in a soothing manner, he stopped when he touched the fresh scar on my thigh from when Alexandra had torn my muscle out earlier.

Before I could stop him, he sat up and pushed me over slightly to see it better. "What's this? This wasn't here yesterday."

I sighed, knowing that I would have to tell him about the challenge and about my request.

"Alexandra challenged me today," I said, sitting and crossing my legs.

"She did? What happened? Did you kill her?"

"No."

"Why not?"

I gnawed on the inside of my cheek, just knowing that this wasn't right. If Luca asked me to kill Damon, I wouldn't be able to—but that was because I still had some feelings for him. Luca had told me that the bond had diminished, basically that he felt nothing for Alexandra anymore, and if that truly was the case, then I needed to do this.

If Mom was warning me of a betrayal from a man close to me, it must be serious and could affect my leadership as the Moon Goddess. I couldn't put the whole species in jeopardy just for a man that I loved. I needed to think about us all, not just him. *He will understand, right?*

"Because you're going to," I said.

He raised his eyebrows. "I am?"

"Yes."

"Why?"

If he was the man who would betray me, then I couldn't let him know I was on to him. I needed to lie even though it was wrong.

So, I bit back all my annoyance at myself and said, "Because if you want to join the Protectors with Valerio and protect me someday, you will kill her."

Seconds passed.

And then minutes.

Luca didn't say anything for a long time. Too long.

If he didn't still have feelings for her, this should be simple for him.

"I'm not going to kill her," he finally said.

"Why?"

"You should've killed her," Luca said.

I crossed my arms. "That didn't answer my question."

"You should've done it."

Instead of arguing with him, I pressed my lips together and glanced down at the scuffed hardwood floor. In a month, I would ascend as the Moon Goddess. I had so much more responsibility now. I couldn't look out for just myself anymore. My main priority was the wolves. And the only way I could keep the species alive was to destroy every last one of the Challengers, so no pups would ever have the life drained out of them again.

Yet Mom hadn't told me much about what would happen, how I would ascend, what kind of pain I would go through. And as much as I despised her right now, I needed to listen to her. She and Valerio were the only people who knew the extent of what would happen during and after the Ascension and what *could* happen to the wolves if I didn't stay focused.

But for tonight, I would let it go because I wanted to just be happy for once.

I grabbed Luca's hand and pulled him close. Tonight wasn't about who I was destined to be with anymore or who had picked me up when I was broken. I might have made poor decisions before, but at the moment, everything felt right.

Until it didn't.

To be continued in *The Betrayal*.

Order now.

ALSO BY DESTINY DIESS

Next-Door Incubus: https://books2read.com/u/3yEnVn

Demonic Desires: https://books2read.com/u/4XXJ2v

Queen of Lust: https://books2read.com/u/3nWa7x

ABOUT THE AUTHOR

Destiny Diess is an international bestselling author of paranormal romance. With over 28 million story reads online, Destiny enjoys writing novels about werewolves, demons, and gods. She was born and raised in Westerly, RI, and now resides in Pittsburgh.

ACKNOWLEDGMENTS

Credit to Keara Williams for the series inspiration!

Made in the USA
Columbia, SC
02 December 2024